PENGUIN BOOKS
## JACK THE RIPPER

Mark Daniel was educated at Ampleforth and at Peter-house, Cambridge. A reluctant stay in Her Majesty's prisons formed the basis of his first, widely praised novel, *Conviction*. This was followed by *The Laughing Man* and a host of other works ranging from a scholarly edition of the works of Gilbert White to the *Real Ghostbuster* novels. A devoted student of skipping-songs and children's rhymes, he has also compiled *The Golden Treasury of Nursery Verse* and *A Child's Treasury of Christmas Verse*. He is at present engaged in writing the Liberty Hall series of novels for teenagers. Mark Daniel is married to the actress Ann Thornton and lives in a converted stableyard on the Wiltshire Downs.

*Mark Daniel*

# JACK

## THE

# RIPPER

Penguin Books
in association
with

PENGUIN BOOKS

Published by the Penguin Group
27 Wrights Lane, London w8 5tz, England
Viking Penguin Inc., 40 West 23rd Street, New York, New York 10010, USA
Penguin Books Australia Ltd, Ringwood, Victoria, Australia
Penguin Books Canada Ltd, 2801 John Street, Markham, Ontario, Canada l3r 1b4
Penguin Books (NZ) Ltd, 182–190 Wairau Road, Auckland 10, New Zealand

Penguin Books Ltd, Registered Offices: Harmondsworth, Middlesex, England

First published 1988

Copyright © Thames Television PLC, 1988
All rights reserved

Filmset in 10 on 12 pt Ehrhardt
Made and printed in Great Britain by Richard Clay Ltd, Bungay, Suffolk

Except in the United States of America,
this book is sold subject to the condition
that it shall not, by way of trade or otherwise,
be lent, re-sold, hired out, or otherwise circulated
without the publisher's prior consent in any form of
binding or cover other than that in which it is
published and without a similar condition
including this condition being imposed
on the subsequent purchaser

*For Dr Claire Elliott, M D,*
*and Sister Elizabeth Webber, R G N, R S C N,*
*dear friends in much traduced professions*

# Contents

# Acknowledgements

*M*any guides are needed in the Ripper maze. I would like to thank David Wickes, the producer of Thames Television's series, his wife Joanna and his researcher Sue Davis for their assistance and for giving me so free a rein. Donald Rumbelow has been unfailingly helpful on matters of City police history and procedure, and Bill Waddell, curator of Scotland Yard's Black Museum, has put up with my telephone calls with generous tolerance. I am grateful, too, to the Superintendent Registrars of Whitechapel and Southwark for ferreting out death certificates and to Michael Woodley of the Met. Office for compiling accurate weather records of 1888 for my benefit. Andrew Cook of Devizes has performed disgusting experiments on pig carcases in order to ascertain the timing of the Ripper murders. Joanna Sarstedt has made many invaluable suggestions and contributed much to research.

# *1988*

❧

Chief Inspector George Godley was eighty-five years old when he recounted this story to my father in the spring of 1941.

My father had received a serious stomach wound when serving with Wavell's expeditionary force in Cyrenaica the previous December. Pneumonia had followed. He was sent to recuperate at Beldale Hall, near East Grinstead in Sussex.

❧

At first I felt too damned ill to do anything but sit in the conservatory and stare into space. I didn't even have the energy to read a newspaper. But, as the weeks passed and I started to sit up and take notice, I simply became bored. My parents were at home in Cornwall. My friends were off in Tobruk or Somaliland or gadding about at Al Burnett's Stork Rooms or the Bag o' Nails. They didn't have time to visit a second lieutenant who'd left half his innards in Libya. The nurses weren't pretty, the weather was foul and the only other servicemen at the place were fliers and either much sicker or much fitter than I. There was bugger all to do.

It was the matron who encouraged me to play draughts with George Godley. 'The man who caught George Chapman. You know. The poisoner.'

Godley, although dependent upon two sticks and largely chair-bound, was surprisingly fit. His hands hardly shook as he moved the pieces around the board, and his voice was unwavering. For three afternoons I played and lost in a desultory fashion, exchanging with Godley little but conventional niceties and speculation as to the course of the war. On the fourth day, however, when I dragged myself over to the table at which Godley always sat after lunch, he chuckled. 'You don't want to play this damn fool game with an old crock like me, do you?'

'It's not my favourite game, I admit, sir.'

'Nor mine. Haven't got a pack of cards about you, I suppose?'

'Yes, as a matter of fact, in my room ...'

'Get them. We'll play brag. Halfpenny a point. Could do with a little excitement round here. You know, sometimes when those Hun bombers pass over, I think, "I wish they'd drop one on this place." Nothing too serious, you know. Just a little bomb to shake this place up a bit.'

'I know the feeling,' I grinned. 'You must be used to a lot more excitement. I gather that you nabbed George Chapman.'

'Yes.' He nodded. 'Yes, I got Chapman. Lot of people thought he was Jack the Ripper, you know. Rubbish, of course. A ripper doesn't turn poisoner. Chapman killed slowly, ruthlessly and secretly. If it hadn't been for a bit of bad luck, he would have got away with it. The Ripper, though – the Ripper was quick, humane and anything but discreet. He wanted the world to know what he was doing. To some extent at least, that was his motive.'

'You must have known people who were on the Ripper case,' I said, thinking that even the boring reminiscences of an old man were better than re-reading the *Punch* almanacs in the library.

'Isn't it funny,' Godley said, smiling, 'the way that the world seems to come to an end when a century ends or there's a war or a king or queen dies? We divide history conveniently into nineteenth century, Victorian, pre-war, post-war, so that it seems inconceivable to you, for example, that I was a 32-year-old sergeant back in 1888 when the Ripper was at large.'

'So you were actually involved in the hunt?'

'I worked hand-in-glove with Fred Abberline. In fact,' he said, and his eyes twinkled, 'I was there when we caught the Ripper.'

'When you ...?' I gawked at him.

He grinned happily. 'Yes. I may tell you about it some time. Go on. Get the cards, lad.'

I thought that he was swinging the lead, of course, and, for a long time, the subject was forgotten. By the end of two weeks of brag and shoot pontoon, however, Godley owed me the princely sum of £4 13s. 6d. and we had become, in so far as an 85-year-old and a 20-year-old can be such things, fast friends. Although Godley always wore good-quality tweed suits and highly polished brogues, I doubted that his police pension would run to gambling debts such as he had incurred, and I was reluctant to ask him for the cash. On the other hand, I knew that he would be insulted if I should offer to waive the debt. At last, after a particularly successful afternoon of three-card brag, I thought of a way out.

'Tell you what,' I said, 'I've got more than enough money. I'll let you off the debt if you'll tell me the story of the Jack the Ripper investigation.'

'Hmm.' He cocked an eyebrow. 'Seems like a bargain. Tell you the truth, I'd be glad to tell someone before I kick the bucket. Don't like to sacrifice an iota of history if it can be avoided. Suppose you'd want to write it all down and publish it and make a fortune out of it, eh?'

'One day, perhaps,' I admitted, 'but why don't *you* do that, anyhow? If, as you say, you actually know who the Ripper was ...?'

'Oh, I know who he was.' Godley nodded. 'I know who he was, but I'm sworn to secrecy, that's the trouble. Fact is, of the three men who knew the truth, I'm the only one left. Fred Abberline's dead, Sir Charles Warren's dead, and I'm on my last legs. The truth dies, as they say, with me.' He considered for a moment. 'Let me sleep on it,' he said. 'I'll see if I can think of a way.'

The following afternoon – for some extraordinary reason we never spoke when we bumped into one another of a morning – Godley had some papers on the table before him. He smiled mysteriously and mischievously as I approached. 'I think,' he said, 'that you have got a deal. I've decided to tell you the truth, but, if you'll excuse me, I'll also tell you some lies. I will distort no essential facts, but – don't know if you've read some of the barmy books about the Ripper – I will furnish you with some red herrings. I'm not a very good liar, so you should be able to distinguish the truth from the nonsense without too much difficulty. I promised never to reveal the Ripper's identity, and I won't – or rather, I will, but I shall also name several other people as the Ripper. Give you more than one ending, if you see what I mean. Again, if you pay attention – and you seem like a bright young fellow – you should find no difficulty in discovering which is the true ending, the true solution. I shall rather enjoy this,' he said gleefully. 'It'll be a kind of game: concealing while revealing, what do you say?'

I confess that I was still sceptical, but I had flicked through the bound editions of the *Illustrated London News* in the library and confirmed that Sergeant George Godley had indeed been at the centre of the Ripper investigations. Whether or not the Ripper had really been identified, Godley must surely have some interesting details, even if only incidentals, to reveal. Until the war had become inevitable and I had enrolled at Sandhurst, I had intended to go up to Oxford to read history, so the thought of a few weeks spent in listening to genuine Victorian reminiscences was not disagreeable to me.

'Seems like a good deal to me.' I grinned and extended my hand. 'Just try to avoid too vivid descriptions of the disembowelments, if you would, sir. A little too close to home.'

He laughed and took my hand. 'Oh, and just one more thing,' he said. 'I'm afraid that I must ask you not to publish any of this until the Home Office and Scotland Yard files are opened. By then, it can do no harm.'

'When's that?' I frowned.

'One hundred years after the murders, I'm afraid. Quite a long time to wait.'

'1988.' I whistled. 'A long time indeed.'

'I'm sorry.'

'Ah, well.' I shrugged. 'I'm more interested in the story on my own account. Perhaps I'll pass it on to some young man when I'm your age, or maybe I'll write it all down and some avid historian will come upon the manuscript and publish it in years to come. It doesn't matter.'

❦

My father never had a chance to pass the tale on directly to 'some young man'. He was to die in a car crash in 1967 when I was just thirteen. His handwritten transcript of Godley's reminiscences lay in his bureau, untouched and almost forgotten, until 1981, when my first novel was published. My mother recalled the manuscript and presented it to me. 'Horrible ghoulish stuff,' she said. 'I've never read it all the way through. Far too gory for me. You may be able to do something with it, though.'

I have not had to do much. Godley's descriptions were vivid, his policeman's eye well trained. All that I have sought to do is to give cohesion to a sometimes rambling, sometimes disjointed account. The bulk of the Mansfield story, for example, was told in the course of one afternoon, without regard to the chronology of the rest of the tale. I have woven it, therefore, into the fabric of the story. Occasionally, too, where Godley's memory as to detail failed him, I have been able to obtain information from the Scotland Yard and Home Office files and from the transcripts of the inquests. I have also ventured on occasion to assess Godley's testimony in relation to modern theory. I trust that such interventions will not be resented.

The name 'Netley' is used here for convenience's sake. The real name of the coachman in this case was at no point revealed by Godley on the grounds that he had many living relatives, many of them 'surprisingly successful people'. John Netley was a scratch-coachman at the time and has been associated, for no particular reason, with certain Jack the Ripper theories. If, in fact, Netley was not the coachman in the case, I apologize to his much maligned shade.

*MD*
*September, 1988*

# *1888*

❦

*F*red Abberline's snores made the cell walls hum. It seemed a shame to awake him for nothing better than a dead whore.

Not commonplace leavings, perhaps, on the Whitechapel streets, but not exactly a rarity either. There were 80,000 full- and part-time tarts on the streets of London, and the Whitechapel and Spitalfields rookeries had more than their share.

If there was a hierarchy in that profession – and God knows, in those days there was – the denizens of the East End cunny-warrens were the basest of prostitutes. They dossed in common lodging-houses. They formed brief, brutal attachments, then broke them for a more pervasive passion: the gin. They lurched from stew to stew, looking for sailors, dockers, lumpers or slumming toffs who would give them a shilling – sometimes less – to flick their skirts up over their rumps for two hot minutes of *plen*. and *coit. abs.* against a piss-streaked wall.

They were no strangers, these women, to blackmail, brawling and betrayal, and if one night some soused tar or embittered Sundayman drew a blade to avenge a slight, no one could be much surprised. Few would mourn.

If this should seem heartless to a more liberal age, one accustomed to paying others to do its dirty work, I apologize, but I've dragged them white and bloated as puffballs from the stinking waters of the Thames. I've found them with their throats turned inside out and larvae flowing from their splayed

17

bodies like bubbling tar. One dead bang-tail more or less was not likely to bring a tear to my eye.

I knew little enough about the case, nor why I had been charged with this mission. A tart had been found prematurely deceased in the early hours of the morning. That was all.

There had been two other such murders in the same area within the past month and the scandal sheets had been fomenting trouble, but that, so far as I could see, was no reason to call in the most senior and experienced East End man on the force.

In his sleep, the most senior and experienced East End man on the force gave a little snort. His whiskers flapped and settled. His fumbling fingers pulled the collar of his ulster tighter about his throat. Something glinted and rattled on the wooden bench. I had leaped forward and caught it one-handed before I even knew what it was.

A whisky bottle. Empty save for the last finger's width.

Abberline was not going to like this. Whatever the problem, he would be considering it with a very sore head.

I reached down and grasped his shoulder. 'Fred.' I shook him. 'Fred . . .?'

Abberline's heavy, veined eyelids fluttered. He scowled and pulled away with a long, low, clogged sound like that of an old pug when he takes a good shot in the dumpling-depot.

'Fred!' I urged, exasperated. I reached behind me, grabbed the door and swung it shut with all my strength. The echoes of the crash pursued one another like bats from cell to cell. Abberline's eyelids snapped open, then sank again.

'George?' he croaked.

'Come on, governor,' I sighed. 'Arnold wants to see you. Now.'

Abberline growled again and swung his legs from the bench. He blinked painfully at the blue flicker of the fish-tail lamp. He ran his hand over his unshaven chin. He opened his mouth wide, just to ascertain that it still worked.

18

'Oh, God!' he moaned. His fingers fumbled at his fly-buttons. 'Arnold wants me? Does he know where I am?'

'No, not yet, so far as I know,' I said briskly, 'but he's about the only man in the Yard who doesn't. He wants us down in Whitechapel. Some tickle-tail got croaked in Buck's Row this morning.'

'So? What's that to do with us?'

'Dunno.' I shrugged. 'Seems ridiculous to me. We're on the case, that's all.'

'Oh, God . . .' The voice seemed to rumble up from somewhere deep in his belly. He slapped his thighs and pulled himself to his feet. He was a good four inches taller than me. The whites of his eyes were stained with yellow. They were very wet. 'Right, George,' he said. 'Get me a razor. Fast.'

As if we did not have enough to worry about.

No doubt by now it is all history and, like most history, vivid only when it has had time to become inaccurate. Perhaps only some few bright students are now told of the many factors that made the policing of London's streets a Sisyphean task in the eighties, and that were to give the Ripper the opportunity to perform his deeds with such apparent impunity.

London was the hub of the world then, administrative and symbolic capital of the greatest empire in history. When people did not know where to go, they came to London. Over the last thirty years, the population of London had more than trebled. First it was the Russians, then the Poles, Austrians, Irishmen and Jews from all over the world and many others, all seeking labour, easy-pickings or merely refuge. London expanded westward, but the builders could not keep pace. When the American Civil War ended with the total defeat of the cotton-producing South, 3,000,000 Manchester cotton labourers lost their jobs. Many of them, too, moved southward to the capital.

America and Ireland had exported another evil that drained police resources and forced us to concentrate in the respectable centre of town rather than in its lawless environs. From the safety of New York, O'Donovan Rossa sent funds and explosives to the Irish Dynamiters, who terrorized the capital by placing bombs in railway stations and public buildings.

It started when I was just a nipper with the bombing of Clerkenwell Prison back in 1867. A prison officer died. Many passers-by were maimed. A Fenian called Michael Barrett was hanged for the crime. I remember the avid crowds that filled Old Bailey from Newgate Street to Ludgate Hill, but I was too small to see anything of the hanging or of the other deaths that took place that day. Nineteen people were crushed or suffocated in their eagerness to see Barrett perform the dance of death. It was Britain's last public hanging.

The bombings continued throughout the seventies. The city lived with constant fear. In the eighties, the campaign increased in intensity. London was frankly terrified.

I was a constable on that beat just a couple of streets away when they blew the Mansion House to bits in 1881. We managed to foil attempts to dynamite *The Times*, the House of Commons, the Nelson Monument and London Bridge.

They had more success with parcel bombs in the stations. One such 'abandoned' parcel crippled or disfigured sixty-two people at Praed Street. Another, in 1884, killed two cloakroom attendants at the new Victoria Station. On 30 May in the same year, Scotland Yard itself was attacked. The detective department was badly damaged. The public house next door was reduced to rubble.

Every copper in the metropolis was on constant alert. We watched stations, theatres and gentlemen's clubs, the residences of prominent citizens and the gay-houses in which they diverted themselves, the docks, the waterworks, the hospitals. There was no time to worry about minor thefts or murders in the Ratcliffe Highway.

East of Aldgate Pump, if truth be told, there were areas where the law was maintained by the law-breakers and where no policemen would venture.

Another funny thing about the eighties. People disappeared. Not just handfuls but hundreds of people, mostly from East and West Ham. Nothing linked them. There were children, middle-aged and old men and women. They just vanished from London's streets, never to be seen again. The extraordinary thing is that they seemed to know that something was about to happen and were torn between terror and irresistible attraction. They loitered on street corners, clearly apprehensive. Friends would advise them to go home. They would nod, walk off as though heading homeward, then return to the same point. And vanish.

Eliza Carter was typical. She was patently terrified, but she refused to go home. Her blue dress was later found on East Ham football field. All the buttons had been removed. Eliza was never seen again.

For nine years, from 1881 to 1890, we were to receive reports of these disappearances. It was reported that many of the victims, like Eliza, had been seen with 'an unprepossessing woman with a long ulster and a black frock'. In January 1890, three girls became the last victims. One, a fifteen-year-old named Amelia Jeffs, was found strangled in an empty house overlooking West Ham Park. Nothing more was seen of her companions. These girls, too, had been seen talking to a woman. It was not my patch, so I do not know the details, but the coroner obviously knew more than he was prepared to reveal when he delivered his verdict. 'Women,' he said, 'are as susceptible to the lower forms of mania as men.'

This, then, was the London in which Abberline and I had been summoned to attend to the last rites of a single tart who would no doubt have died of cirrhosis or syphilis within a matter of years.

*

Abberline, now scrubbed, shaven and with his hair flattened with water, had spent the last ten minutes in Detective Chief Superintendent Arnold's office. I sat outside on a hard-backed chair and studied my hands. From inside came the deep rumble of Arnold's pulpit tone, with the occasional characteristic twang as Abberline answered. I could make out no words until at last the voices grew louder and the door-handle turned. I jumped to my feet.

Abberline swept out first. The tweed of his ulster grazed my cheek as he strode past. Behind him, Arnold stood in the door-way. He was a brisk man of medium height with bug-whiskers and a greying moustache that looked like two quick dabs with a paintbrush. His chest was constantly flung out, presumably so that the world could see his medals the better. His voice was deep, his vowels flat, his sentences clipped, save when he got a bee in his bonnet – which happened not infrequently, usually about the morals of the men under his command. Then he would turn bright pink and beat the table and deliver himself of long, rolling, blood-and-thunder speeches that bordered on the hysterical.

It was widely maintained at the Yard that Arnold held direct consultations with the Almighty and considered himself responsible for the moral welfare of every man on the force. The merest rumours of unmarried officers' liaisons, of visits to knocking-houses or of coarse language were sufficient to send him into one of his fine towering rages.

'Abberline,' he rapped, and he made it sound like 'Ebberline', 'Abberline. I want this one solved. I want this man brought to justice.'

'I had assumed that, sir,' Abberline said drily over his shoulder. 'It is the usual procedure.'

He did not check his stride. He pushed open the double doors into the vestibule. I saluted Arnold and said 'sir' as quickly as I could before setting off in pursuit.

Abberline was already at the main doors when I emerged. I caught up with him only as he reached the pavement. 'Tom!' He waved to the constable who stood to attention by the door.

'Sir.' Tom nodded and stepped into the street. He blew two high-pitched blasts on his pea-whistle.

'So,' I said impatiently. 'What's it to do with us?'

'We're coppers, aren't we?' Abberline said lightly. He did not turn to look at me.

'Yes.'

'And someone's been murdered.'

'Yes, but all the . . .'

'*Quod erat demonstrandum*,' said Abberline.

A growler, pulled by a bay High Mettled Racer Shortly Before Its Demise, drew up beside us.

'But why us, for the Lord's sake?' I asked Abberline's back as he climbed in.

'Two reasons, it seems, George.' Abberline sat. 'One, Superintendent Arnold is of the opinion that I need a rest. Maybe this is his idea of a holiday. Two,' he said, shoving a newspaper into my hands as I clambered after him. 'Take a dekko at that.'

I unfolded the newspaper. Abberline leaned forward and called over my shoulder, 'Buck's Row, Whitechapel! And see if Eclipse there can get into a trot, would you?'

The growler lurched forward. I was looking at this morning's edition of the *Star*, the new radical newspaper, which bore as much resemblance to a real newspaper as a defence counsel's speech does to a true character sketch. In fairness to O'Connor, its editor, he had declared his bias from the outset. I have before me now the first ever edition, published on 17 January of that year:

> The Star *will be a Radical journal. It will judge all policy —*
> *domestic, foreign, social — from the Radical Standpoint . . .*

*The effect of every policy must first be regarded from the stand-point of the workers of the nation, and of the poorest and the most helpless among them. The charwoman that lives in St Giles, the seamstress that is sweated in Whitechapel, the labourer that stands begging for work outside the dockyard gate in St George's-in-the-East – these are the persons by whose condition we shall judge the policy of the different political parties . . .*

*The House of Lords, the Property vote, the monopoly of parlia-mentary life by the rich – these all belong to the edifice of Privilege and must be swept away. We hope to help in bringing the day when, as in the United States and in France and in Switzerland, every citizen stands exactly equal before the nation . . .*

*Londoners are ruled by one of the worst and most corrupt oligar-chies that ever disgraced and robbed a city . . . Recently, the want of popular control, particularly over the police, has encouraged, on the part of the Government and of the police authorities, a system of violent suppression of popular rights which would be impossible in a self-governed city . . .*

Such, then, was the considered and avowed opinion of the *Star*. It was a product – and a remarkably well-financed product at that – of Bloody Sunday, the well-orchestrated 'phossy jaw' strike at Bryant & May, the rabble-rousing of such as Burns, Tillett and Crooks, and the ever more prevalent doctrines of subversives such as Engels and his friend Marx. I was not therefore surprised to read the banner headline before me: MURDER IN WHITECHAPEL: HAVE POLICE LOST CONTROL?

'So?' I shrugged. 'Is Arnold going to let himself be goaded by this sort of rubbish?'

'Seems so,' Abberline nodded. His eyes were almost closed. 'Reckons that the East End is a tinder-box, and this sort of thing could just be the spark. Could be right at that. Bloody Sunday's just a year away, George.'

I grimaced, recalling the havoc of that day.

The summer of 1887 had been the hottest on record. This did not make it the pleasantest. The Thames in those days was London's sole sewer. No one opened windows when hot weather came. Resentment festered, the people sweated and the rats treated the streets as their own. Autumn came, and large numbers of unemployed pitched camp in the West End parks and gardens. The Chief Commissioner, Charles Warren, closed off Trafalgar Square.

On 13 November, soon after the weather first broke, the regimented unemployed, many of them armed, gathered and marched. Against the commissioners' orders, they headed for Trafalgar Square. Three hundred constables, foot and mounted, halted them, but the mob was in no mood to be halted. In blinding rain, the police fell back, but the Foot Guards were behind us, with rifles loaded and bayonets fixed. Warren, a military man rather than a policeman, ordered two squadrons of Life Guards up Whitehall to disperse the crowd.

It is, I think, the very sight of mounted cavalry that gives rise to vastly exaggerated myth. Only one man died on Bloody Sunday. One hundred and fifty were injured. Three hundred were arrested. That twice as many were arrested as were even injured seems to me to argue good and moderate policing, but the public – the mass of unskilled unemployed, the trouble-making ranters among the skilled unemployed, the sentimental middle class – did not choose to see it that way. Bloody Sunday had already become a byword for police oppression. You could turn nowhere without seeing REMEMBER BLOODY SUNDAY scrawled on walls or on placards.


'But why this particular whore?' I demanded of Abberline.

'I dunno, George,' he droned. 'I dunno.'

'Is there something special about her?'

'Not so far as I know.' The corners of his lips twitched downward. 'Maybe there's something special about the murderer,' he said. 'That ever cross your mind?'

'You don't mean it?' I leaned forward, my forearms on my thighs. 'Did Arnold say anything . . .?'

'Nah. Just joshing.' Abberline grinned. 'Fact of the matter is, the muck-raking journals like the *Star* mould public opinion. The people who live in these respectable parts like to get sentimental about the poor and the Social Evils. The poor and the Social Evils like to claim they're hard done by. Neither of them means it much, but that, Sergeant Godley, is public opinion, and we're public servants, so Arnold says. They want us to investigate a tart murder? We say "Yes, sir" nicely and we investigate.'

The growler swung round into the Strand. I leaned back and stared out of the window. The morning sky was of the sheerest sugary blue. Every cornice and keystone on the new law courts and on Haxwell's, Horrocks's and the other great hotels, every cobblestone and gable was streaked with brilliant white. A light veil of mist still floated around the spire of St Clement Dane's. It was going to be a fine cold day.

Fleet Street, as ever, was chaotic and crowded. The traffic was thick. Already the street-traders were out with their constant chorus of 'Meolk!', 'Chairs to Mend!', 'Knives to Grind!' A tin-smith's traveller clanked close by the window with some twenty or thirty pans over his back. On the other side of the street, a butcher's boy dodged in and out of the kerbstone traders with a wooden meat-float on his right shoulder. The float seemed as broad as the boy was tall. Blood trickled from the back on to the kerbstones.

The flow of traffic was not helped by the usual collection of males gathered beneath the iron lattice-work bridge, or 'pedestrian crossing', which spanned the foot of the hill. They could be found at any hour of the day, gazing hopefully upward, showing particular avidity and interest whenever a typewriter passed over in her broad skirt.

This was a new city superimposed upon an old one. Dark medieval alleys and mews survived unchanged just behind the new stuccoed squares and avenues and the Queen Anne terraces out west. Here, in the centre of the world's commerce, we were only yards from networks of narrow, unlit alleyways.

Beneath the Mansion House, now lit with the new electric arc lamps, one of those accursed hurdy-gurdy men stood with his hated Italian droning and rattling machine. Abberline clutched his forehead, screwed up his eyes and groaned deeply. 'Do you think, George, that there is any excuse for arresting that – that person?'

'I wish there was, gov.' I grinned. 'Still suffering, are you?'

'What do you think?'

'Er – well . . .' I hesitated, then plunged. 'Why the hell do you do it?'

Abberline sat up straight. His eyes were suddenly very cold. ''Cos I like it,' he said. ''Cos I'm not one of your lickspittle, roll up your trouser-leg, leather-apron, Rule Britannia and of-course-it's-all-right-if-you-went-to-Eton-and-shake-hands-right coppers. I'm human, God save us. Things hurt sometimes, George, and it's agreeable to go on a bend. Forget everything. You should try it one day. Do you a power of good.'

'Not with our bosses.'

'A fig for our bosses.' Abberline crossed his hands in his lap and leaned back against the cracked leather seat. He closed his eyes again. 'The likes of you and me, George,' he said patiently, 'are not going to end up as commissioners of the Metropolitan police if we stay dry as lime-baskets from now till doomsday. Do your job as well as you can. Enjoy yourself when you get the chance. Our bosses don't have to see what we see. They don't have to pick up the shite; they just tell us where to put it and look the other way with perfumed kerchieves to their snot-boxes.

27

Occasionally, just occasionally, a drop – all right, a quart – of the booze is as good as a week in the South of France. Better, if you ask me. Left here!' he called to the driver, 'then past the station and left again just before the hospital.'

'Well, just you look out, Fred,' I persisted, ''cos a few more bends like this and they're gonna send you back here to White-chapel permanently. End of a brilliant career. I've been with you for three years now, gov, and this is the umpteenth time you've . . .'

'Oh, don't start, George.' Abberline flapped away my lecture. 'Not now, for God's sake. Anyhow,' he sniffed, 'I like White-chapel. It's my patch. Why should I worry? Here we are.' He pulled himself forward in his seat and pointed. 'This is it. Buck's Row.'

It was his patch all right. You could see it in the glint in his eye as he sniffed the air and took in the scene, the sudden confidence and ease with which he moved. At the Yard he seemed sham-bolic and scruffy. Behind his desk he had the air of something badly folded. But here, where everyone else glanced over his shoulder with every other stride, his height was imposing rather than ungainly. His long strides seemed purposeful and assured.

Buck's Row is a long straight street with unrelieved red brick tenements on the left-hand side and nothing but a low brick wall on the right. At night, it was unlit save by a single globular lamp at the far end. A crowd of the curious and the ghoulish was gathered at the point where the street narrowed as it neared Brady Street. The trains of the East London Railway passed directly beneath on their way from Bethnal Green to Whitechapel Station. Pro-vided that the residents of the tenements were asleep or minding their own business, it was a nice, isolated spot for a bit of murder-ing.

The crowd was characteristically East End. Nowhere else could you see the shape of women's legs beneath their skirts, but here there were three or four middle-aged women with neither crinolines nor bustles. In the middle of the street, another typical Whitechapel sight: an old woman with a bun on her head and a bustle at her rear, her cottage-loaf body tightly encased in muddy green, berated her cringing husband in Polish.

No one turned as we approached, but Abberline's quick eye caught something that I missed. He tapped the greenish shoulder of a frock-coat that had seen better days. 'Put it back, Whizzer,' he said softly.

Whizzer jumped. His left hand flew up to his absurd stove-pipe hat. He turned. He could not have been much more than sixteen. A toothless grin drew a diamond on his pale, pocked face. 'Oh, hello, inspector,' he said cheerfully, but his voice quavered. 'I just wanted to know what the time was.' He opened his right hand and looked wistfully down at the gleaming half-hunter.

'Yeah, well. Now you know.'

Whizzer's lips twitched. He sighed, reached forward and dropped the watch into the black barathea pocket in front of him.

'There's a good boy,' said Abberline. 'Excuse me . . .' He turned sideways in order to ease his way through the crowd. I followed. 'Excuse me. Thank you. Sorry. Excuse me, ma'am . . .'

The objects of the crowd's avid attention were a bucket and a solitary police constable. The constable was on his hands and knees beneath one of the tenement windows. He was scrubbing the cobblestones with considerable vigour. He tried hard to pretend that he was alone. He hummed a casual tuneless tune as he worked, but his cheeks were pink as pippins.

'What are you doing, sonny?' demanded Abberline.

'Getting rid of the blood.' The constable looked up. He pushed back his helmet with the hand that held the scrubbing-brush. 'What's it to you, anyway?'

'This,' I said sharply, 'is Inspector Abberline from the Yard. On your feet, lad.'

'Oh, sorry sir.' The young man stood and flapped his hands uselessly at the sodden knees of his trousers. 'It's – um – it's Dr Llewellyn's orders, sir. Keep the place clean, you know?'

I exchanged a quick glance with Abberline, then pointed down to the winking brown bubbles between the cobbles. 'Know what you're actually doing, constable? Disposing of evidence, that's what.'

'Sorry, sir.' The constable bit his lower lip and shifted nervously from foot to foot. 'Inspector Spratling said . . .'

'I know,' broke in Abberline. 'So where'd they take the body?'

'Workhouse mortuary, sir.'

'We're not gonna learn much more here, thanks to the good doctor's touching concern for sanitation. Best see the corpse first.'

He turned away. The crowd parted to let us through, but one man at its outskirts stood in our way. 'Morning, inspector,' he beamed. Abberline set his jaw and bore on regardless. The man skipped backward, gabbling, as we headed back towards the growler. 'Am I to assume from your presence that the local police force is incapable of keeping the peace? Would it be fair to say that the Yard has been called in as a sop to the Radicals? Is it not unusual for a senior officer from the Yard to investigate the murder of a mere Whitechapel market-dame?'

'And who might you be?' Abberline asked casually but through gritted teeth.

'Benjamin Bates. The *Star*.' He was twenty-six, twenty-seven, perhaps. His body was lean, but his face was plump and flushed. His jowls shook with each hasty backward step. Unkempt, colourless hair flapped over his brow.

'Are you aware . . .?' Abberline began, reaching for the door-handle of the cab, 'are you aware, Mr Benjamin Bates, that your sort of penny-dreadful moralizing, your readiness to glorify poverty and murder for your own ends, can actually cause poverty and murder? And can I take it, Mr Benjamin Bates, that *your* presence here at the scene of the murder of "a mere Whitechapel market-dame" indicates that you have some personal interest in this crime?'

'No . . .' For a moment Bates was flustered, then, 'I mean . . . yes! All right, yes! I and our readers have a personal interest in all crime on the streets of our city.'

'So have I, sonny.' Abberline climbed into the cab. I brushed past Bates and joined him. 'So have I.'

The door slammed shut. 'The workhouse!' ordered Abberline. The cab rocked and ground slowly forward.

Bates smirked smugly as he watched it go. There was a bright glint of excitement in his eye, like that of a soldier before the battle.

I didn't like it.


'Let me see if I understand you correctly, Dr Llewellyn.' Abberline spoke in a dangerous monotone. 'You examined this woman by the light of three . . .? By the light of four bull's-eye lanterns, and you concluded that her throat had been cut. You failed to notice, however, that she had also been dis-embowelled.'

'Yes.' Dr Llewellyn's voice was clogged and reedy. He did his best to sound efficient. 'Conditions, you will understand, were far from favourable, and it was only a perfunctory initial examination. Furthermore . . .'

'The inspection of the corpse at the scene of the crime was perfunctory,' Abberline repeated, still in that mechanical monotone, 'not to say downright casual. The body is then brought here, where it is stripped, washed and laid out by an idiot who just happens to be a workhouse inmate, before any further examination is made. Then, and only then, when all evidence has been washed away, do you notice by chance that this poor bitch has had most of her insides removed. That is what you are telling me?'

'Yes.' Llewellyn nodded sadly. 'It was unfortunate . . .'

'It was bloody disastrous,' announced Abberline dismissively. He turned back to a perusal of the doctor's report.

I have said that you got used to dead bodies in the course of police work. So you did, but I had never seen one quite like this. Somehow the very fact that she had been washed made the injuries more obscene. Blood would have masked much. There was no blood here, just flesh of different shades of pink.

The body lay on a bare wooden table in the workhouse mortuary. The corners of the room were deep in shadow, but the cold light from the two windows made the naked corpse seem very white, very dead. The sweet, rotten smell was strong. I knew that it would stay in my nostrils long after I had left the room.

It was the body of a drab. There could be no other word for her. She had been, perhaps, forty, forty-five. Her hair was dark and shot with pewter-grey. Her eyebrows were thick, her cheeks so heavy as almost to be dewlaps. The lips were drawn back in a sneering rictus revealing that several teeth were missing and that those which remained were stained and crooked. There was a circular bruise on her left cheek, another running beneath her right jawbone.

It was only thanks to the delicacy of the doctor that the head rested sedately on the neck. The slightest push would have caused it to roll to one side in a position unknown to nature. The killer had slashed through all the throat tissue down to the spine.

' . . . left-hand side of neck, one inch below jaw from point

immediately below ear,' read Abberline, 'a four-inch incision
. . . same side, one inch below and one inch in front, a circular
incision terminating three inches below the right jaw, the incision being eight inches in length . . . several incisions running
across the abdomen . . . knife used violently and downwards . . .
injuries were from left to right and might have been made by a
left-handed person . . . all injuries were caused by the same
instrument, to whit . . . let's see . . . a long-bladed knife, moder-
ately sharp, used with great violence. Seems to be about it.
Except – here you say that she's been operated on. What do you
mean by that, doctor? Abortion?'

'No, no.' Llewellyn shook his long thin head. 'Nothing like
that.'

'But you say "operated".'

'Yes, well.' The doctor waved towards the thing on the table.
'It's hardly just a stabbing, is it? A police surgeon in Whitechapel sees enough of those, I can promise you.'

'I was here for fourteen years, doctor,' Abberline sighed. 'Go
on.'

'Well, the flesh has been torn apart with great force, and
yet . . .'

'Yes?'

'And yet the cuts are quite deliberate. Almost – you might
say – well – clinical.'

'Was he a surgeon?' asked Abberline quickly.

Llewellyn started. The question had evidently already occurred to him. He frowned sternly and drew himself up. 'Surgeons
save lives, inspector. They do not destroy them. No member of
my profession would make incisions like that. There is no conceivable medical purpose in them.'

'No conceivable purpose, medical or otherwise,' hummed
Abberline, 'but he knew the workings of the human body.
You'd go that far?'

'Where to find the organs, yes.' The doctor walked towards

33

the window, his palms joined as though in prayer. 'But that does not make him a physician, inspector. Any butcher would know as much. There is a slaughterhouse just across from where she was murdered. You knew that?'

'Yes,' said Abberline. 'It will be looked into. Thank you, doctor. I won't keep you any longer. You've had a long morning.'

'Yes,' said Llewellyn rather plaintively. He bobbed from the waist and dry-washed his hands. 'Yes, it has been a trifle harrowing. Thank you, gentlemen.' He pulled on his frock-coat, picked up his bag and, still bobbing, made his way to the door.

'That man,' said Abberline as the door closed, 'is either an idiot or a criminal or both. It's bleeding incredible! First he fails to notice that this poor old dear has had most of her bread-basket hacked out, then he systematically destroys all the evidence! I mean, Christ! We're supposed to present evidence at the inquest tomorrow!'

'Tomorrow?' I gaped. 'How can we present evidence tomorrow?'

'We can't.' Abberline's voice was like a muffled drum.

'You mean someone doesn't want us to.'

'I don't know yet.' Abberline slowly shook his head. 'I just don't know. But something stinks, and it's not just this place. Come on, George. Let's have a word with this fellow who washed her down.'

'You don't think – well, that the mutilations happened here?'

'Nah, shouldn't think so. Still, we'll have to check it out. Now, listen, first thing tomorrow, I want a list of all butchers, veterinarians, doctors, feldschers, cork-cutters – anyone within a three-mile radius who uses a knife for a living. I want to know where they were last night and why.'

'Right.' I nodded. There'd be no sleep tonight. 'And the usual pimps, bully-boys, money-lenders and so on?'

'Yup. And the Old Nichol gang. All the usual suspects. And while you're at it, check up on our friend the doctor, will you?'

'Ah, come on, gov. He may be incompetent, but he's the police surgeon.'

'And by his own admission, whoever did this little lot knew his way round the human body. Put him on your list, George. I'd like it to be him.'


Our interview with Robert Munn, the pauper inmate who had laid the old girl out, was brief. Munn was aged, frail, hare-lipped and subject to convulsive fits. One look at him was sufficient to tell us that he was not our man, but we asked him a few questions none the less. Yes, he had washed the body. He washed all the bodies in the workhouse. He liked washing bodies. He was good at it. He didn't like this body because it was messy. He said this as though the murderer had deliberately hacked up his victim in order to offend Munn's aesthetic sensibilities and pride in his work.

When Munn had gone, the matron of the Lambeth work-house arrived in a cab and in high dudgeon. Abberline had sent for her in the hope that she might be able to identify the corpse, for the Lambeth Union's mark was stencilled on the dead woman's petticoats.

The matron grumbled and flounced and said a great deal about how much she had to do already without being summoned halfway across London in this high-handed manner, and no, she didn't know the dead woman from Eve, though that wasn't saying much, seeing as how the drink completely changed the appearance of these unfortunates and anyhow they came and went in their thousands and how was she to know every one of them by sight, she'd like to know, and as for the clothes, they could have been issued to any inmate in the past three years and if the good inspector would be kind enough to allow an honest woman to return to her labours, which were thankless enough, God knew . . .

The room seemed to sigh as she bustled out.

'Right,' said Abberline, shaking his head as though to awaken himself from a dream. 'We've done all we can here. Let's go and find ourselves a place to live.'


'Afternoon, Bill.' Abberline swept into the charge room of Bishopsgate police station and past the startled sergeant.

'Er, Inspector Abb . . .' The man stared after him, but Abberline had already passed through into the squad room like a wind.

The ceilings of the long, low room were split and flaking, the walls and windows coated in blistered paint. Loosely bound files lay everywhere – on the floor, on desks and on windowsills. Dead flies were heaped in the corners. The windows were half covered with 'Wanted' bills, so that, although it was still light outside, it had already been necessary to light the gas.

There were five desks in the room, but only one was occupied. A uniformed sergeant sprawled in an oak revolving chair, his booted feet crossed on the desk, his hands crossed in his lap. The gold buttons of his tunic were undone. His crested helmet with its City coat of arms and dragon supporters lay on its side by the feet of the chair.

'God,' muttered Abberline. His steel-capped shoes rattled on the bare boards as he strode over to examine one of the offices that led off the squad room. I sat on the sergeant's desk, picked up his feet and swung them off the desk. His jaw dropped. His bum slid forward. His arms flapped at the non-existent arms of the chair. 'Hey!' he croaked. His eyes fluttered open. 'What's all this about?'

'We're looking for a policeman,' I told him. 'Looks like we've come to the wrong place. Name of Spratling.'

'You've found him.' The voice from behind me was hard and sharp. It made the windows buzz. 'And who might you be?'

I turned. Spratling was a short, terrier-like man with twin clouds of bluish-grey hair on either side of a sallow face. His lips were very thin and powder dry.

'Sergeant Godley, sir.' I stood to attention. 'Scotland Yard.'

'Scotland Yard, is it?' Spratling strolled around me like an expert appraising a much fêted exhibit that he knows to be a fake. 'Scotland Yard. Well, well, well.' He turned to the sergeant, who was now standing and smiling unpleasantly. 'A real detective from Scotland Yard, come to tell us how to do our job, Kerby. *Sergeant* Godley is it? Hmm? Oh, dear, oh, dear. Round here, sergeants make the tea.'

'And what do inspectors do?'

I had seen Abberline strolling back into the squad room and leaning against the door frame. Spratling had not. He spun around. Some people look scared when surprised. A few, like Spratling, look savage. 'Abberline . . .' he growled.

'I shall need a clean office.' Abberline raised his eyebrows and sauntered into the middle of the room. 'That one's filthy. Oh, and *Sergeant* Kerby, is it? Godley takes sugar in his tea. I don't. Now, then, Jack.' He turned to Spratling. 'How's the collecting business? Still showing a profit, are we, or shouldn't I ask?'

'What are you doing back here, Abberline?' snapped Spratling.

'Dead whore in Buck's Row.'

'What?'

'You should pay more attention to what goes on in your patch, Jack. Common prostitute, murdered last night. Examined in your presence by Dr Llewellyn a mere sixteen hours ago. Half her insides were hanging out. Ring a bell?'

Spratling scowled. 'We can clean up our own messes, thanks.'

'Not what DCS Arnold thinks, I'm afraid. Come along, sergeant, where's our tea?'

*

By midnight, we knew the identity of our victim. Several women examined the body where it lay, now mercifully clothed, in a shell at the mortuary, and identified it as 'Polly'. Surnames were harder to come by, but at last Ellen 'Nelly' Holland came forward and named her as Mary Ann or Polly Nichols. Not long afterwards Edward Walker, an unemployed smith, confirmed the identification. Mary Ann was his daughter. He had not seen her for two years, but his identification was positive, ''Cos of her missing teeth, and the scar on her forehead. Got that when she fell down. Just a nipper she was then.'

I have been in the force for over thirty years now, and still I get a thrill at the moment when a case suddenly becomes an investigation. Not even the moment of arrest or of conviction can equal that. It's like a steam locomotive starting up. At one moment it is heavy, like an old man puffing and pulling himself along the platform. The next, it is a thing of grace and immense power and complexity.

Within hours, the previously deserted squad room was such a machine. Orders were barked. Constables saluted and barged into one another as they set about their business. They came in with reports and were dispatched at once to investigate something else. A thick strand of pipe-smoke hung above our heads. Mugs of tea and chocolate steamed on every desk. Remingtons clattered. Witnesses were bustled in and out of offices.

Slowly, a picture of the victim emerged. Of her kind, Mary Ann Nichols appears to have been a decent sort. There are discrepancies between her own statement (made on admission to Mitcham workhouse on 13 February that year) and her father's evidence. According to Nichols, she was born in Shoe Lane off Fleet Street in August 1851, which would make her thirty-seven or thirty-eight. Walker, however, claimed that she was forty-two. Her husband, William Nichols, declared, truthfully as it turned out, that she was married in January 1864, when she was only twelve. Walker, on the other hand, maintained that she had been married for quite twenty-two years. Given a woman's vanity, it seems reasonable to assume that she was, in fact, born in 1846 or 1847, which means that she would have been seventeen or eighteen when she married.

Her husband, whom we found later that night at his home in Cobourg Road off the Old Kent Road, had been a Fleet Street printer's machinist and now worked for Messrs Perkins Bacon & Co. in Whitefriars. The newly-weds at some point lived in Blackfriars Road. They had five children, the oldest of whom was now twenty-one. Mary Ann's problem, however, was a weakness for the gin. According to Nichols, they separated several times. Each time, he took her back in. Each time, after a short period of good conduct, she went off on another binge.

The final break seems to have taken place in 1880 or 1881. For some time, he continued to pay Mary Ann five shillings a week, but when he learned that she was living as a prostitute, he withdrew his support. She therefore became the charge of the guardians of the parish of Lambeth. They summoned William to show cause why he should not be ordered to contribute towards her support. When he had shown to their satisfaction that she was a drunkard and a whore, the case was dismissed. William had not seen her since.

As for Mary Ann, she had become one of the many drabs that roamed from workhouse to common lodging-house, from common lodging-house to workhouse. Since 1882 she had been an inmate of Edmonton, the City of London, Holborn and Lambeth workhouses.

On 12 May of this year, she made one last attempt to drag herself from the quicksand. She took a job as a domestic servant in Rosehill Road, Wandsworth. It lasted just two months. On 12 July she absconded with clothing to the value of three pounds and ten shillings.

It is difficult for many who live in a more civilized age and a more privileged world to understand how or why the likes of Mary Ann so loved and needed this world of stinking streets, sweaty, diseased bodies, cheap gin, ordure and violence. But those streets were exciting. Life was short. Everyone knew everyone else. There was gossip and speculation in every alehouse. From the moment that she awoke of a morning, Polly Nichols had a purpose to her day. She would see friends, meet new people, get drunk and aim to have enough pennies left to rent a truckle bed in a lodging-house. Every day was a grotesque adventure.

And somewhere at the back of her mind, no doubt, adding spice and even perhaps hope to the daily round, was the idea that something or someone might be waiting for her in the shadows with a well-ground blade.

Domestic service could not compete with that.

A few days after her departure from Wandsworth, she turned up at home again. 'Home' meant the lodging-house at 18 Thrawl Street, Spitalfields, and occasionally another such house at 55 Flower & Dean Street (or Flowery Dean Street as commonly, and probably correctly, we knew it).

These lodging-houses were the only places left for casual prostitutes and drunks, thanks to a whole series of laws supposedly introduced to control prostitution – in fact, mere sops to the disapproving middle classes. I'll just run through those that I remember. There was the Vagrancy Act, which made vagrants of common prostitutes but left the 'pretty horsebreakers' to ply their trade with impunity. Then another Act, the Metropolitan Police Act, made loitering an offence, forcing the tarts off the streets and into the public houses. Chased from pillar to post, the poor girls started to recruit their customers in the alehouses and take them to shared rooms in lodging-houses.

In 1858 that, too, became illegal. The police were given the right to search lodging-houses. If more than one prostitute was found 'in residence', we were obliged to declare the premises a 'disorderly house'. Then publicans were banned by law from allowing prostitutes to 'assemble and continue' on their premises. Finally, the Contagious Diseases Act, one of the most unfair, unworkable and undignified laws ever to pass through the Mother of Parliaments, made medical examination of all prostitutes compulsory.

The net result of these laws, of course, was to fill the streets and the lodging-houses with bawds. Had they been permitted to club together in order to rent premises, the streets, and the girls, would have been considerably better off, but the law in its wisdom sought to be seen to discourage prostitution without, of course, in any way inhibiting the rights of their customers.

In Whitechapel alone, there were 233 common lodging-houses, each of which boasted, by way of accommodation, a crowded, squalid kitchen and a dormitory for both sexes. Such dormitories teemed with vermin. Although strictly speaking there were restrictions as to how many people at any one time could sleep in the fourpenny singles and eightpenny doubles, we all knew that, on the average night, we might find two or even three times as many dossers crowded on to the beds or on mattresses on the floor.

This, then, was the world to which Polly Nichols returned after her brief attempt at health and respectability.

One thing must be understood about that world. The Empire was mighty and widespread. The sea was full of fish. England's fields were green. No one starved in 1880s London. Food and gin were cheap. If deficiency diseases were widespread, it was only because the poor preferred to live on stale bread and broken biscuits rather than pease-pudding and faggots and thus save another ha'pence for beer or spirits.

And if, at the end of the day, a Polly Nichols did not have the fourpence necessary for a bed, she had two choices. She could sleep in the parks or the streets without being disturbed by the police, or she could go a-hunting for a quick shilling-shag.

It was this latter course that she chose on the night of 30 August.

We do not know for certain where she spent the last eight or ten days of her life. Before that, she had lived for some six weeks in Thrawl Street, sharing a bed with an eighteen-year-old called Jane Oram. Jane, another inmate of the lodging-house, testified that Mary Ann had turned up in Thrawl Street on the night of the murder. She had been reeling drunk. She told Jane that she had been staying at the White House, another lodging-house in Flower & Dean Street. Jane attempted to persuade her to stay with her, but Mary Ann refused and lurched off into the night.

At 2.30am, Ellen Holland saw her at the corner of Osborn Street and Whitechapel Road. She was, said Holland, 'staggering against the wall'.

'I've had my lodging money three times today,' she drooled, 'but I spent it.'

Holland, too, tried to persuade Mary Ann to return to Thrawl Street with her, but she belligerently refused. She was going to earn her doss money, she said, and set off laboriously in the direction of Buck's Row.

At 3.45, she was found dead. That was all that was known.

All through the night and the following morning our men scoured the streets, interviewing coffee-stall keepers, prostitutes, night-watchmen and the inhabitants of Buck's Row. No one had seen Mary Ann on her last walk. No one had heard a cry for help or the sounds of a struggle.


I managed to sleep at my desk for two hours that night. I do not know about Abberline. When I walked into his office at eleven o'clock on the Saturday morning, his eyes were red, his hair once more untended, his face pale, but still he talked fast and coherently. His movements were quick and decisive. He, too, was enjoying the familiar excitement of seeing a picture developing on a blank sheet of paper, a picture of a life, a death.

'This,' he announced, 'ain't going to be easy. Seems we've got no motive, no witness.'

I nodded. 'We've had a few girls come in and make accusations. Shouldn't think they'll come to much.'

'Piser seems to be a name that recurs.' Abberline sipped his coffee, sat back and sighed.

'Yeah. I've ordered a search. Seems he likes to extort money from tarts and assaults them if they won't pay up. No record of this sort of thing though.'

'We all have to start somewhere.' Abberline smiled. He pulled out his fob-watch. 'Right,' he said. 'I reckon we've done enough for now. Let's go and find something to eat before the inquest.'


The inquest on Mary Ann Nichols was held at the Working Lads' Institute in Whitechapel Road on Saturday, 2 September.

As with most coroners' inquests, it was a makeshift affair. We entered the plain stone second-floor room and took our seats at the back of the crowd, immediately on the right of the door. The coroner, Wynne E. Baxter, sat facing us at a trestle table at the centre of the room. Behind him, at another table, sat the jury that had already been sworn and taken down to the mortuary to see the body. Witnesses came forward from the crowd to answer the coroner's questions.

Usually, the attendance at such events was sparse. Today, however, the place was packed. The East Enders, I noticed – the friends and relations of the deceased – huddled together as if by some instinct in the lower left-hand seats. The press, who were there in force, occupied the front seats on the right.

Edward Walker was the first to give evidence. He had once been a big and strong man. His neck was thick, his fingers like saveloys. But what had once been muscle now sagged like some loose brown fabric about his skeleton. There were heavy bags beneath his eyes. His hair was of the same colour as his daughter's. His clothes, which exhibited some lingering pretensions to respectability, were several sizes too big for him.

He identified the body as that of his daughter. He had not seen her, he said, since 1886 when, respectably dressed, she had attended the funeral of her brother, who had been killed in a paraffin-lamp explosion. No, she was not a particularly sober woman, which was why he and she had fallen out. He did not believe that she was fast with men. On the occasion that she had lived with him, she was not in the habit of staying out late. He had never turned her out of doors. They had merely argued and she had left home. He did not think that she had any enemies. 'She was too good for that.'

Then came John Neil. I knew John. He was a good, quiet, reliable sort of copper of some thirty years' experience. His voice was soft, his words carefully chosen.

'On Friday morning,' he said, 'I was going down Buck's Row in the direction of Brady Street. I did not notice anyone about. I'd been round the same spot about half an hour before that, and I didn't see anyone. I was walking along the right-hand side of the street when I noticed a figure. It was dark at the time, though there was a street lamp at the end of the row. I walked across and found the deceased lying outside a stable gateway. Her head was turned towards the east. The deceased was lying lengthways, and her left hand touched the gate. I examined the body in the lamplight – that's my lamp – and saw blood oozing from a wound in her throat. She was lying on her back, with her clothes disarranged. I felt her arm, which was warm from the joints upwards. Her eyes were wide open. Her bonnet had fallen off her head and was lying at her right side, close by

44

her left hand. I heard a constable passing Brady Street and I called out to him. I told him, "Run at once for Dr Llewellyn." Then I saw another constable in Buck's Row, and I sent him off for the ambulance. Dr Llewellyn arrived a very short time afterwards. He looked at the woman and said, "Move the woman to the mortuary; she is dead. I will make a further examination of her." We then placed the deceased on the ambulance.'

'You did not notice at this time that she had abdominal injuries?' asked the coroner.

'No, sir. That happened later. Inspector Spratling came to the mortuary and was taking a description of the deceased. He raised her clothes and discovered she'd been disembowelled.'

'What of the victim's personal effects, constable?'

'Just a piece of comb and a bit of looking-glass, sir, and an unmarked white pocket handkerchief in her pocket.'

'Was there a great deal of blood?'

'Well, sir,' Neil considered, 'not as was immediately obvious, sir. There was a big pool where her neck had been, but that was all I could see.'

'Did you hear any disturbances that night, constable?'

'No, sir. Nothing at all. I was never far away from the spot. The furthest that I went was up Buck's Row to the Whitechapel Road. As you are probably aware, the Whitechapel Road is very busy in the early morning. There were a number of women passing along it, presumably on their way home. At that time, anyone could have got away easily.'

'Excuse me.' A heavily moustachioed juror leaned forward. 'Did you see a trap or carriage of any sort in the road?'

'No, sir,' Neil answered promptly. 'I actually examined the ground while the doctor was being sent for. There were no marks of wheels on the road.'

'Who were the first people to arrive on the scene after you discovered the body?' asked another juror.

'Two men who worked in the slaughterhouse opposite,' said

45

Neil. He frowned and looked about him nervously as a murmur spread through the crowd. 'I questioned them. They said that they knew nothing of the affair and that they hadn't heard any screams or anything like that. I'd seen them both at their work beforehand, at around a quarter past three.'

'Half an hour, that is,' said the coroner, scribbling, 'before you found the body.'

Next Llewellyn came forward, bobbing up and down and rubbing his hands with a dreadful sort of keenness. Not unnaturally, he made much of the fact that it was very dark when he made his preliminary examination. He estimated that the deceased had not been dead for more than half an hour.

'There was very little blood around the neck,' he said. Beside me, Abberline suddenly straightened in his chair. '. . . and no signs of a struggle, or of blood as though the body had been dragged.'

'Which is in direct contradiction to Neil's evidence,' muttered Abberline.

'Why are you letting this go on?' I whispered.

'Just interested in seeing who's here.' Abberline's eyes flickered over the crowd. 'I see our young reporter has found a friend . . .'

I followed his gaze. Benjamin Bates of the *Star* was not with his fellow-journalists. He stood against the left-hand wall of the room. His head was bowed. He nodded and muttered to a large, bohemian-looking character with a broad felt hat and heavy walrus moustaches. Pink spots sprouted in Bates's cheeks. The usual bang of hair hung over his eyes.

His companion had protuberant eyes, hard and grey as acid drops. They swivelled about the courtroom while he talked, as though independent of his brain. His complexion was dark and his cheekbones cast still darker shadows.

'Looks like an artist.' I shrugged.

'Or an anarchist,' added Abberline. He turned back to the coroner.

'Were the abdominal injuries caused after the fatal injuries to the neck, doctor?'

'It is my view that the abdominal injuries were inflicted first.' Llewellyn breathed so softly and intently that I wanted to hit him. 'They would have caused instantaneous death.'

'What is he talking about?' Abberline hissed in my ear. 'What is the maniac talking about?'

I was as bemused as Abberline. 'I dunno.' I shook my head. 'I really do not know.'


The inquest was adjourned until the following morning. As we walked out into the cold grey afternoon, ignoring the questions of the press, Abberline was seething.

'What's that man's game?' He spread snuff on the back of his thumb and sniffed hard and loud. 'First he denies that there was much blood, yet Constable Neil observed plenty.'

'And Phail,' I said.

'What?'

'PC Phail. The second cop on the scene. I talked to him last night.'

'Have him brought in to the station as soon as we get back.'

'Right, governor.'

'And then – then he asks us to believe that our murderer killed the woman – in total silence, mark you – by ripping open her Berkshire hunt – and then, by way of diversion, he half cuts her head off. They may do it that way in the Welsh valleys, but they sure as hell don't do it that way round these parts. Am I going mad, George, or does your normal maniac simply kill by cutting throats, then mess about with the remains?'

'You'd have thought so.'

'And that's what Neil's evidence indicates?'

'Yup. And Phail's.'

'And the fact that it was all done silently. So why is Llewellyn

47

trying to persuade us otherwise? I want that man watched, George. Either he's got something of his own to hide or he's hiding something for someone else – or he's the most incompetent, short-sighted police surgeon it's been my misfortune to encounter. Either way, I want his every step double-checked.'

'Right. What's the next step, then?'

'Bring in this Phail and the slaughterers – what were their names?'

'Er . . .' I consulted my notebook. 'Tomkins, Britton and Mumford.'

'Right. Take their statements separately. Make sure that their stories match up. Then go back to bed.'

At St Katherine Cree, we swung round to the right into Leadenhall Street, still at a cracking pace, and so, past the synagogue and the Leather Market and into Bishopsgate once more.

By the time that Abberline had talked to John Phail, he was more than ever convinced that Llewellyn was insane. According to Phail, as he helped to raise the body on to the ambulance, his hands slithered in blood – sodden clothing that stretched from her neck to her waist. There was a mass of congealed blood where her torso had been lying and further blood trickling towards the gutter where the legs had been.

As for Tomkins, Britton and Mumford who had been working at the slaughterhouse on the night of the murder, they stank, but each independently corroborated the other's story. They had slaughtered and disembowelled horses enough that night, but no whores.

It was half past seven when I left the station and, unseeing and half asleep, suffered myself to be borne back to Panton Street, where I kept rooms.

Mrs Callaghan, my landlady, was as usual lying in wait to pounce out at me as I came through the front door.

'Evenin', Mr Godley, sir.' She folded arms as plump and

puckered as flaccid balloons. 'Didn't come home last night, then?'

'No, Mrs Callaghan,' I said wearily. I grasped the turned wooden ball at the foot of the banister and pulled myself on to the first step.

'Enjoying ourselves, were we?' she croaked after me in indulgent tones.

'Police work,' I hummed. I trudged resolutely upward.

'Oooh. Anything interesting, would it be?'

'No, no.' I stopped on the landing and looked down on the few smoky wisps of hair on her scalp. 'Just a murder, Mrs Callaghan. Just another murder.'

# 1988

George Godley's account of the Nichols murder omits little of importance. The curious interest of the Radical press may, of course, have been merely coincidental or it may simply have been stimulated by the appointment of Abberline to investigate so commonplace a murder. That interest was, however, considerable, and soon spread to all the newspapers, whatever their political allegiances.

The *Star* led the way, deliberately setting out to shock and revealing details that would usually have been glossed over:

> *No murder was ever more ferociously and brutally done. The knife, which must have been a long and sharp one, was jabbed into the deceased at the lower part of the abdomen and then drawn upwards not once but twice. The first cut veered to the right, slitting up the groin and passing over the left hip, but the second cut went straight upward along the centre of the body, and reaching to the breastbone ...*

The clinical post mortem descriptions of the incisions are subtly changed. 'Ferociously', 'brutally', 'jabbed', 'drawn', 'slitting' – these are carefully chosen emotive words. The reader is invited to see the murderer at his work.

The more lurid journals such as the *Illustrated Police News* had a field day with illustrations. Under the heading REVOLTING AND MYSTERIOUS MURDER OF A WOMAN – BUCK'S ROW, WHITECHAPEL, in the issue of 8 September, there is a large drawing of Polly Nichols in her mortuary shell. Her eyes are closed and she is clothed, but the artist has carefully delineated the livid bruises on her face, the jagged scar at her throat. There are representations, too, of the finding of the body and of the inquest, and portrait sketches of the coroner, of John Neil, of Dr Llewellyn and of Abberline, whom the newspaper wrongly identifies as Inspector Helston.

As for Llewellyn's incompetence or deliberate obfuscation of the evidence, Godley is perhaps a trifle harsh, but there can be no doubt that the Nichols investigation was handled incompetently from the outset. This, however, probably shows more clearly than any other factor the 'unimportant' and unexceptional nature of the crime. So far as Llewellyn was concerned, a whore with her throat cut was unworthy of serious and painstaking examination. What blood there was could be washed away so as not to offend passers-by. The police, after all, would never find the killer, and would not look for him very assiduously.

And yet, within twenty-four hours, this corpse undeserving of a police surgeon's attention had become the centre of a major police investigation and was elevated almost to the status of a holy martyr by the popular press.

Of pertinent facts, Godley has omitted only one. The body of Mary Ann Nichols was, in fact, first discovered by one George Cross, a carman on his way to work. He at first took the huddled pile in the gateway for a tarpaulin, but discovered it to be the body of a woman and hailed another carman, Robert Paul, who was walking on the other side of the street. The dead woman's clothes were raised 'almost to her stomach'. Paul pulled them down. The two men set off in search of a constable. P C Neil happened along the row shortly after this and independently discovered the body.

Godley also fails to record the fact that, at the time – at least officially – the police regarded the murder of Mary Ann Nichols as the third of a series. On 3 April, Emma Smith, a common prostitute, was attacked, so she said, by four men. She staggered into her lodging-house, plainly in pain, and did everything in her power to resist being taken to the London Hospital, where she died the following day. She had been savagely raped with a jagged instrument, probably a broken bottle. The fact that she claimed to have been attacked by four men, the nature of the assault and her fear of attracting official attention makes it almost certain that she was the victim of a gang punishment – probably by the notorious Old Nichol gang – for failing to pay her protection money.

The second case was that of Martha Tabram, discovered on 7 August on a first-floor landing in George Yard. Tabram's body had been *punctured* – probably by a bayonet – thirty-nine times. This was a frenzied killing – the sort that we have come to associate with opiate or hallucinogenic intoxication – not the methodical butchery that was later known to be the Ripper's trade-mark.

The man, John Piser, or Pizer, also known as Leather Apron, was already being sought by police after the Tabram killing. Many prostitutes came forward to complain that he 'ill used' them and that they lived in fear of him. For the time being, at least, Piser was lying low.

# *1888*

❧

*T*he inquest on Polly Nichols continued on the Monday, and the coroner, much to Abberline's satisfaction, tore Spratling off a strip for not ascertaining whether her clothes – a reddish ulster, a new brown linsey dress, the two Lambeth workhouse petticoats and a pair of stays – were properly fastened. Abberline then announced that the police did not propose to offer any further evidence at that time. The inquest was adjourned for a fortnight.

There were no dramatic developments in our investigation. We did not expect them. On the Wednesday, however, we had two distinguished visitors. The first, who merely strode through the squad room to Abberline's office with no more than a superior sniff for us, was DCS Arnold.

Abberline's office door, which had thus far remained open throughout the investigation, swung shut. A minute or two later, Abberline peered around the door and beckoned. 'George . . .?' he called. 'Come in here, will you?'

I pushed aside the latest batch of statements and got to my feet. Abberline held the door open for me with mock gallantry, closed it behind me and resumed his normal seat behind the desk. Arnold was already seated. I stood at ease, trying not to seem too large and imposing in the tiny room.

'George,' said Abberline casually. 'You know DCS Arnold?'

'Sir.'

Arnold nodded.

'He's worried about these papers.' He indicated several

53

newspapers that lay open on the desk top. The *Star*, of course, was the most prominent. 'You've seen them?'

'Yes, sir. Of course.'

Abberline picked up the *Star* and read, '"Police Baffled . . ." Are we baffled, George?'

'Utterly, sir.' I shrugged.

'Quite right.' He selected another journal. '"Is the East End Lawless?" Well, George? Straight question. Is it?'

'No, sir. Certainly not in the past few days. The whole of Whitechapel is crawling with reelers — with policemen, I mean.'

'There you are, Chief Superintendent.' Abberline flung down the newspapers and reached for his snuff-box. 'All we need is time.'

'Time?' Arnold placed his thumb beneath his chin. His forefinger hooked and waggled frantically at his moustache. 'There is no time, Abberline. I had a personal interview with the Commissioner this morning. He needs an arrest. Not next week or next month. Now.'

'Do you want the killer, sir?' Abberline sniffed snuff and snapped the bone box shut. He blinked ingenuously over a large red handkerchief. 'Or will just anyone do?'

'Don't be ridiculous, Abberline,' said Arnold stiffly.

'Well, look. I'm sorry, sir, but what you seem to be saying is, "Commissioner Charles Warren is getting a touch embarrassed 'cos he's really unpopular after last year's shindig and the newspapers are making a fuss about this Nichols case, so we don't want good police work, we want an arrest." Is that right?'

'Of course not, but equally we don't want a three-act tragedy made out of the death of a shilling whore. Look, Fred.' Arnold leaned forward, his forearms on the desk. This was the chummy approach. 'We're two of a kind, you and me. We came up the hard way. How long have you been an inspector?'

'Fourteen years.'

'You should be a superintendent by now. It's all a game, you know. We're pawns, that's all – you, me, even the shilling whores. Our kind never wins against the kings and queens and bishops. The best we can do is play safe, hedge our bets.'

'I don't really understand a word of all that, sir.' Abberline shook his head, resigned.

'Just bury this case.' Arnold stood, straightened his tunic and blew out his chest. 'Bury it quickly and quietly and we'll see you back at the Yard and a lot further up the ladder, Fred. Right? Good. Splendid.' He swung round, stamped his right foot and marched from the room without a backward glance.

I frowned, questioning, at Abberline. He shrugged and smiled on one side of his mouth.

There were two sharp knocks on the door. 'Come!' called Abberline.

'Sorry, sir.' Francis Wensley, one of our youngest constables, stuck his chubby face around the door.

'Yes? What is it, Wensley?'

'A Mr Robert James Lees to see you, sir. Says as he's got some very particular and important information for us.'

'Lees?' Abberline frowned. 'Christ. Well, I suppose we might as well try anything once. Show him in, will you, Wensley?' He grinned at me and shifted forward in his chair. 'This should be very interesting. Stay where you are, George. You'll learn something here.'

Robert James Lees was a short man with a big beard and broad shoulders that would not have looked out of place on someone of Abberline's height. Were it not for the paunch that strained his waistcoat, he would have been entirely top-heavy. His dark, bloodshot eyes were like those of a small rodent, forever darting this way and that, afraid, alive, alert.

'Mr Lees.' Abberline stood and extended a hand. 'Inspector Abberline. This is Sergeant Godley. Thank you, Wensley. That's all.'

Lees leaned very close to Abberline as he shook his hand. 'You know who I am?' His voice was like sandpaper.

'By reputation, yes, Mr Lees. Please take a seat.'

Lees pulled back the chair just vacated by Arnold, and sat. He leaned forward avidly, his fingers clasped. His breathing was heavy. Between every other phrase, he licked his glistening lower lip with a curious crackling sound.

'My visions have been of use before, Mr Abberline. To the police, I mean.'

Abberline nodded. 'The boy in the river. I remember it.'

'And – and other cases.'

'So I've heard, so I've heard, Mr Lees.' Abberline tapped the table with his silver pencil. 'Now,' he coaxed with a big grin, 'do you think that you might be able to help us?'

Lees gulped and leaned so far forward over the desk that his bum rose from the seat. He gulped. 'I've seen him. Your killer. Oh, no.' He sat back, both hands now raised, fingers extended. 'Not his face, you understand – well, yes, his face, but not clearly. My visions, you see, they're symbolic – intuitive, like memories rather than photographs, if you see what I mean.'

'You saw the killer?' Now it was Abberline's turn to sit forward, still showing his teeth amiably to Lees. 'You actually saw him? In one of your visions?'

'Yes, yes.' Lees took one big rasping breath, and suddenly his hands were painting pictures in the air. 'Imagine two windmills turning . . .' He looked up suddenly, as though afraid that I might be smiling. 'Like two wheels.' He turned back to Abberline. 'Each is a face, together yet apart. Like the wheels of a coach, but two faces. You understand?'

'You mean that we are talking about two killers?' prompted Abberline.

'No, no, no, no, no. One killer, but with two faces. Two faces, but the same man.'

'I'm sorry.' Abberline still beamed. 'I think you've lost me.'

'All right.' Lees's lip crackled. He bounced forward in his chair. 'All right. Listen. His victim had a black straw hat with a green feather. A brown dress with two patches. And one of her shoes wants a heel. Am I right?'

I put on my best poker face as Abberline's eyes met mine. The man was right.

'I'm right, aren't I?' breathed Lees. 'I am right. That's all I have to tell you. Look for a man with two faces. That's – that's all I can say. I'm sorry I have bothered you . . .' He stood and twice hit the pockets of his astrakhan-lined overcoat. 'Good day.'

He flung open the door and swung it shut behind him with such force that it bounced open again. I closed it quietly and turned to Abberline.

'Those,' he smiled, 'are two of the strangest interviews that I've ever had in my life. Not full moon or something, is it?'

'But he did know . . .' – I pointed at the door – '. . . he did know about the clothes.'

'Yeah.' Abberline nodded. 'But don't forget. Lees is a journalist. He's got friends among journalists. Any one of the vultures who examined the corpse could've told him that. No. Lees interests me all right, but not because he sees visions of broken shoes. Remember what I said to you on Friday when you were wondering why we'd been called in? I said, "If the dead trug-moldie ain't important, maybe the killer is," or words to that effect. And you know who Lees is, don't you?'

'Well, yes, sort of.' I shrugged. 'Seances, isn't it? Spiritualism. Bringing back the dead for lonely, rich old women. He's dippy.'

'No, George.' Abberline pulled himself to his feet. He turned and stood tiptoe to peer out of the window. His voice thudded on the glass. 'He's more than that. Robert James Lees is the close friend and psychic medium of one particular lonely, rich old woman. Has a nice little place at the end of the Mall. Name of Victoria. Queen.'

'Bloody hell, we've come a long way from a dead trug-moldie, haven't we?'

'Haven't we just?' sang Abberline on a rising scale. Then, on a grim monotone, 'Hav-en't-we-just.'


Spratling had not been idle. As Abberline and I walked out into the rain that evening to continue our investigations on the streets, a constable splashed up to us and saluted. Water dribbled in a quicksilver chain from the peak of his cap. His cape puddered like a flag in a gale.

'Yes, constable?'

'Inspector Spratling says there's eight suspects in the old Army Drill Hall, Flowery Dean Street, sir. They're waiting for you to examine them.'

'Suspects?' Abberline snapped. 'What suspects? You pulling my leg, son?'

'N-no, sir.' The constable blinked pearled eyelashes. 'It's Mr Spratling's orders, sir. Sorry, sir.'

Abberline cast a despairing glance in my direction. 'All right,' he said gently. 'Lead on, son.'


Abberline shrugged his coat off and flung it down on the bench just inside the door. It steamed. I removed my bowler and regretfully smoothed the felt with my sleeve.

'Well?' Abberline glanced around the hall. It was dark and cavernous and cold. The rain beat a frenzied tattoo on the vaulted ceiling. Each time that the tattoo became faster and louder, the naphtha flares wavered and dimmed.

'Over here, sir.' The constable gestured. His boots squelched and his cape shed spangles as he led us over to the brick wall at the far end.

'Here you are, sir.'

Abberline's eyeballs slowly shifted from side to side, like bluebottles dying in a bottle. 'What the hell are these?' he hissed.

'Er, Mr Spratling's murder list, sir.'

'His – murder list?'

'Yes, sir.'

Abberline shook his head. 'God albleedinmighty.'

The eight men who slouched against the dark bricks had eyes only for the gleaming vat of soup in the far corner of the hall. There was a young lad with a topper, yellow hair and honey-coloured acne. He could not have weighed more than five stone. 'Evenin', Jan.' Abberline nodded to him.

'Evenin', Mr Abberline, sir.' The young man touched his forelock.

'But he's a dip, for Christ's sake!' Abberline muttered. 'We're looking for a murderer!'

The second man, a typical London beggar, sat hunched and trembling. He was somewhere between forty and Methuselah. He crooned and jabbered to himself. Saliva bubbles formed, grew and burst by the dry sores at the corner of his mouth. His hair was dark and thickly matted. His left eye stared fixedly at the floor, his right at the ceiling.

'And Charlie here is a mutcher.' The policeman indicated a big man with skin like risen dough.

'What?' Abberline struck his brow with the heel of his hand.

'A mutcher is a man who robs drunks, sir.'

'I know what a mutcher is, lad, but why's he here?'

'I donno.' The constable shrugged. 'He's on the murder list.'

'What in God's name is a murder list?'

'Well, we round them up, sir. Whenever there's a murder.'

'Always the same people?'

'Mostly, yes. Keeps the public happy, Mr Spratling says.'

'Yeah? And then what?'

'We let them go,' said the constable with a little nervous giggle. 'They don't mind, you know. Most of them volunteer.'

''Course they bleeding do,' Abberline said patiently. 'Most of them would sell their ballocks for a mug of soup.'

At that moment something that looked like an overgrown trout fly with a shaggy red hackle flung itself at Abberline's feet. What little was visible of skin beneath the whiskers was puce and scaly as though burned. 'I did it, sir.' The creature clutched at Abberline's trouser cuffs. 'As God is my witness. I did it. With my bare hands. These self-same soiled hands it was, sir. He was a Roman, sir, a filthy Roman spy in the pay of the accursed Pontius Pilate. He deserved to die as he did, pleading for mercy from the Almighty, but the Almighty, he says to me, "No, John. Show no quarter. Strike!" Take me, sir. Do with me what you will. I forgive you all.'

He released Abberline's trousers and prostrated himself, arms flung out wide, as though awaiting the descent of the axe.

'God almighty . . .' Abberline fastidiously stepped over the body. 'Give them the soup and let them go, son. Come on, George, we've got work to do.'

As we picked up our hats and coats, we heard the waffling and growling of a pack of animals released to feed. 'Get back there!' The constable's voice slapped at the ceiling beams. 'No! Stop that! Form a line! Come on, please? Form a line! . . .'


The rain had stopped. It was dark now. The wet pavements sounded like tissue paper beneath our boots. There were just two small gas lamps that made the street seem darker.

This may seem a paradox to those who never knew the age of gas, but, except on the big, well-lit thoroughfares such as the Embankment, gas lamps did not so much light the streets and alleys as cast small clouds of misty, milky light that served to make everything else seem darker by contrast. The shadows in doorways and narrow passages seemed deeper than if there had been no light at all.

Gaslight was diffuse. For all the candle power of, say, a crystal gasolier, the light seemed to evaporate only yards from its source. Only now, as the fizzing, clicking arc lights appeared before the grander houses and theatres, did we see that gas was in league with the dark.

We were constantly alert – I suppose, without realizing it. Every one of those dark doorways could hide a man with a knife in his hand and nothing to lose. Many of them did.

'Time to go round the pubs, George,' said Abberline, as we walked down towards Aldgate.

'I thought you weren't drinking.'

'Not me. You. Get your ear to the ground. Hang round the Britannia, the Ten Bells. Make yourself pleasant to some of the prozzies. See what they know. I'm going back to Buck's Row.'

'Think there's something to find?' I asked.

'Nah. Just thought I'd try a little experiment. See you later.'


The Britannia, on the corner of Dorset Street, was, quite simply, a typical East End public of the sort that admitted women (many others had a strict 'no ladies' rule). It was large and smoky and noisy. The mouldings at the ceiling were heavy and ornate, but already the red and gold paint was flaking. There was sawdust on the floor and engraving on the windows, and a man with a pipe plunked out an old Vance favourite on the piano while a large blonde woman sang:

> *The Stilton, sir, the cheese, the O K thing to do*
> *On Sunday afternoon, is to toddle to the zoo;*
> *Week-days may do for cads, but not for me and you,*
> *So dressed right down the road, we show 'em 'oo is 'oo. . .*

Everyone joined in a raucous, ragged chorus:

*The Walking in the zoo,*
*The Walking in the zoo,*
*The O K thing on Sunday is the*
*Walking in the zoo!*

I narrowed my eyes against the smoke, looking for a familiar face. There were several, and most of them were ugly, but one stood out from the rest: a fresh face, a young face, flushed with drink and a little on the plump side, but still animated and attractive. I strolled over, noting the way that the prismatic light from the gasolier glinted blue off her long black hair.

'Hello, Mary Jane.'

She looked up, wide-eyed. 'Well, hello dere!' Her Irish accent was soft. 'If it isn't Mr Devilish himself come to visit us. Sit yourself down and buy us a scoop. You know Fanny, don't you?'

'We've met, haven't we, Fanny?' I grinned at the gaunt, wild-eyed woman on the other side of the table. Her hair was dark and thin and spiky. There were absurd spots of rouge on her sunken white cheeks. She nervously bared a mouthful of jagged brown teeth.

I clicked my fingers at a pot-boy and sat. 'So, Mary Jane, how do?'

'Full of fuck and half starved, dear,' she said happily.

'Long time since your fair form graced Whitechapel. Where've you been?'

'Oh, here and there,' she replied airily. 'I've got meself a place in McCarthy's Rents.'

'Miller's Court?'

'Yeah. It's not exactly like the old days in the Haymarket, but a girl's got to live.'

'Here she goes again!' hooted Fanny. 'Haymarket my arse. More like a knock on a slab at Smithfield Market, if you ask me. Go on, Mary Jane, tell him about Paris while you're at it. It's the Irish talking,' she confided to me, 'full of piss and wind, the lot of 'em.'

'It's true, actually, and what'd you know, anyhow?' Mary Jane said casually. 'Beautiful this time of year, Paris. The music, the dancing. You think you've seen the cancan? Nothing like it. I saw it all. Gentleman took me over there for a while. I was an artist's model. Honest, whatever she says. Marie Jeanette, they called me. Posed for Mr Poynter. I did.'

'Go on, my tulip!' Fanny urged sarcastically. 'Good as a book, she is.'

'Of course, I didn't like Paris in the end.' Mary Jane cast a quick dismissive glance at Fanny. 'So I came back to London. Bad mistake, the whole thing. Come back broke to the wide. Before den, oh sure, I knew 'em all. Laura Bell, Skittles – "pretty horsebreakers" dey called 'em. Still at it, I make no doubt, respectable as can be and wedding earls and dukes and all. So I'll give yez a riddle, Mr Devilish, and good health to yez, and here's me riddle. What's the difference between a respectable duchess and a Whitechapel market-dame? Shall I tell yez? Love, dat's what. I could've been dere still, living the life of Riley, but oh, no. I had to get mashed on a fancy-bloke, and here I am, while dose who had more sense and kept deir minds on de job, dey're looking down deir noses and calling us Social Evils and praying for the welfare of our immortal souls. We're all of us sitting on the rent, Mr Devilish, one way or another, and it's a wise girl as never forgets it. Love's a scullion's luxury and dat's a fact.'

She supped her ale and wiped foam from her upper lip. 'And what are you doing?' She pointed accusingly at me. 'What are you doing about dis feller who carved Polly Nichols, I'd like to know?'

'Who says it's a feller?' I asked, just trying the idea out for size.

'What?' Mary Jane frowned, 'Ah, come on!'

'Well, it could be, couldn't it? One of your back-street abortionists that call themselves midwives, or a jealous wife crazed by the pox and out to get the girl who clapped her man. It's possible.'

'Nah!' Fanny sounded like a rocking ship's timbers.

'Get along wid yer.' Mary Jane smiled. 'Ye're a mivvy for the tall tale-telling, but ye'll not persuade me. No. I'll tell you what. You look out for the Jews. Good with a knife, dey are, and always chopping up animals in peculiar ways.'

'Funny about fucking, Jews.' Fanny nodded sagely. 'Got their meat and two veg just like other blokes, but they don't like to admit it.'

'Thanks for the tip.'

'Right, mister . . .' A hand fell on my shoulder. I stiffened. In my pocket, my right fist clenched. I could feel the man's hot breath on my ear and could smell his bitter sweat as he continued in a low voice. 'Time is money, mister. She's not cheap, but she used to be an acrobat.'

'Gawd save us,' Fanny sighed.

I reached up and removed the offensive hand. I turned as casually as I was able. The man was clean-shaven. He had a pug's spread nose, broad black bugger's grips and a mouth twisted in a permanent sneer. 'You wanted something?' I asked.

'Yeah, Johnnie, I wanted something. Come on, cull. These girls ain't in it for love. Make up yer mind. Which one d'ye fancy? You can have the dewey if you've got the dinarlee. Bionk peroon. Whaddye say?'

'Bleeding cheek!' Fanny squawked. 'You don't run Mary, does he love?'

'Not fucking likely,' Mary Jane sniffed. 'What'd I want with the likes of him? I've got me own letty, I'll have ye know.'

'Oh yeah? Well, she'll need a protector. You'll all need protectors, the way things are going.'

'Protector!' Fanny smirked. 'What *things* are you talking about?'

'I hope you never find out, that's all,' said the pimp with a knowing leer.

I frowned. 'Find out about what?'

'I'm not talking to you.'

'No.' I pushed back my chair and stood. He was the same size as me. His brown eyes were dead. It was like looking into a mirror and seeing no reflection. 'I am talking to you. What do you mean, you hope she'll never find out?'

'There's a smell in here . . .' the pimp said without opening his mouth. He backed away.

'Hey. I asked you a question,' I barked. 'Find out about *what*?'

'Sod off.' The pimp turned and moved off towards the door.

It took me two quick strides to catch up with him. I grabbed his collar and pushed. 'Right. Outside. You and I are going to have a little talk.'

'Take your hands off me.' The oily, easy voice was suddenly hard as a single piano note played again and again. With no soft pedal. 'Or you'll be coughing up teeth.'

I should have got a proper grip on him. Suddenly his elbow hit me hard in the stomach and he wrenched free. His hand reached out to a table on his right. Something smashed. The people at the table leaped up and stepped back to the walls. The pimp turned, crouched. His nose tugged up his upper lip. In his hand the jagged edges of a broken brown bottle gave off a phosphorescent light, like oil on the Thames.

'Now that,' I said through my teeth, 'is a big mistake.'

'Gerrout,' the pimp growled. 'Scarper, cull, while you still gorra face.'

There was silence then save for the pimp's fast breathing and the soft hiss of the gas. Then a woman's voice from behind me called, 'Get him!' and the crowd came to life again. There were whistles and hisses. Something soft and damp hit my cheek. I vaguely realized that it was a pig of an orange. Someone shoved me in the small of my back. I did not turn. I just stared at the bottle, then at those blank brown eyes.

'What's the matter, reeler?' the pimp hissed. 'No guts?'

'That's right,' I said softly. 'That's right.' Out of the corner of my eye, I saw the landlord hefting a vicious-looking knobkerrie.

'Come on, then.' The pimp grinned. He feinted with the bottle. 'What are you waiting for Joh . . .'

That's when I moved. The bottle shot up too late. My left hand grasped the wrist. My right knee jerked upward, hard and fast. He bent forward to avoid it. My right forearm smashed into his already smashed nose. I got him a good one in the stomach, but his right hand still strained against mine. If he could just get that bottle free . . .

The crowd had exploded into jeers, shouts of encouragement and jovial obscenities. I swung the pimp round by his right arm, curled my left leg around his, raised my knee to the elbow and pulled, hard. He let out a howl as much of fury and frustration as of pain. Those eyes rolled upward. The bottle dropped from his hand and rolled.

'All right,' I panted. The man's greasy hair was against my mouth. The smell of his sweat was strong. His body had sagged and was shaking violently. Little whipcrack whimpers seeped from his sneering mouth. 'All right, son. You want to keep the other arm, you come with me nice and quiet and we have a little chat like I said in the first place. Come on.'

I half pulled, half carried him to the door. Behind me the crowd booed and hissed, but it seemed that he didn't have friends good enough to come to his aid. At the doorstep, I gave him one extra hard shove. He fell forward through the door and collapsed like a stringless puppet on the wet Dorset Street pavement.

'Who's he, then?'

I pushed the hair back off my brow and frowned at the darkness on the opposite side of the street. Abberline detached himself from the wall and strolled into the light from the pub windows.

'I dunno,' I said, gulping air, 'but I'm taking the little bastard in.' Then I thought. 'Wait a minute,' I said. It came out as a squeak. 'How long have you been there?'

'Long enough.' Abberline smiled. 'I looked in, matter of fact, but you seemed to be doing all right.' He looked down at the pimp who clutched his broken arm and keened. 'Hello, Billy.'

'I – I didn't know he was one of yourn, Mr Abberline.' The pimp drew up his legs and did his best to look appealing. He needed practice. 'Honest I didn't.'

The piano started up in the pub once again. 'But *you're* one of mine, ain't you, Billy boy?' Abberline soothed.

'I don't know nuffink, Mr Abberline. I was just trying to scare the girls. I'd tell you if I knew somefink, honest I would.'

'Oh, yes, Billy boy, you'd tell me, all right. Nothing more certain. And now you're short one arm. Teach you to be a little more polite, won't it? Come on, George. We'll pick him up tomorrow if we need him.'

We turned away and walked slowly down the street. The noise from the pub faded, but even at the far end of the street we could hear occasional outbursts of laughter.

'One of your noses, was he?' I said, still out of breath and a trifle aggrieved.

'And his father before him,' Abberline said smoothly. 'Still, you needed the exercise.' He was silent for a minute, then, 'There's something wrong, George.'

'What?'

'Nobody heard her scream. I went along there tonight. Buck's Row. I dropped some soldi on the pavement. Just a few pennies. Within seconds, there was a face at every window. There's at least eight families living opposite. Nobody heard a dicky-bird.'

'Yeah, well.' I shrugged. 'That's Whitechapel. Hear no evil, speak no evil. Even with murder.'

'You're teaching your grandam to grope ducks,' Abberline nodded. 'But – I dunno. There's something wrong about the

67

whole thing. I just get this feeling. This isn't just murder. It's something – well, it *feels* – like something bigger.'

We may have begun to feel that we were engaged in a futile hunt, but the newspapers gave us no let-up. The following morning the *Star* had a new angle. QUEEN'S MEDIUM SEES KILLER, it declared. Beneath, it recounted that, at the instigation of your ever vigilant, crusading newspaper, Mr Robert James Lees had gone to see the famous American actor Robert Mansfield playing Jekyll and Hyde at the Lyceum theatre.

Of course, we had heard of Mansfield's performance. Everyone in London had. The scene in which he was transformed from the gentle doctor into the maniacal monster Hyde was a celebrated *coup de théâtre*. In full view of the audience, so it was said, everything about him changed. His face became unrecognizable. His voice, his gait, his mannerisms – even his size, it seemed – appeared to be transmuted. Women were said to have fainted at the sight, men to have shouted defiant abuse at the monster. Lees, reported Mr Benjamin Bates, had been deeply affected by the resemblance between this performance and his earlier vision of the killer.

Abberline summoned Lees to the station.

'So.' He paced before the nervous medium. 'What's all this about *Jekyll and Hyde*, Mr Lees?'

'I told you,' Lees puffed, 'two faces. A killer with two faces. It's him.'

'But *Jekyll and Hyde* is a fiction, Mr Lees. There is no Dr Jekyll. There is no Mr Hyde. There was a very real dead harlot on Buck's Row.'

'No, no, you don't understand.' Lees leaned forward, his big hands scratching at his thighs. 'The *actor*! You must see the actor! It's my vision, to the life. You must come to the theatre, I beg you. Come and see for yourself. I know you think I'm mad, but . . .'

68

'No, no.' Abberline smiled consolingly. 'It's interesting, isn't it, Sergeant Godley?'

'Fascinating.' I nodded obediently.

'We'll come to the theatre if you like,' Abberline said, perching on the corner of his desk, 'if you really think that we would find it instructive. But – keep it to yourself, all right?'

'You're afraid of mockery.' Lees smiled. 'I've lived with it all my life, inspector. What people don't understand, they try to destroy . . .' He paused, then his eyes grew suddenly bright. 'They're trying to destroy you, inspector,' he said softly. 'Aren't they?'

The corner of Abberline's lips twitched. He looked away. 'Well, thank you, Mr Lees,' he said, too lightly. 'We are always interested in anything that might lead us to the killer, however . . . out of the ordinary. I wish you good day.'

When Lees had left, Abberline sat stock still, frowning for a minute or more. 'Is that it?' he said slowly. 'Is that the aim?'

'Ah, come on, governor,' I laughed. 'You can't take all this hocus-pocus seriously.'

'No, but hold on a moment.' Abberline held up a hand. 'Maybe it is in someone's interest to have us fail in this case. All the publicity. The evidence covered up or washed away. Think, George. Our Chief Commissioner is a thoroughly unpopular man, right?'

'Yes.'

'Unpopular with the public and the Home Secretary and Assistant Commissioner Anderson, right?'

'Yes.'

'Well, now. If we fail in this case and the publicity goes on like this – London's police out of control, undisciplined, ill equipped and so on – Commissioner Warren's position would become untenable. Anderson would step into his place. It is possible. You'll admit that.'

'Yes, it's possible,' I agreed. 'It's also possible that the Queen killed Mary Ann Nichols. I don't believe it, that's all.'

'And there's another thing. If Warren goes and we're all left looking stupid, the whole autonomy of the Metropolitan police will go. They've been trying to place us under the control of this London County Council as it is.'

'No, Fred,' I said firmly. 'You're letting this thing run away with you. This is a murder case. That's all. Some maniac is out there with a knife and a down on trollops. It's happened before. It'll happen again. I admit that there have been odd things in this case. I'll even admit that maybe some people are not being overly helpful to our investigation and wouldn't mind if we were to fail, but I will not believe that the powers that be are all involved in a big conspiracy. Neither Mary Ann Nichols, nor we, are important enough.'

'No.' Abberline closed his eyes and slowly nodded. 'No. You may be right.' He flung himself into his chair. 'You may be right, George.' He pulled open the top right-hand drawer of his desk and pulled out a full bottle of whisky. I just sat still and watched, expressionless.

Abberline licked his lips and stared at the bottle. 'Oh, damn it,' he said quietly. 'You don't get me as easy as that.'

He grinned and shoved the bottle firmly back into the drawer.


'And now to settle what remains. Think before you answer, Lanyon, for it shall be done as you decide. If you say yes, a new province of knowledge and power will be laid open to you. Here, in this room, upon the instant . . .'

Richard Mansfield had a voice that resounded through a great theatre, then resounded through your skull long after he had finished speaking. He was small and sturdy, yet somehow contrived to persuade you that he was tall and elegant. His movements were quick but always graceful.

I had started by appraising Mansfield with a trained police-man's eye, registering details of his appearance – the broad high forehead, the finely cropped hair, jutting jaw, broad shoulders and athletic figure. I rapidly discovered, however, that I could read nothing of his character in his mannerisms. He revealed nothing of himself, everything of Dr Jekyll. I would not have liked to interrogate this man. He could readily have convinced me that he was a monster, a saint or even a woman if he chose.

A few moments later, I had stopped thinking like a policeman at all. I am no theatre-goer as a rule. The Sod's Opera or the Old Mo are more in my line, but the fine, majestic music that rolled from Mansfield's lips would have stirred the seven sleepers. Now, as the transformation scene approached, I sat on the edge of my seat with the best of them. Abberline looked cooler than me, but his eyes, too, glittered and never left the man at the centre of the stage, who poured foaming liquid from a phial into a glass.

'. . . your sight shall be blasted by a prodigy to stagger Satan himself.'

'I have gone too far to pause before the end,' the actor playing Lanyon intoned.

'Very well,' snapped Mansfield – Jekyll. 'You – who have denied the virtues of transcendental medicine, you, who have derided your superiors . . . behold!'

Mansfield drank.

For a long moment, nothing happened. Mansfield stared out at the house with wide white eyes. Then his hands trembled and formed claws. A great shudder shook his shoulders. He reeled, steadied himself, reeled again. A deep, rumbling growl forced its way up from deep within him, and suddenly he was shrieking – a mighty, shrilling, shivering, purely animal sound like a hare's scream amplified many times.

What followed was among the most extraordinary and dis-comfiting sights that I have ever seen. Before our eyes, Mans-field was transformed. His eyes seemed to bulge until they threatened to burst. His mouth twisted and drooped. His tongue lolled. By some bewilderingly ingenious trickery, his very hair seemed to have grown.

He snarled at the audience, and something about the man made each of us feel that he was snarling at us alone. Several women yelped. Several men rose to their feet.

I turned to Abberline. He frowned deeply. He shook his head very slowly. His mouth was puckered in a silent whistle of admiration and incredulity.

Lees's point was well made. We had just seen a man turning into a monster.


'Mr Mansfield sees no one after a performance.' The dresser, a very thin little man, with smooth sandy stoat's hair and a stoat's sharp nose, shifted from foot to foot before the dressing-room door. 'Never. He's overwrought after a performance. It's always the same with talent. Dressed Irving once, I did, and he was the same. Total collapse after a show. Total.'

'He'll see us,' said Abberline.

'I've asked him and he says no, not even if you were the Prince of Wales. Sorry, gents, but you'll have to leave . . . Hey!' he trilled. I pushed him aside with a straight arm and threw open the door. 'You can't go in there! No! Ooh!'

We ignored him. Abberline swept in. I followed and slammed the door behind me. The dresser pounded and whimpered.

Abberline stopped so suddenly that I bumped into him.

The dressing-room was a plain square cell of shiny pale blue that looked grey in the lamplight. Mansfield sat in his vest before a large mirror. His face was streaked with white cream. The muscles at his shoulders were cabochon stones, his spine like twisted rope. The smell of paraffin cut the thicker, meadow-sweet aroma of grease-paint.

In the corner, her sketch-book now laid on her lap, sat a

woman. Her pencil was raised in a childish gesture to the corner of her mouth. It was Abberline who had caused it to spring there. It was she who had made Abberline so suddenly to stop. I knew her. Abberline knew her somewhat better.

'Who the devil are you?' Mansfield thumped the littered dressing-table. Sticks of grease-paint spurted across its surface. He stood and turned, those round hard shoulders lowered. 'John!' he called. Then, 'Leave this room at once, or I'll call the police.'

'I am the police, Mr Mansfield,' said Abberline casually. He turned to the woman in the corner. 'Emma.' He nodded.

'Hello, Frederick.'

Mansfield glanced quickly from one to the other. 'Oh, isn't this cosy! So you know each other.'

'Richard . . .' Emma stood. The rustle of her long green evening-gown seemed very loud. 'I should go.'

'No!' cried Mansfield, exasperated. 'I ordered supper!'

'Please forgive me.' Her eyelids drooped. 'I really am very tired.'

Mansfield sank back into his chair. His mouth was a thin straight slit. 'Very well,' he said huffily, 'but I wanted to see your sketch.'

'I'll leave it here, and collect it in the morning. Good night, Richard . . . Frederick,' she murmured. I held the door open for her. She looked up at me. She frowned quickly, then smiled her recognition. 'Thank you, Sergeant Godley.'

Her teeth flashed. Her hair gave off a glimmer like a racer's rump. The scent of violets made a pleasant change. Something tickled my tonsils as I closed the door behind her. I had forgotten how beautiful she was.

'All right,' barked Mansfield. 'I've had enough of this. What in hell is all this about?'

'We would merely be grateful if you could assist us in our investigations.' Abberline sat in the chair that Emma had just left. I stood with my back to the door.

'Investigations into what?'

'A murder.'

'Oh, for Christ's sake!' Mansfield turned back to the mirror and resumed the greasing of his face. 'That damned clairvoyant didn't say that I was the murderer. All he said was what I do out there is just like what he saw in his visions, that's all. He dreamed of a guy who turned into a monster. I play that part. Later this year I play Richard III. Am I to expect you guys round every time a child gets killed?'

'No, Mr Mansfield.' Abberline thudded. 'What I'd like to know is just what goes through your mind as you make that transformation.'

'What?' Mansfield laughed. 'You come barging in here, demanding to know how I turn into Hyde? Half the actors in the world would give their right arm to know that.' He pointed flamboyantly to the door. 'Out.'

Abberline studied his nails, unmoved. 'We are conducting a police inquiry, Mr Mansfield, and Mr Lees has been very helpful to us in the past. He was very startled by the resemblance between your monster and his vision. Do you want us roasting you brown until we are satisfied that you are being a good boy?'

Mansfield nodded. 'All right. For what it's worth. I observe and I imitate. Over and over until I become the character I want to be. What else would I do?'

'You play a doctor, so you observe doctors. Is that right?'

'Bravo.'

'And the other one – Hyde? How do you create a creature like that?'

'Same technique.'

'Observe. Maniacs?'

'Yes. Well, people I feel could be . . . would be . . . people from that sort of world.'

'Rumour has it that you like to visit the stews of the East End. Is that in the spirit of research, Mr Mansfield?'

'Yes. That sort of thing. Partly. Where do you get these rumours?'

'It's our business,' sang Abberline. 'So? Is this Hyde of yours someone that you met on one of these little sprees?'

'He's several people,' said Mansfield wearily. 'A criminal I met in New York gave me the voice, a man here in London was responsible for the face . . .'

'The face that Lees saw?' said Abberline sharply. 'In the East End?'

Mansfield rubbed his face vigorously with a small white towel. His eyes emerged above it. He remained like that, the towel over his nose and mouth, staring defiantly at Abberline in the mirror. 'I don't have to answer these questions,' he said.

'Yes, you do,' Abberline said mildly. 'When did you last see this man, this real Hyde? Last month? Last week?'

'I don't keep a diary.' Mansfield was uncomfortable.

'Or last Friday, perhaps?'

Mansfield pulled on his shirt. 'Exactly what are you trying to say, inspector?'

'Our woman was killed last Friday night. If your Mr Hyde was in the East End at the time, I'd be fascinated to meet him. So, seeing as you have no supper engagement tonight, why don't you come along and introduce us, hmm, Mr Mansfield?'

Mansfield muttered several curses that sounded unfamiliar but nasty. He was not a happy man.


We stood waiting at the stage door while Mansfield finished dressing. It was a mild night, and only a few clouds shifted across the moon like a veil.

'What are you playing at, governor?' I asked Abberline. 'I mean, it seems we're here 'cos of a loony clairvoyant's visions and a good acting job. Not exactly standard police procedure.'

'Nope.'

'You don't really think Mansfield has anything to do with it?'

'Dunno. He's a toff who likes low-life. That's all. He's strong, and ... who knows how far he'd take his research? It's possible.'

'Bleeding unlikely, if you ask me.'

'Maybe. But we're not wasting time. Like I said, he's a toff who likes low-life. You, me, we're out of date. God knows what delightful new diversions Whitechapel can offer to the curious. Mansfield's gonna show us. He's our guide. Ah! Mr Mansfield,' he effused. 'How kind of you to assist us. Come. Let's seek a Hyde.'

Mansfield did not seem to be in the mood for jokes. He brushed between us and into the hansom without a word.

'Are you certain this time?' Abberline droned sarcastically. It was two in the morning now.

'Yes. Yes. I recognize the door.'

'You said that last time.'

'Yes, well.' The actor flapped his hands. 'There are so many of them.'

'And you've visited them all?' Abberline raised his eyebrows. 'You do keep busy. Come on, then.' He reached across me and threw open the cab door.

We climbed out into the dingy street. The gaslight made the brick houses seem pale grey. It cast deep, guillotine blade shadows across the cobbles. It caught the few wispy strands of mist that stretched and floated like gossamer from one side of the street to the other. In the doorways further down the street, you could see the occasional strange shadow or the soft glow of some fabric as it protruded into the light. The girls were there, waiting for custom. Abberline hammered loudly on the door indicated by Mansfield. 'And you say he'll recognize you?' he checked with Mansfield as the echoes died.

'He, or the girls will.'

'Ah, yes.' Abberline nodded. 'The girls.'

'Women often *do* remember me, inspector,' the actor bridled, 'and I'm tired of these endless remarks. Sure, I'm an active man alone in a big city. So what's so strange about that? If I'm under any sort of suspicion, you just say so and have done with it, but let me remind you, I'm not just anyone. I'm a friend of royalty . . .'

Shuffling footfalls drew nearer. A bolt was drawn. The door opened just a crack. 'That's him!' Mansfield pointed. 'That's the man!'

I had raised my foot to kick the door before I even noticed that it was closing again. So had Abberline. Our boots struck the wood at the same moment.

There was a loud clatter as the door swung in. 'Ow, you fucker!' squawked someone from inside.

'Language, Rodman, language.' Abberline bent and pulled the man up. 'This is a friend of royalty, I'll have you know.'

'Oh, bloody hell,' the man moaned. 'It's Abberline. Thought you was dead.'

'No such luck, Rodman. Surprised you still know me.'

'I never forget a voice, Mr Abberline.'

Abberline swung the man round and pushed him down the narrow, unplastered corridor. He stood him up against the wall beneath a naphtha flare. 'This your man, Mansfield?' He turned the man's face round.

I took a rapid step backward.

The man, who could not have been more than forty, was very seriously ugly. His jaw pushed forward like that of an ape. His tongue seemed too large for his mouth and hung, spittle-coated, from between his teeth. His bulbous bright red nose appeared to grow sideways rather than forwards. What hair he had sprouted in random little clumps from his scalp, like twitch-grass on a rubbish tip. His neck was not a neck but a vast purple

77

swelling, broader than his face at its broadest point. Had a fisherman pulled this creature from the depths of the Atlantic Ocean and exhibited it as the missing link between fish and man, I would have found it less surprising than to see him walking and talking and running an East End flophouse. John Merrick, the Elephant Man, resided only three hundred yards away in Whitechapel Hospital. I had never seen him, but even he, I felt, would have won a bathing belles contest with Rodman.

'Yes.' Mansfield's voice was less assured now. 'Yes, this is the man. Good evening,' he said with characteristic New World old-worldliness. 'We've never spoken, but I was here last Friday. You remember me, of course.'

Abberline shook his head. Very gently, he placed his finger and thumb at the spot where a chin should have been, and pushed the face further upward towards the flare.

The eyes cast back the light like cloudy moonstones.

'Not your lucky day, Mansfield.' Abberline released the man. 'Rodman is stone blind. Let's hope you're right about the women, shall we? Foreign girl,' he said sharply to Rodman. 'Name of Anna? Anneka? Does a duet.'

'There'sh a genn'leman in, Misher Abberline,' drooled Rodman.

'Well, we'll have to get him out, won't we?'

Abberline trotted up the stairs. I pushed Mansfield after him. Abberline did not even check his pace at the first-floor landing. He just opened the door and strolled in.

Have you ever looked at a medieval cathedral and thought how it must have seemed to the peasants of the time? Those vast towering buildings, peopled with a pantheon of carved figures, filled with brilliant colour from the stained-glass windows, must have seemed proof positive that God existed and halfway to heaven itself. No man who dwelled in daub and wattle could have constructed so rich and so mighty an edifice.

The room into which now we stepped must have had some-

78

thing of the same effect on young girls when first they came here. This was luxury greater than a Mary Ann Nichols, for example, could ever have imagined. Any twelve-year-old girl who had seen this, and been offered it in exchange for a little not unpleasant labour on her back, would have been hard put to it to tolerate a sweated life of finishing gents' trousers, button-holes, buttons and all, for twopence apiece.

Here, a lazy girl could be a princess.

The walls were covered in deep-red flock. There were large gilt mirrors and chairs that glittered in the light from an ornate gasolier at the centre of the room. A half-full bottle of champagne stood on a marble-topped table beneath an oil painting of ancient gods and goddesses behaving in an ungodly manner. The carpet was thick, the rugs of silk.

On a huge brass bed, one girl, who might have been fourteen, yapped and cowered beneath the sheets as we entered. The other – older, naked, blonde and heavy breasted – could not immediately do so. She first had to raise herself off the plump, grey-haired man beneath her, who bore no resemblance to the gods in the picture, but was doing his best.

She did so, and turned to face us without shame.

'Evenin', milord,' said Abberline. 'Warm night.'

'Um,' said the man. 'Er, excuse me, um . . .' He snatched up his tailcoat, his white shirt and tie and, clutching them to his genitals and bent almost double, rushed red-faced for the door.

I let him go. I knew who he was. So did half of Whitechapel.

'Which of you is Anneka?' demanded Abberline.

'I am Annette,' said the blonde girl, still making no attempt to cover herself.

'Ever seen this man before?' Abberline indicated Mansfield. 'No need to be frightened.'

'Non,' said Annette, who allowed her eyes to linger lustfully on each of us in turn. 'I never seen him.'

Mansfield smiled slowly. He reached up and fumbled with

something at his brow. I knew a split second of terror as I saw the hair – the whole scalp – arising from his skull, then I realized, and sighed my relief: some sort of actor's hairpiece or wig.

'Ah!' The girl's eyes lit up. 'Dixie!'

'Well, good ole Dixie,' Abberline droned. 'How many more layers can you pull off, Mansfield? When do we get to the real Richard Mansfield?'

Mansfield ignored him. His eyes flickered appreciatively over the girl's body. 'I was here last Friday,' he croaked, 'around eleven. You said it was your birthday, right?'

'Oh, yes,' the girl purred, 'but how could I forget?'

'How long did he stay?' Abberline coaxed. 'Last Friday. How long?'

'All night.' Annette shrugged. 'Sometimes Monique was sleeping. Sometimes I was sleeping. *Il est épuisant, celui-là.*'

'All right.' Mansfield nodded smugly. 'And that, inspector, is why girls remember me. I gave you a present, Annette. Do you still have it?'

The girl lay back casually, revealing what had hitherto been hidden in her lap. I licked my lips and looked up at the ceiling.

'This, you mean?' She held up her right hand. A ring gleamed dully on the middle finger. 'You say it is gold. Now it is green. *Salaud pris de merde.*'

Abberline grinned happily. 'Or perhaps that's why they remember you. Goodnight, Mr Mansfield.'

Mansfield gritted his teeth and flounced from the room, for all the world like a dowager affronted by a fart. We wished the girls goodnight and followed slowly.

'You take the cab, George,' Abberline told me as we stepped on to the street again. 'Get back round the pubs. I need to think.'

I wondered how much licence I would be permitted. 'You wouldn't be thinking about a certain young lady at the theatre tonight? Emma Prentice?'

'See you tomorrow, George.'

'Don't get caught up again, Fred,' I begged. 'She's trouble. You know she is . . . Last time, she almost . . .' But Abberline was out of earshot and walking briskly. I cursed and sighed and muttered 'bloody fool' several times as I climbed back into the cab. As I did so, I saw a hansom, further down the street. A man's arm emerged from it, then half of a face in profile. Mansfield. A woman in a long black jacket emerged from the shadows, smiling. She took the proffered hand and climbed up into the cab. The door closed. The driver whipped up his horses.

I turned back, to see if Abberline had seen, but he was still walking away. Just as he was about to round the corner, I saw something glint in his right hand. He raised the something to his lips and tipped back his head. The moonlight painted a slippery sheen on his nose, his closed eyelids, the silver hip-flask.


It was half past six. The sun was up. I was thinking of home and just nodding off to the peaceful motion of the cab when suddenly there was a jolt that made the back of the seat hit me hard. I supported myself with one hand and called up to the driver, 'What the hell is . . .'

The door was thrown open. I blinked, bemused, at the brightness of a police lantern outside. A hand reached in and grabbed my wrist. A voice that I vaguely recognized said, 'Out. You. Out of the cab! Now!'

I stumbled out. The lantern swung to one side. P C Wensley's face emerged from the darkness, then receded, emerged, receded. 'What the bloody hell do you think you're doing, Wensley?' I demanded.

'Oh, sorry, sarge,' Wensley said without the least trace of sincerity. 'We've been told to stop everyone in the area. There's been another one in Hanbury Street.'

'What?' I said stupidly.

'And it's worse, this one, by all accounts. Kerby saw her and threw up his accounts.'

'Get me there,' I said, suddenly awake. 'Quickly.'

# METROPOLITAN POLICE
# CRIMINAL INVESTIGATION DEPARTMENT
# SCOTLAND YARD

Central Officers
Special Report

Subject Hanbury
Street murder of
*ANNIE CHAPMAN*

I beg to report that the following are the facts respecting the murder of ANNIE CHAPMAN on 8 September at 29 Hanbury Street. 6 am, 8 September 1888. The body of a woman was discovered in the backyard of Hanbury Street, Spitalfields, by John Davies of that address who immediately informed the police, and Dr Phillips the divisional surgeon was sent for, who stated that in his opinion death had taken place *two or three hours*. Examination of the body showed that the throat was severed deeply, incision *jagged*. Removed from but attached to the body and placed above right shoulder were a flap of the wall of the belly, the whole of the small intestines and attachments. Two other portions of wall of belly and 'pubes' were placed above left shoulder in a large quantity of blood. Abrasion of head of first phalanx of ring finger, distinct marking of ring or rings, probably the latter on proximal phalanx of same finger. The following parts were missing: part of belly wall including naval [*sic*], the *womb*, the *upper part of vagina* and greater part of *bladder*. The doctor gives it as his opinion that the murderer was possessed of anatomical knowledge from the manner of removal of viscera and that the knife used was not an ordinary knife, but such as a small amputating knife, or a well-ground slaughter-man's knife, narrow and thin, sharp and blade of six to eight inches in length.

9 September the body was identified as that of ANNIE

Annie Chapman was a bruiser. She was five foot tall, forty-seven years old, thick-set and plain as a yard of pump water.

In her life, she had been anybody's. Now she was all mine. No one, had she had such a thing, would have attended her funeral, yet a thousand lives had touched hers and had made her who and what she was. She, no doubt, directly or indirectly, had affected many more – her husband, her children, her fellow-whores, those with whom she fought, those with whom she drank, her clients, their wives, their children – many thousands of people, of whom perhaps ten would remember her by name and none would miss her.

To me, had I seen her on the streets, she would have been just another ugly face, another still-sow on the game. Now, thanks to a nameless butcher with a long knife, I was to come to know her better – or know more about her, at least – than any man alive.

Annie Chapman, a sharp, intelligent woman, had once been married, and to a skilled and intelligent man at that. Veterinarians were not so highly prized or paid as today, when they are regarded as nigh professional people. Back in the eighties, they were little more than experienced head lads or livery-men. John Chapman had none the less shown the bottom and the acquisitiveness to bob to the top of his class.

He had a sizeable military pension that he supplemented by working as a coachman. He and Annie lived in the shadow of the castle at Windsor. They had a son and a daughter. The son was a cripple. The daughter, so they say, was living in an institution in France.

Gin had been Mary Ann's problem. Rum was Annie's. She must have craved the stuff. In 1884 her increasingly dissolute habits brought about her separation from her elderly respectable husband. He paid her an allowance of ten shillings a week, but she none the less flung herself headlong down the primrose path. Hers was no gradual degeneration from respectable married life to drunken whoredom. With what looks like a desire for damnation, she moved at once from the fresh air and stillness of the royal borough to the stinking stews and common lodging-houses of Spitalfields and Whitechapel.

I rapidly conjured a picture of Annie's more than usually complex nature. Ever aware of her former standing, her intelligence and her seniority to the sillier, more attractive chits who surrounded her, yet ever driven by her bewildering addiction, she bullied, browbeat, grumbled and sneered like a demented hospital matron.

Nobody liked Annie much. Her temper was too volatile, her conviction of her own superiority too marked, her disdain for human weakness and human passion too evident. I spoke to some of the men who had used her. They recalled the incidents with no pleasure. No one went to Whitechapel looking for love, but a degree of courtesy always helps. Annie was the kind who would look bored and scornful throughout, ask, 'Have yer done, then?' in a bored tone, lower her skirts and go on her way without another word.

Not that she did not have her gentlemen friends, to whom, no doubt, she showed some greater courtesy. Two years ago, she was living in Dorset Street with a sievemaker (in consequence of which several witnesses identified her as 'Sievey' or 'Siffy'), and, for the past few weeks at least, she had regularly spent the weekend in the Dorset Street lodging-house with one Edward Stanley, significantly known as 'The Pensioner', a smoked fish of a man who claimed to have been in the Essex Regiment and who spun a good yarn about his experiences fighting the fuzzy wuzzy.

Last Saturday evening, all the gossip in the dormitory at

85

35 Dorset Street had been about the murder of Mary Ann Nichols.

'Wadde wanna pick her for?' Amelia Farmer sounded almost affronted. 'Ugly as sin and always full to the bungs, she was.'

'Don't worry, doll,' said another woman, shovelling broken biscuits into her mouth as she talked. 'You just hang about and I'm sure you'll get your chance.'

'Slit her, they say, all the way up.' Eliza Cooper flapped a plain grey blanket above the fourpenny single. She was a fair-skinned, freckled redhead of thirty-six, thirty-seven. 'I'm not going out there tonight, I'll tell you. Done a couple of dog's rigs in daylight, and I've got me dook for tonight. That'll do me.'

'Not me.' Amelia sighed. 'Got nants for the dook and me stomach thinks me throat's been cut.'

'May be right before the night's out,' cackled an old man already in bed at the far end of the room.

'Nah.' Amelia brightened. 'There's enough of us to go round. I'll be all right. Whole area's crawling with reelers, anyhow. Safe as houses out there.'

Heavy footsteps sounded on the stairs. Annie Chapman appeared at the open door. 'Anyone got any soap?' she asked. 'The Pensioner wants a wash.'

There was a lot of shaking of heads. 'Ask Liza.' Amelia nodded at Eliza Carter, who was undoing her bodice. 'She's got all the soldi round these parts.'

Annie waddled up the aisle of beds. 'Excuse me,' she said with refinement. 'You haven't got a bit of soap for the Pensioner, have you? Pay you back.'

Eliza laid off her bodice. 'Yeah, all right,' she sighed and opened her locker. She fished out a bar of carbolic. 'But it's called Pete, right?'

'Yeah, of course,' said Annie huffily, her dignity affronted by the very suggestion that she might do anything dishonest. 'You'll get it back. Don't know what you're worried about.' She strutted a little as she left, but Eliza noticed that she had to support herself on one of the beds on her way out.

Ten minutes later, Annie returned, this time with the Pensioner in tow. He wore baggy trousers and a flannel vest. His braces hung looped at his waist. He was a strange fellow, the Pensioner. His eyes were pale porcelain blue, his skin creased and tanned. He walked, like Arnold, with his chest thrust out, only he did not have much chest to thrust. His thin arms swung at his sides. 'Hello, girls,' he said briskly.

A desultory chorus of 'hellos' answered him.

'Filthy business about this Nichols woman, eh? Met her a couple of times. Pity. Like to get hold of the bugger who done it. I'd show him a thing or two.'

'That's right, dear,' Annie laid a chubby hand on his naked forearm. 'Come on, let's get down the carsey. I need a drink.'

'Right, yeah.' The Pensioner buttoned his shirt and carefully tied a red scarf around his neck. 'Tell you what.' He reached into his pocket. 'You take this down to the deputy for the bed. Two nights. Time you're finished, I'll be all ready.' He handed Annie a florin.

She smiled broadly and turned to leave, the coin clutched tightly in her hand. 'Here, Annie!' called Eliza from her bed.

'Yeah?'

'What about that soap, then?'

'Don't worry,' Annie sang. 'I'll see you by and by.'

That night the Pensioner and Annie returned rolling drunk and singing. The springs of their eightpenny double creaked for five or ten minutes, then fell silent. Annie was still contentedly snoring through her flat nose when Eliza left in the early morning.

It would be Wednesday before they met again, this time in the lodging-house kitchen. Again Eliza demanded the return of her soap. Annie, who had already had a few drinks, played Lady Muck. 'Here.' She stood and contemptuously flung a halfpenny bit on the floor at Eliza's feet. 'I have no desire to spend my time arguing about anything so trivial with the likes of you. If it's so important to you, go and buy ha'pence worth and good riddance.'

Colour rose into Eliza's pale cheeks. Her eyes grew bright. 'Who the fuck you think you are?' she demanded. 'What are you on about, the likes of me? Something so high and mighty about being a plain old farting crone, is there?'

'I'm not going to listen to this.' Annie turned away and walked to the door. 'You're no more than a poxy skin-the-pizzle, best of times. Silly cow,' she murmured, and slammed the door behind her.

'Filthy *bitch*!' shrieked Eliza. She too stood and – remembering first to pick up the halfpenny – rushed off in pursuit.

She caught up with Annie at the door of the Ringers public house. She grabbed her by the shoulder, but Annie wrenched free. 'Piss off, pinchgut,' she snarled. She bustled into the public. She nodded with grotesque graciousness to people whom she knew or imagined that she knew.

'But by then I'd got my shirt out proper,' Eliza told me. 'I mean, how dare she? Coming the nob with me! I've never been near a workhouse in me life! Never have, never will. She was in and out of them like the old thing you have at a wedding, and there she was lardy-dah-ing it over me! I grabs her again and she turns round with that ugly old face all sort of crinkled up like a sea-boot, and she clouts me across the chops. "Think yourself lucky I don't do more," she says, all snooty. Well, I let go the painter, didn't I? Got her a beauty on the left eye and another to the old bawd's dugs, and a couple of kicks as well. Ooh, she didn't half squeal! Well, when I saw the bruises on the poor old totty's carcase, and her with her grumble and grunt all ripped out, I thought, my gawd, you know? I done that – the bruises, I mean. Mind, if it hadn't been for Harry the Hawker, who dragged me off her, I reckon as I'd have killed her and saved your murderer the trouble.'

Annie was already, to quote the coroner, 'far advanced in disease of the lung and the membranes of the brain', and it may have been the beating that she received at Eliza's hands that so gravely dispirited her. For some days afterwards, she complained of feeling unwell and of having no energy. Unable to work, she admitted herself to the casual ward for a day or two.

At five o'clock on Friday, just twelve hours before her death, Annie was again seen in Dorset Street. She was listless. 'It's no use my giving way,' she said dully. 'I must pull myself together and go out and get some money or I shall have no lodgings.'

By seven o'clock, however, she still had not mustered the energy to set off in search of a client. She dragged herself into the lodging-house where she had lived for the past four months. 'I haven't got the rent,' she told Timothy Donovan, the 29-year-old deputy of the house. 'I've not been well. Been in the infirmary. Can I just sit in the kitchen for a while?'

Donovan had known her for a long time. He consented. A habitual drunk himself, he believed that she had been drinking, although she was still able to walk straight. Annie sat slumped and silent in the kitchen as the lodging-house filled up. At two in the morning, however, it was plain that she had no intention of raising the rent, and Donovan was obliged to turn her out.

'I haven't the money now.' Her speech was slurred. 'But don't let the bed. I'll be back soon.'

'Can't get enough for the rent,' Donovan called after her, 'but I see you can get enough for a lush.'

'Just went up the Ringers for a pint o' bitter beer,' she protested. 'Nothing wrong in that, is there?'

Her dragged feet scraped on the bare boards. The door creaked and banged shut. It creaked and banged, creaked and banged again and again in the light breeze.

John Evans, the night-watchman at the lodging-house, saw Annie heading slowly and ponderously off in the direction of Brushfield Street. She then seems, quite literally, to have vanished. Although it was a warmish night with only intermittent cloud and there were many other people abroad in Whitechapel and Spitalfields, no one else appears to have seen her in the next three hours, the last of her life.

Hanbury Street is another long narrow street that runs straight from Spitalfields meat market to Whitechapel. At half past five on the Saturday morning, Elizabeth Long, a park-keeper's wife, was passing down Hanbury Street towards Spital-fields in search of the early morning's bargains. As she passed 29 Hanbury Street, she saw a man and a woman talking. She was sure that the woman was the same as she who now lay in the shell that Polly Nichols had occupied just a week before.

She did not see the man's face 'except to notice that he was dark'. He wore a brown deer-stalker hat and (she thought, but was unsure) a dark coat. He was a little taller than the woman with whom he conferred, and Mrs Long estimated that he was over forty. He appeared to be a foreigner, she said, and had a shabby genteel appearance. She heard him say, 'Will you?'

'Yes,' said the woman.

Mrs Long thought nothing of this and proceeded on her way.

Mrs Long's evidence was frankly unsatisfactory. She was respectable enough, and I never for a moment doubted that she saw such a couple in the crepuscular light, but she was one of those witnesses who grew increasingly certain of details the more often she repeated them. It may merely be that she was, in fact, searching her memory and seeing ever more clearly, but that is not the impression that she gave me. The improbably brief overheard conversation became louder as she related it to me, nor could I ascertain, despite repeated questioning, on what evidence she maintained that the mysterious man, though unseen in all but outline, was a foreigner.

None the less, the one point in her evidence of which she seemed certain was her identification of the woman as Annie Chapman. If she was correct, Annie had spent three and a half hours somewhere, unseen, on the East End streets, yet ended up just four hundred yards from home. If she was correct, too, the murderer had accosted his victim on a busy street in daylight, led her into the yard behind No. 29 and, again in daylight and at a time at which many labourers were arising, had spent at least fifteen minutes in methodically peeling off her flesh as a gardener peels turf from soil, and plundering her of the very particular treasures that he sought.

Because, supposedly just half an hour after Mrs Long saw murderer and victim together, John Davis found the work done.

No. 29 Hanbury Street incorporated a barber's shop on the ground floor and a home for seventeen people crammed into the few rooms on its three storeys. Access to the residential parts of the building was attained through a door to the left of the barber's shop door. This door was commonly left open, day and night. It led through a narrow dark passage to another door, also left open, then three stone steps leading down to the little backyard.

John Davis, a carman who shared a single room on the third floor with his wife and three sons, had had a sleepless night. The last of his three sons came home at a quarter to eleven. Davis awoke again at three and stayed awake until five. He heard nothing but his family's snores and slow breathing and the usual sounds from the street: banging doors, footfalls of men and women going to and from work, the occasional curt greeting, the grinding and bumping of cartwheels. At five o'clock, he again nodded off. He dragged himself from his pallet bed and soon before six, his trouser belt still hanging from his hand, strolled down the stairs, into the passageway and turned right into the yard.

That was when he saw the body.

He turned and staggered back, past the staircase and into the street, struggling to find words for what he had seen. Neighbouring workmen ran up to see what the fuss was about, peered into the yard and backed nervously away. One of them, James Kent, rushed off for a large glass of brandy before returning with a length of canvas. Averting his eyes, he threw it as best he could over the dead woman.

A crowd quickly gathered and filled the narrow passageway. People peered out of the windows surrounding the yard. Many of them worked at Spitalfields; blood, raw meat and intestines were the very fabric of their daily life, yet they had seen nothing like this before.

On Commercial Street, Detective Inspector Chandler saw several men running up Hanbury Street. Chandler was a first-class officer. He knew from the men's expressions that whatever made them run was police business. He beckoned them over.

'What is it?' he demanded.

'Another woman . . .' The man panted and gulped and pointed. 'Another woman has been murdered!'

'All right.' Chandler took a deep breath. 'I'm a police officer. Come on. Show me.'

By the time that Chandler arrived, the crowd in the passageway was already speculating as to the identity of the murderer. In common with Mrs Long, they were of the opinion that no Christian could have done such a thing. Already the word 'Jew' was passing from one sagely nodding head to another.

'Police!' called Chandler's guide. 'Make way! Police!'

Chandler was the first man to venture into that yard since John Davis rushed babbling from it just two or three minutes before.

Annie Chapman lay on her back. Her head, which was turned to the right, was no more than six inches away from the bottom step. Her left arm lay across her left breast. Her legs were drawn up so that the soles of her feet rested on the rough paving-stones. Her right arm was flung across her body. The hand lay limp by her left hip. Her long black skirt and jacket had been pushed up, revealing the origin of the ghastly red slashes that crossed her bodice.

The fence beside which the poor drab lay was intact. There was no evidence that anyone had entered or departed by that route. There was a spattering of blood on the wall of the house, and larger stains on the palings near the victim's head.

Inspector Chandler did things by the book. He sent for the divisional surgeon, the ambulance and further police assistance. He ordered that Abberline should be notified at once. When the constables arrived, he had the passageway cleared.

At half past six, Dr George Bagster Phillips arrived. I was there a mere five minutes later.

'Hello, Godley,' said Chandler briskly. 'Not a pretty sight, I fear.'

I looked down at the bundle beneath the steps. Dr Phillips still knelt at the head. He was a shiny, cheery-looking man with locks of white hair above his ears. I nodded to him. He pulled back the sacking and canvas that covered the body.

The blood left my face so fast that it felt as though a layer of skin had been pulled off. Something cold wriggled down my spine and my arms suddenly stuck to my sides. I badly wanted to sit down.

'So.' Spratling's satisfied voice grated at my shoulder. 'You've got a monster on your hands, sergeant. What's your oh-so-clever governor going to do now?'

'Find the bastard,' said Abberline grimly, doing his usual appearing-from-nowhere trick. 'That's what, Spratling.' He indicated to Phillips that he should lower the covering once more. 'George,' he said. 'I want you to find me the best man there is on madness. I don't care where he is, I want the top man. Understood?'

'Understood, governor.'

*

93

Two more discoveries were made that morning, discoveries that would cost us a great deal in time, effort and annoyance. First one of the young constables instructed to search the yard found a sodden leather apron hanging on the yard-tap. John Piser, whom we had been seeking without success since Martha Tabram's killing, was known in the area as 'Leather Apron'.

For his own sake as much as for ours, John Piser would have to be found.

The constables then bent to pick up the body and to load it on to the ambulance. As they raised it, the head jerked backward: further backward than any head should go. Above Annie's kingsman – the scarf worn about the neck by costers and their girls – the tubes and the flesh of her throat glistened like some ornate enamel and ivory plaque.

'Hold on to the damned thing!' Abberline pointed and grimaced. 'Hello . . .' He looked downward and frowned. 'What's all this, then?'

He knelt. I bent over his shoulder. 'Her belongings, I suppose.'

On the cracked paving-stones somewhere close by where her feet had been, a piece of coarse folded muslin and a small pocket haircomb-case had been laid side by side. Where her head had been, there was a folded scrap of paper containing two pills and a section of an envelope, bearing the seal of the Sussex Regiment on one side and the letter M scrawled in a man's hand on the other.

'Hmm,' mused Abberline. 'Well, they didn't just fall out like this, did they? All very carefully laid out. Very exact. Almost like – I dunno – like a priest performing some sort of ritual . . .' He stood with a grunt. 'So what sort of man is this? At one minute, he's an animal, ripping up a woman like a sack of grain. At the next, he's carefully folding bits of muslin and laying things out all neat and tidy like nanny said. What do you make of that, Dr Phillips?'

'I am no alienist, inspector.' Phillips dusted down his hands and shook his head. 'Though I have often observed almost religious fastidiousness in the insane – washing hands a lot, things like that, you know? And anyhow, I'm not at all sure that this man did just indiscriminately cut her open as you imply. We won't know till after the *post mortem*, of course, but I have a fancy that he might have been just as precise and fastidious in his cutting. We shall see.'

Abberline nodded and pulled on his gloves. 'Thank you, doctor,' he said, and his tone told me that he approved of Phillips. 'Let us know as soon as possible, will you?'

'Of course.'

We turned and followed the bearers of the body towards the passageway. Abberline stood back to allow Phillips to pass up the steps, but, just as Phillips laid his foot on the first step, another man, his cheeks red, his breathing short, emerged through the yard door. 'Ah,' he said, and ran his long left hand back over the glossy dark hair at his temple. 'Yes. Good morning, gentlemen.'

Abberline gave me a sideways glance. 'Morning, Dr Llewellyn,' he said. 'And what are you doing down here?'

Llewellyn set down his bag and started the usual apologetic dry-washing of his hands. 'I heard there was another murder,' he gulped, 'another woman.'

'That's right, doctor.' Abberline smiled a thin smile. 'But Dr Phillips here is the divisional surgeon. You get an official summons, did you?'

'No, no.' Llewellyn gave a little laugh that sounded like something falling downstairs. 'Phillips.' He nodded.

'Llewellyn.'

'No, inspector, as I was saying . . .' Llewellyn took one more casual step downward, but none of us stood aside for him. He found himself face to face with Phillips. 'No, it's just that I thought you might be glad of a second opinion. Seeing as I saw the first girl, that is.' He craned his neck, peering over Phillips's shoulder for a glimpse of the spot where the murder had taken place. Abberline moved an inch across — just far enough to ensure that he stood between Llewellyn and the bloodstains. He watched Llewellyn's eyes very closely.

'No,' he said, 'thank you, doctor. We have ascertained that this killing was done by the same man and with the same weapon. Oh, and Dr Phillips here very cleverly noticed that the poor old bawd had lost a large number of internal organs. I don't think we have any need of a second opinion. Now, if you will come with me, doctor,' Abberline said as he laid a hand on Llewellyn's upper arm and turned him round, 'these gentlemen have important business to attend to. I'd just like to ask you a couple of questions. Perhaps you'd like to tell me just where you were last night, hmm?'

# 1988

There are several points of interest in Godley's account of Annie Chapman's murder. First, and most significant, it omits several of the myths invented by later Ripperologists and accepted by their successors as facts. It will be found, for example, to be positively asserted by the majority of modern chroniclers that Chapman's rings and several small coins were laid in line at her feet. This is nonsense, invented initially by a venal author who wished to stress the ritualistic nature of the Ripper's murders. Chapman did habitually wear three brass rings on the third finger of her left hand, and someone – probably the murderer – did wrench them off, but they were never found. There were no coins found at the murder site.

Ripperologists also have a habit of giving credence to a witness, however unreliable, if that witness's evidence supports their theories. Godley rightly casts doubt upon Elizabeth Long's supposed sighting of Chapman and her killer at 5.30 am.

Long's evidence is at best vague. It has the inconsistencies of much suspect testimony. She was certain of the time, because the brewer's clock had struck at the moment when she passed 29 Hanbury Street. Why, given that No. 29 was, until half an hour later, merely another house among thousands and that she might have seen a hundred men and women together at that hour, did she particularly observe the time? She did not, after all, turn round in order to see the man's face, although she 'thought* he had on a dark coat, but I'm not quite certain of that

... couldn't say what his age was ... but he looked over forty,' and 'he *appeared* to be a little taller' than Chapman and '*appeared* to be a foreigner'.

The dialogue that she claims to have heard 'Will you?' 'Yes,' is not impossible, but is it not just a little too pat and predictable? Are these not precisely the words that an unimaginative woman would have put into the mouths of a fictitious punter and whore?

When Dr Phillips examined Chapman's body at 6.30 am, he estimated that she had been dead for *at least* two hours. 'The stiffness of the limbs was not marked, but was evidently commencing,' he told the inquest. Phillips was an expert and singularly meticulous witness, yet the coroner preferred the conflicting evidence of Mrs Long and of Albert Cadosch, a carpenter who lived at 27 Hanbury Street.

Cadosch stated that, on the morning of the murder, he had arisen at 5.15 and had wandered out into the yard of No. 27 (such yards, of course, frequently served as urinals). Returning towards the door, he said, he heard a voice 'quite close to him' saying 'No.' He *believed* that it came from No. 29. He then heard 'a sort of fall against the fence'. He heard no other noise, nor was his curiosity sufficiently aroused for him to peer over the fence.

We therefore have three conflicting testimonies. If we believe Mrs Long, Chapman was alive at 5.30. She was killed, presumably, shortly afterwards. Phillips stated that he could not have mutilated a body as Chapman's was mutilated 'even without a struggle' in less than a quarter of an hour. We therefore have the picture of the murderer at his work for fifteen minutes in growing daylight, overlooked by many windows at a spot and at a time at which any number of people might have been expected to pass on their way to or from work. We also have to believe that rigor mortis started to set in within three quarters of an hour.

98

Cadosch, on the other hand, fixes the supposed time of the murder at 5.20. This, too, conflicts with the medical evidence, and again supposes that the murderer calmly and carefully hacked up his victim, careless as to whether such people as Cadosch himself might appear on the scene. A far more likely explanation of Cadosch's evidence, if it is to be believed, is that someone else – perhaps the worse for drink – came upon the corpse at 5.20. The faint cry of 'no' and the lurch against the fence are entirely in keeping with such a supposition.

The coroner, however, was cavalier about the matter of the time of the murder, dismissing the variation in evidence as 'not very great or very important'. He seems almost to have twisted himself inside out in his attempt to make Cadosch's evidence coincide with Long's at the expense of Dr Phillips's. 'If he [Cadosch] is out of his reckoning but a quarter of an hour, the discrepancy in the evidence of fact vanishes; and he might be mistaken, for he admits that he did not get up till a quarter past five . . . It is true that Dr Phillips thought that when he saw the body at 6.30, the deceased had been dead at least two hours, but he admits that the coldness of the morning and the great loss of blood might affect his opinion, and if the evidence of the other witnesses is correct, Dr Phillips miscalculated the effect of those forces . . .'

This is, frankly, an astonishing judgement. On the basis of the vague and inconclusive evidence of two fallible witnesses whose accounts might be explained in a hundred ways and are, in any case, mutually contradictory, the cold fact of rigor mortis is ignored and we are asked to believe in a murderer at once clever and reckless to the point of stupidity.

Two other minor points: Godley supposes that the fight between Chapman and Cooper took place on the Wednesday before the murder. This tallies with Cooper's evidence. Subsequent chroniclers, however, have sided with Amelia Farmer, who maintained that Chapman showed her the bruises on the

Monday, and that the injuries were sustained on Saturday, 1 September. This appears to be more likely.

The envelope bearing the seal of the Sussex Regiment was to lead the police down a blind-alley. As Godley states, the initial M was written on it in a bold male hand. There was also a postmark (London, 28 August 1888) but no stamp, and the letters *Sp* on the other side. Intensive police inquiries at the Sussex Regiment's Farnborough camp yielded nothing. The regiment's stationery was sold at the canteen and at the Lynch-fords Road Post Office where the letter had been posted.

It was not until 15 September that William Stevens, a painter, came forward and made a statement. On the last day of her life, he said, Annie Chapman had walked into the Dorset Street lodging-house and declared that she had been to the hospital and intended to go to the infirmary the following day. She held a bottle of medicine, a bottle of lotion and a box with two pills in it. 'As she was handling the box it came to pieces; she then took out the pills and picked up a piece of paper from the kitchen floor near the fireplace and wrapped the pills up in it. I believe the piece of paper with Sussex Regiment thereon to be the same. I do not know of any lodger in the house who has been in the army.'

'35 Dorset Street,' appends Inspector Chandler, 'is a common lodging-house and frequented by a great many strangers and it is very probable it may have been dropped there by one of them.'

# *1888*

⌒⌒⌒∞⌒⌒

**T**here were a thousand things that had to be done, but first I had my own bit of policing to do.

I took a cab to the Inns of Court Hotel on Holborn. I strode through the swing-doors of bevelled plate-glass and across the huge, echoing entrance hall lined with alcoves, pillars and potted palms. The hall porter looked disapprovingly up at me as though striding were immoral.

'Mr Mansfield's room number,' I barked.

'I'm sorry, sir,' the man intoned. 'I am not empowered to give you that intelligence.'

'I am a police officer. Mr Mansfield's room number. Now.'

'I am sorry, sir.' The man's expression did not change. His voice sounded as though he were chanting through a drainpipe. 'Our clients enjoy absolute confidentiality. Mr Mansfield has given express instructions . . .'

'Two seconds,' I said. A few heads turned in the alcoves.

'Sir?'

'You have two seconds to give me that number before I declare this hotel to be a disorderly house and close it. For good. One . . .'

'Three five two, sir,' the man said quickly and quietly. His expression still had not changed, but his skin looked a trifle greyer and something pulsed at his temple.

'Thank you.'

I could have taken an ascending room, but I did not like or trust the things. Instead, I ran two steps at a time up the curving, thick-carpeted stairs.

Thanks to the usual eccentric numbering of rooms in grand hotels, it took me a few feverish minutes to find No. 352. By the time that I did, I was in a thoroughly nasty mood. I hammered on the door, regardless of Mansfield's reputation. 'Police!' I shouted. 'Open up!'

Various other doors along the corridor opened. Curious heads peered out. There were sounds of movement from Mansfield's room. The door did not open.

'Mansfield! Open this bleeding door before I break it down!'

'All right, all right!' Mansfield's voice grew louder as the door swung inward. He stood in the doorway naked to the waist, his arms folded, his legs set wide. 'What the hell is it now? I've been up the whole night with you people already . . .'

I brushed past him as he spoke. Mansfield's crumpled clothes lay on a chair at the foot of the bed. I picked them up and examined them for stains. 'Are these the clothes you wore?'

'What is this?' Mansfield slammed the door and walked back into the room.

I did not turn. 'I said, are these the clothes you wore? Last night.'

'Yes, but . . .'

'Good. Put them on again. Now.' I flung them at Mansfield's feet.

'Now, look here . . .' Mansfield's face was suddenly very ugly.

'No, Mansfield. You look. You are in trouble. You had better help us or we'll take you in for questioning and there are going to be a lot of disappointed customers at the Lyceum over the next few weeks. Put them on.'

'Very well,' Mansfield said, punching his arm into his shirt-sleeve, 'but it may interest you to know that later today, I'll be seeing the American ambassador. He's a personal friend. And when I tell him about this, he'll . . .'

'He'll be delighted to hear how you gave us your fullest co-operation, for which we are most grateful.' I strolled to the head of the bed and laid the back of my hand on the pillow. There was a dent in the pillow, but it was cold. 'Been out all night, have you, Mr Mansfield?' I hummed, 'or have you just got bad circulation?'

'Now listen, sergeant,' Mansfield hissed. 'What I do with my time is my business, and so far as I understand your law, I'd be perfectly entitled to throw you bodily out of here.'

'You could try,' I agreed amiably. I cast an eye over the clothes. They were sorely in need of laundry, but there were no tears, no blood stains. 'All right. Thank you, Mr Mansfield. Just don't change your lodgings without letting me know. Good day.'

'Is that it?' Mansfield had recovered his great voice. It pursued me to the door and down the corridor. 'Is that all that you wanted? Is it for that that you storm in here, menacing an American citizen? Is it for that . . .'

Maybe I was being fanciful, but so many vivid images conspired to make me suspect Mansfield: the transformation from man to monster on stage, the cocky lasciviousness with which he regarded women and, above all, the memory of that woman in a long black jacket who had stepped from the shadows and taken the actor's hand soon after three o'clock that very morning.


With the second murder – we were certain by now that the Smith and Tabram killings were not by the same hand – hell broke loose and ran amok. Speculation, suggestions and criticism of the police abounded in the newspapers and in thousands of letters. Every tip-off had to be followed up. Commissioner Warren, as Abberline had supposed, found himself the butt of much of the criticism. Thousands of constables, both City and Metropolitan, patrolled the streets day and night, many of them in plain clothes. The worst of it – such is human nature – was that there was an almost tangible air of excitement in the East End. Laughter in the pubs was more frenzied, singing more spirited, flirtation more pointed. I have not seen the figures recorded, but I'll warrant that more children than usual were born in the summer of 1889.

We solved two pressing problems quickly enough. The leather apron was ascertained to be the property of John Richardson, son of the woman who let out the lower half of the house. She had washed it on Thursday and left it hanging over the tap to dry.

This did nothing to assuage the conviction of a frenzied section of the crowd that 'leather apron' and the killer were the same. John Piser was at last arrested on the Monday at 22 Mulberry Street, where he had been hiding in terror both of the police and of the mob. His alibi for the nights of both killings was corroborated and confirmed. He had learned that he was the prime suspect and, on his brother's advice, had 'gone underground'.

Lees, of course, was back at Bishopsgate before the blood on Annie's corpse had dried. 'I saw it,' he breathed in the hushed, awed tones of one who has noticed in the midst of a funeral that the church is on fire. 'A tall man . . . in the yard. I saw the blood, everything, but it was too late, too late . . .'

'That's the trouble with the spirit world, isn't it?' Abberline did his best to conceal his irritation. His best was not very good. 'Always telling us after the event, never before. And I suppose you'll be rushing off to your friend Mr Bates at the *Star* to give him your description, right?'

'Mr Bates is deeply concerned,' Lees reproved.

'We are all deeply concerned, but some of us are interested in stopping destruction and some of us in encouraging it. By the way, Mr Lees, where were you last night?'

'At . . . at home. I went straight home at eleven o'clock.'

'Very well, Mr Lees. Thank you for your, um, assistance. Good day.'

'You think I'm a charlatan, don't you?' Lees blinked up at Abberline. 'I can see it in your eyes . . .'

'I'll just tell you one thing, Mr Lees,' said Abberline, his eyes marble, 'and in case you can't see this in my eyes, I'll say it out loud for you. If you did see the killer, I'd be very careful whom you tell, savvy? 'Cos if he believes in the spirit world, he might just come looking for you, mightn't he?'

Lees's lips twitched a couple of times. His eyebrows meshed as he thought it out. He stood and waddled out without another word.

I whistled. 'Steady on, governor.'

Abberline grinned nastily. 'Yeah,' he said.

I wandered to the window and peered through the grimy glass. Outside, a mob had gathered. They chanted something incomprehensible and waved knobkerries, life-preservers, even bottles above their heads. The large, moustachioed man whom we had seen in court stood at their centre, his mouth opened wide as though roaring, his bulging grey eyes like those of a Tussaud's waxwork.

'There he is again,' I murmured. 'He's the ringleader.'

'Who's that?' I felt Abberline's words on the back of my neck. 'Oh, *him*! And there, of course, is the omnipresent Mr Bates.'

I nodded. To the left, Lees appeared at the front door and, rather apprehensively, scurried down the steps into the street. Benjamin Bates came forward from the crowd. He smiled, took Lees's hand and, still smiling, led him away.

'What about the *people*!' yelled the big man at the head of the crowd. 'Who will protect the *poor*, the exploited, the downtrodden . . .?'

The crowd gave a loud but inconclusive answer and shook their weapons.

'Who *is* that man?' I frowned.

'Dunno,' said Abberline. 'Doesn't look too poor and down-trodden to me in his fancy velveteens. Find out, George. Who-ever he is, he's a troublemaker. Oh, and check out Lees's story, will you, and find out if there was a baby born in Old Montague Street round six o'clock this morning.'

'A baby?'

'Yeah. Llewellyn tells me he was delivering a baby there. Jewish woman. Says he can't remember the name. Oh, and don't forget what I said about madness, George. The best man. I don't care if he's in Inverness. I want to see him on Monday.'


It may seem from this account that we spent all our time in indulging eccentric whims related to such as Lees and Mans-field. While it is true that in the absence of clues, we were prepared to follow any possible scent, however faint, the greater part of our days – and nights – were passed in common-or-garden methodical police work.

The principal reason for our eclecticism was that we did not even know what type of man we were looking for. Nowadays, particularly with the advances in psychiatry made during this war, we would doubtless be bombarded with suggestions by experts in the vagaries of the human brain. Not then.

Certainly there was nothing in my ken to compare with these apparently motiveless murders and mutilations. Ruthless cruelty for its own sake, of course, I had encountered, but this killer was not cruel. He killed with greater humaneness and dispatch than most slaughterers, not cutting with the honed edge of his knife but plunging it deep and dragging, causing instant death. He was neat, too, not merely in his arrangement of Chapman's possessions but also in his killing and his mutilations.

For those who did not see Chapman's body, this concept of neatness may be hard to understand. Certainly it was a messy sight, but there was unquestionable method in the murderer's madness. His object had been access to the stomach cavity and the internal organs. The stomach itself and the intestines had lain in his way. He had not hacked at them, therefore, but had carefully removed them; one length up and on to one shoulder, the other on to the other. Add to this the almost incredible coolness, so it seemed, with which these crimes had been committed in spots where at any time witnesses might have happened upon the killer, and we had a composite picture of a man such as I, at least, had never encountered, nor even dreamed of.

The immediate shocked reactions to the sight of Chapman's body turned out to be as close to modern-style psychoanalysis as the police were to come. Phillips declared, shaking his head as though he might rid himself of the image, 'She's been . . . *plundered*!'

'Gralloched,' said a down-to-earth Scottish constable.

Abberline had spun round. 'What?'

'Gralloched, sir. It's what we do to deer. Cut them up the middle, remove the stomach, cut out the fry. Stops the stomach swelling.'

'Do you, now? And would most Scotsmen know how to do this?'

'Aye, the countryfolk, sir, aye.'

'Christ! That's half the British army you're talking about, son.'

'Aye.' The constable gave a small, proud smile.

'George,' sighed Abberline, 'add ghillies to the list.'

'Aye, sir.'

Abberline shook his head. 'Leave it to George Leybourne, Sergeant Godley,' he said briskly.

But the word that immediately occurred to me was 'ransacked'. Phillips's 'plundered' implied that the murderer had known what he wanted and had found it. I felt that he had been seeking something – some answer that he believed to be concealed within a woman's belly. I never believed, throughout the series of murders, that the killer knew precisely what he sought, and somehow, seeing Nichols's corpse, then Chapman's, I knew that his search was only just beginning. His depredations to me recalled nothing so much as those wrought by a resentful or envious burglar on a well-kept home.

Abberline's response, however, was the most grotesque and the most interesting. He eyed the washed body in the workhouse and said, as though puzzled by the word that came to his lips, 'Playful.'

'You what?'

'Playful. Child-like. It's ridiculous, I know, but that's the thought that comes to my mind. The man felt liberated. Irresponsible. Having fun dipping into the ottoman. When I was a nipper, down in Dorset, I used to spend a lot of time digging for treasure, you know? And exploring my grandfather's old trunks in the attic. Do you remember the excitement of it, George? Never knowing quite what new playthings you'd find? That's what this reminds me of. The bastard's been let loose in the sweet-shop.'


I learned the identity of the mysterious rabble-rouser early on Sunday evening, though by then I had often heard his name.

I was standing at the corner of Fashion Street and Brick Lane with one of those little groups that always lined the East End alleys when the sun shone. A Jew with a pointed black beard and a battered hat atop a mass of curly black hair sat huddled on the road, clutching his knees to his chest. A long, emaciated Indian in oversized clothes stood slouched on one leg. His empty clay pipe popped. At my feet, an old woman with a sprouting mole on her cheek and a three-strand beard alternately crooned and cackled and cursed to herself. Beside her, a dirty-faced girl of eight or nine sat with a sleeping infant in her arms. Children's clothes were unheard of among the poor in those days. The girl wore a tatty black bonnet and a brown dress and shawl ten times too big for her. Her feet were bare. She sang softly to the baby.

Just a few feet away from this desultory group, dissociating himself from it by his cocky air and the self-conscious elegance, stood Joe Plater. Joe Plater was a coster. He could not have been anything else. Everything about him proudly declared his membership of the tribe – for tribe it was, rather than merely profession. You were born a coster and you died one, whether you had a barrow or not.

He wore a blue kingsman at his throat and a long corduroy waistcoat with ornate carved bone buttons. His trousers were tight at the knee and flared below. His boots, now scuffed and welted, had once been his pride and joy. You could still just trace the vestiges of a stitched hearts-and-flowers pattern in the leather.

Costers were renowned for their dandified dress and for their hatred, instilled from birth, of the police. 'Serving out a crusher' was for them a point of pride, and a coster would die sooner than report a threat or a crime to a policeman. Hard times and fluctuating markets, however, had forced Joe to adapt his talents to other means of making a dishonest living. He had become a high-class beggar.

The word 'high-class' is indicative only of the imaginative nature of his begging. Not for him the whine and the outstretched hand. Joe worked with accomplices. One of the approaches that yielded rich pickings was the starving stranger routine. In a crowded place, Joe's accomplice would keel over, ashen and unconscious. Joe would solicitously examine the poor fellow and spend his last few pennies on a glass of brandy to bring him round. He would declare, his eyes blazing with righteous indignation at the surrounding revellers, that the poor wretch was suffering from malnutrition. With dignity, he would remove his hat and pass it accusingly about the assembled company. They paid up readily enough.

He did not content himself with on-the-spot begging. He had a host of testimonials from vicars and churchwardens and good ladies declaring that he was a crippled soldier, a misused father, or a respectable merchant cheated by his creditors. These he posted to suitable 'marks', pointing out that there was no reason why they should send him money, but if they didn't, he would commit suicide, and, if they did, he would remember them in his very regular prayers. They usually did.

Another angle was that of the poor, ill-used girl who, strangely, seemed to write to men only when they had recently died. No sooner had an obituary of one who had died young appear in the newspapers than the grieving family would receive a heart-rending letter, addressed to the deceased, saying that the girl should never have been so rash and foolish and had only herself to blame, but now she was with child and the workhouse was a mere breath away, and if kind sir (who had had his pleasure of her and rightly abandoned her as a wicked woman) could find it in his heart to take responsibility for the infant to the tune of, say, ten pounds there would be an end to the matter and she would remember him in her prayers and teach their child that his father had been a good and generous man.

Ten pounds was not much when winding up a man's estate. The already dispirited family found it easier to pay than to argue.

In such a trade, Joe had no further reason to continue his hereditary vendetta with the police. He was anxious now to appear in every way a model citizen. His widespread contacts in the East End, however, made him a useful source of casual information. He had been of some assistance to me before now.

Joe spoke in a language that you seldom hear today and that I will not try to reproduce. Parlyaree, or parlary, it was called. With back-slang, it served to make a coster's banter incomprehensible whenever he chose. It was largely based on

Italian, so a halfpenny was a 'medza' and a half crown 'medza-caroon'. I can still count in parlyaree: una, dewey, tray, quattro, chinqua, say, setta, otta, nobba, daiture, lepta . . . That's where words like 'letty' came from for 'bed', too, and 'dinarlee' for 'money'.

'Everyone's saying as it's one of your lot, Sergeant Godley,' Joe sniffed. 'The girls trust whoever it is, don't they? Makes sense. And how does cully get to know as no one's going to interrupt him while he's doing his butching, eh? Simple. He's a crusher, that's how.'

'Could be right,' I said, nodding, 'but wasn't anyone meant to be protecting the poor old troll? She must have had some sort of prosser or pimp.'

'Well, there's prossers and prossers, ain't there, sarge? I mean, no one's exactly gonna devote his working hours to watching an old pinch-prick like Annie Chapman, now is he? Couldn't be worth more than fourpence a day, and then only when there's a thick fog. I'd have broken a lance with a pig sooner than her, I can tell you.'

'It's somebody terribly 'portant,' croaked the bearded old woman. 'You mark my words. Somebody terribly, terribly, 'portant. Probly has half the brigade of guards looking out for him as he does it. It's a 'spiracy, that's what it is, a 'spiracy.' She inhaled deeply. 'Probly the Prince of Wales himself,' she cackled. 'Probly the Prince of Wales himself . . .' She went off into her crooning again.

'Not quite, mother.' Joe smiled. 'Could be his son, though.'

'What?' I glanced quickly over my shoulder and drew closer to the coster.

'You a crusher and you haven't heard the *on dit*?' he sneered. 'Oh, yeah. You look out for our Eddie. He's been down here often, and it ain't' 'cos he likes herrings, neither.'

'You watch your tongue, Joe Plater,' I ordered. 'That's treason, that is.'

'It's not treason, sarge. It's truth.' Joe shrugged. 'Seen him meself. Leastways, seen his carriage outside the knocking shops. Seems from what they say as he's gonna be the last of his line, and all. Word has it as he prefers little boys to little girls. My mummy told me you don't get babies that way. That right, is it?'

'Thank you, Joe,' I said drily. 'I'd keep that sort of intelligence to yourself, if I were you. You just keep your ear to the ground and let me know if you hear anything – *anything*, all right?'

'But of course, sergeant.' Joe made a leg like a Shakespearean courtier. 'I am your obedient, law-abiding servant. Whoops!' He swung around at the sound of approaching music. 'Here comes the Starvation Army.'

'General' William Booth's 'Hallelujah Band' appeared around the corner from Commercial Street. They marched to two different tunes. The ragged band of the reformed at the front played 'Onward Christian Soldiers' on cornets, trombones and side-drums. Behind them, however, strutting and dancing and aping the Boothites' actions, came the notorious Starvation Army, a group of mocking ragamuffins, footpads and children that gathered as soon as the music struck up and followed the Boothites like gulls behind a plough. They clashed dustbin lids and beat on saucepans with sticks, creating a cacophony that easily overwhelmed the strains of the hymn.

This second army was there, of course, for the fun of it and for the chance of a bowl of 'Hallelujah Stew', but on more than one occasion, the Hallelujah Band, in keeping with its 'Blood and Fire' motto, had turned on its deriders and had shown a more muscular form of Christianity than is generally associated with gentle Jesus, meek and mild.

And now, from behind me, I heard still more assertively pounding feet. I turned. Six men approached from Brick Lane, their faces set and grim, their steps purposeful. Five of them carried heavy clubs. The sixth, their leader, swung an ebony swordstick in his large and hairy right hand. It was the same man who had been conferring so closely with Bates at the coroner's court; the same man who yesterday had been working the mob into a fury.

He strode directly up to me. 'Who are you and what's your business here?' he demanded. 'Account for yourself.'

'I will do nothing of the sort.' My fists clenched by my sides.

'All right, lads.' The big man's eyes slid from right to left. The burly men behind him stepped forward to encircle me. 'Now,' he said softly with a broad ugly smile, 'you will do as we say. We are here to protect the people of Whitechapel. If you don't co-operate, we will be forced to assume that your intentions are criminal and act accordingly. Is that understood? Now. What is your name?'

'None of your damned business,' I muttered, 'and I'd remind you that I in common with all citizens have freedom of passage on the Queen's highway, and that if you obstruct it, it is you, not I, who are committing a crime.'

The men growled and jostled closer. One prodded me in the back, pushing me towards the leader.

'He's a reeler, cull!' called Joe from outside the ring. 'What are you, blind, or something?'

The men surrounding me stepped back, but the leader just pushed back his hat, still smiling that smile. His eyes scanned my face as though in search of blemishes. 'Is that right?' he purred.

'That's right. I am a police officer. And now it's my turn to ask you a few questions. Let's start with the ones you asked me. Who are you and what is your business?'

'As a matter of fact,' the man said smugly, 'I am George Albert Lusk, Chairman . . .'

'Of the so-called Whitechapel Vigilance Committee?' I supplied. 'Oh yes. I know all about you. And your business on these streets?'

'I would have thought that obvious, officer.' Lusk's eyes never looked directly into mine. They moved impudently over my brow, my lips, from one eye to another, studying closely as though to remember every detail for some later obscure purpose. 'I am here to do what your people have so signally failed to do and so obviously have no intention of doing. I intend to see that the ordinary people of Whitechapel, people so ordinary as to be beneath your attention, can walk the streets in safety. I have at the moment one hundred armed men at my call. If you will not see that the poor and the unemployed receive the protection given to every other citizen, then I will, is that understood, officer?'

'If you summon one hundred armed men for any purpose, Mr Lusk,' I said quietly, but my voice wavered, 'the poor and the unemployed are going to be without their champion for a very, very long time. If the Guards are not called in again and you manage to keep your head on your shoulders, I personally will see to it that you get twenty years' hard labour.'

'Ah,' barked Lusk, 'the oppressor speaks! Listen, brethren! We try to protect and are threatened with death and imprisonment, but the man who roams the streets with a bloody knife, tormenting the unfortunate for his own pleasure, what of him? He is protected. He is permitted to go about his business . . .' His voice was drowned out by the passing Hallelujah Band and their mimicking followers, but Lusk, regardless, kept talking. Occasional words reached my ears as the whole group backed up against the wall and the bugles shrieked and the dustbin lids clashed in hideous discord. Lusk's face grew darker and darker as he spoke until, at the last, as the last Christian Soldier moved Onward, his voice once more rang out through the street.

'They,' he said pointing, 'oh, yes, they are permitted to assemble and to march because they are the representatives of the oppressors; they bring fine words to the poor, a bowl of soup here, a pat on the head there. But do they bring houses? Do they bring labour? Do they bring hope? Do they bring decency? Do they bring safety? No, no. We do that, and so we are illegal. The people must not have their protectors but the murderer shall! Well, I tell you, officer, the Vigilance Committee will continue to do its work and if you want to try to stop us, you will find all of Whitechapel – nay, all the poor people of London rising up against you. Call in the Guards! We welcome them! Let sabres kill still more of the people, even as this murderer kills with his knife. We do not care, for the poor and the unemployed are a hydra. Cut off one head and there will be a hundred to avenge it, cut off a hundred and there will be a million! Just try it, officer, just tell your masters to try it, and Bloody Sunday will be forgotten in a trice!'

I raised an eyebrow and slowly shook my head. 'You do talk a lot, don't you Mr Lusk?' I said. 'Still, that is your right, just as it is my right to walk along this street without let or hindrance, so stand back, there's a good fellow, or I'll give you an official and legal dot on the boko. And if I find you molesting other people on the street, I shall place you under arrest, Mr Lusk, on suspicion of being the murderer. Good day.'

Lusk caught his breath and stood back. His fist held so tightly to the swordstick that it shook. I turned back as I entered Brick Lane. Lusk still regarded me with pale eyes full of fury. I waved.


'Right.' Abberline paid the cab-driver and turned to me. I was standing on the steps before Guy's Hospital. 'What have you found out?'

'Sir William Withey Gull,' I read from my notebook, 'MD, FRCS, FRS, LLD, Member of the General Medical Council, President of the Clinical Society, books on diseases of the brain, papers on vivisection and cretinoid women, among others. He's the Prince of Wales's doctor . . .'

'And physician to Her Majesty the Queen.' Abberline nodded.

'Right.'

We entered the hospital.

Hospitals in those days were dark and gloomy places, all panelling and staircases and tight rustling clothes. The smell was more of urine than of antiseptic and the whole place teemed at every moment with nurses, patients and visitors. It was like a gigantic down-at-heel hotel, or prison, I suppose.

An impressively uniformed porter took Abberline's card and led us up a narrow flight of stairs and along a landing. He knocked and opened the door without awaiting an answer. 'Mr Frederick Abberline,' he announced, 'and Mr George Godley.' He stood back and motioned us in.

We were in a large, high-ceilinged room with walls the colour of bones. Two large windows overlooked the Thames and provided watery light. Anatomy charts and racks full of specimen jars lined the walls. Two long, scrubbed tables ran almost the full length of the room. At one of these, a youngish good-looking man in a waistcoat and shirt-sleeves sat eating a packed lunch. He was fair, fit and obviously prosperous. He had that sort of fresh, glowing complexion that no amount of money and good-living in later life can supply. You have to be born rich to look like that.

'Sir William Gull?' asked Abberline.

'Not so distinguished, I'm afraid.' The young man smiled. 'I'm Dr Acland. He'll be here in a minute. Do please sit down. Would you like some milk?'

'No, thank you.' Abberline pulled out a wooden chair and sat.

I said, 'Yes, please.'

Acland carefully poured milk from a big jug into a medical measuring glass. He pushed it over to me. I looked at it and smiled my thanks, but somehow the milk did not seem so attractive in those conditions, in that environment. I did not touch the glass.

'Charles Darwin.' said Acland. I looked up, surprised. Acland had followed the direction of Abberline's gaze to a marble bust that stood on a bracket on the opposite wall. 'Fellow of the Royal Society, just like Sir William. Sir William is, shall we say, a disciple.' His perfect teeth crunched into an apple.

'Darwin,' mused Abberline. 'All our ancestors were monkeys. That the man?'

'That's the one.' Acland nodded. '*On the Origin of Species, Descent of Man*. You ever read them?'

'Er, no,' said Abberline, almost apologetically.

'Is there something wrong with the milk?' Acland asked through a mouthful of apple.

'No, no . . .' I grinned. I was spared further explanation. The door swung inward. A man stepped briskly through, turned briskly on his heel and briskly and precisely closed the door. 'Now,' he said. 'I'm sorry to have kept you waiting.' He strode immediately over to Abberline and enfolded his hands in his before Abberline had even had a chance to stand. 'Gull,' he said.

'Abberline, sir. And this is Sergeant Godley.'

I had already stood. Gull walked over and took my hand. His was as soft and dry as a bitch's belly.

'Sit down,' he said. 'Sit down, please.'

He picked up my milk and drank it, for which I shall ever be. grateful, then wiped his beard with a handkerchief. 'Now sir, did anybody offer you luncheon, or are you self-sufficient?'

'We've eaten, thank you, Sir William,' said Abberline, which in my case was untrue.

'Splendid, splendid. Just one moment, please.'

He looked over at Acland, who had quietly stood, donned his frock-coat and was now walking to the door. 'Please don't be late, tonight, Theodore,' he said. 'We have those French people coming.'

'Ah, the French.' Acland winked at Abberline. 'A compelling argument for Darwin's theory. Good day, gentlemen.'

He went out. Again Gull closed the door, then turned to face us. 'Now, gentlemen.' He loudly clapped his hands. 'To business.'


Gull was, as I had already ascertained, seventy-two years old. He wore his hair combed straight across his brow. His eyes were expressive, his lips pale pink and very thin.

He reminded me of Napoleon, except that Gull had a huge barrel chest and broad shoulders and made even larger men feel small in his presence. The strength of the man was palpable — strength both intellectual and physical. You could almost see his mind working like some great muscle, and this, extraordinarily, was *after* his first stroke. The year before, he had suffered slight paralysis of the right side and aphasia after a stroke suffered in Scotland. Although his clothes now hung a little loose on his frame he looked healthy and vigorous. His strength, no doubt, he inherited from the same source as his almost imperceptible accent. This distinguished and wealthy man (he left an unprecedented fortune of £344,000 in his will) was the youngest son of a bargee and wharfinger.

He smiled fondly as he flicked back the skirts of his cutaway coat and sat. 'That,' he said, 'was my son-in-law. First-class mind, even though he *was* born with a silver spoon in his mouth. I don't envy him that, do you, inspector?'

'Not as such,' said Abberline. 'I'd have to know him better.'

'Good answer, good answer. Now, your question.'

'What is madness?'

'What . . .?' Gull started. Both bushy eyebrows jerked upward. 'Well, I could try to answer you, inspector, but it would take me two or three days and my fees for consultation are rather high. Could you be a little more specific?'

'Well . . .' Abberline hesitated. Then, 'Is it possible to be half mad? I mean, normal one minute, insane the next?'

'A question dear to my heart, inspector.' Gull grinned contentedly. 'And the answer – the official answer – is yes, but only in cases where chemicals have been introduced or denied to the body. Thus an iodine deficiency, for example, can result in conduct that can be described only as insane, yet can readily be corrected. Oxygen starvation, of course, has been shown to cause a state of reckless well-being far beyond anything that we include in our definition of 'sanity', but again, return the supply of oxygen to the subject and he will again be his usual cautious, sensible self. Then there are the narcotics – there are several interesting South American chemicals occurring naturally in plants with which we have been experimenting recently – but I take it that this is not the sort of situation to which you refer.'

'No. Is it possible without any outside agency?'

'In my view, inspector, yes, it is perfectly possible. I have stated as much in public. But you will not find that opinion confirmed in any of the textbooks.'

'And why's that, Sir William?'

'Because the concept of a multi-faceted mind is too radical, too complex for the medical profession to accommodate. In time to come, no doubt, it will be accepted as a matter of course. Meanwhile, we lump all such phenomena together under the rather vague and unsatisfactory title *dementia praecox*. You see, inspector, we are hidebound by the concept of the soul. For so long we have spoken of each man as immutable. He is a good man. He is a bad man. That sort of thing. And yet, if you look at the problem rationally, you will find that there is no one constant trait in you, for example, which makes you Inspector Abberline from one day to another, one year to another. We may say today, "Inspector Abberline is well," yet tomorrow it may be, "Inspector Abberline is ill." The same is true of any epithet whereby you might be identified. Equally, I see

Inspector Abberline as an entity essentially different from that which Sergeant Godley, for example, or you yourself identify as Inspector Abberline, d'you see? And every cell of your body and brain will one day die and rot, so by what curious reasoning do we maintain that there is an immortal, immutable soul that is the essential Abberline?

'For all that, we not only think in terms of one man, one nature, but insist that various traits have specific locations in the cerebellum. Like the absurd phrenologists, we maintain that decency lies here or that the tendency to violence lies here, when all the evidence indicates that brain cells are infinitely adaptable and that each impulse involves an intricate chain of multitudinous cells.

'Now, nothing is inconceivable to the human brain. Nothing. We retain in vestigial form all the skills and impulses – perhaps even some of the memories – which served us when we were cavemen and even when we were apes. Once upon a time, it was useful to be able to kill indiscriminately, for example, or to go into a killing frenzy like that of the fox. Now let the series of impulses necessary, say, to sexual union, be interrupted, diverted by, perhaps, hormonal factors, and sexual union and the fox's frenzy become one, d'you see? A man lays his hands upon a woman's throat. The smell or the touch or the feel trigger associations of which he may not even be aware. They set chemical changes in course which in turn make the man react in a certain way. His penis is engorged. He shakes. Suddenly everything – moral considerations, fear, compassion – is forgotten. His fingers tighten.'

Gull mimed, his hands like claws in front of him. Abberline and I were silent. Suddenly Gull heard the echo of his own words and looked from Abberline to me. He mustered a smile. 'And, you see,' he continued, quieter now, 'once it has passed, just like the sexual frenzy itself to which we are all more or less subject, so soon as it is past, he looks around him, astonished and distressed, unable to believe that he was ever capable of such an act.'

'But thereafter,' said Abberline slowly, 'thereafter, surely he wouldn't do it again?'

'Why not?' Gull shrugged. 'Have we not all at one point or another done just that, either in battle or in the brothel? Have we not all lost our selves, our sense of responsibility, our very consciousness in a moment of madness, felt guilty or rueful afterwards, yet, so intense was the experience, returned once more, torn between excitement and apprehensiveness, in search of that same moment of liberation?'

Abberline nodded. 'Yes,' he murmured.

'You, sergeant?'

I looked down at my hands and shifted somewhat uncomfortably in my chair. 'Er . . . yes . . . I suppose so.'

'So, if I understand you correctly,' said Abberline, placing his palms together and leaning forward, 'a man could be a saint and a beast at the same time?'

'Yes. I don't see why not. In fact, it might be said that a saint – that is, someone constrained by a large number of moral obligations – might be expected to crave such freedom more than another.'

'Thank you.' Abberline was pensive. 'Thank you, Sir William, this has been most instructive.' He stood. 'By the way, Sir William, could this apply to a doctor?'

'Oh, yes, yes, in theory, of course. Doctors are subject to a large number of constraints, a great deal of moral responsibility. It is perfectly conceivable that a physician should be the victim of such dementia, but if, as I suppose, you are discussing the recent murders in Whitechapel, I would suggest that a doctor was literally the last person on this earth whom you should be considering.'

'Oh, and why's that?'

'Because, inspector,' said Gull, as he, too, stood, 'a doctor would feel no sense of liberation whatsoever in the anatomizing of corpses. He can obtain a corpse for vivisection at any time. He can perform precisely the same mutilations on a hundred unclaimed bodies whensoever he wishes. There is no mystery for him in the stomach cavity of a woman, nor can he feel an urgent compulsion to kill on handling female flesh. He has handled it too often, and would have betrayed himself a thousand times over in the hospital or the operating theatre had any such compulsion existed. No, inspector. Look for your saint, for a clerk, a sexual invert, a solicitor, even a policeman, but not a doctor, inspector, not a doctor.'

Lees was waiting for us when we returned to Bishopsgate that afternoon. He had been sitting in the vestibule, but as soon as we entered, he flung himself forward. His cheeks looked as though someone had rubbed ash into the pores. His eyes were wide. His empty chicken's crop wobbled. 'You warned me,' he gulped and gabbled. 'You warned me, and you were right. They're out to kill me.' He ran his hands up and down Abberline's silk-faced lapels. 'I know it. They're out to kill me.'

'Calm down, Mr Lees.' Abberline chipped the words off a hard, cold block. He pushed Lees backward, through the incident room and into his office. 'Calm down. Let us not attract further attention from the newspapers, if you please. Now. Sit down and tell me what you've seen this time.'

Lees fumbled in his pocket and produced a folded sheet of thin, rustling paper. 'I've drawn the coach as best I could.' He swallowed a large mouthful of air and washed his mouth out afterwards. 'And there is the crest, you see. There is the crest!'

Abberline sat behind his desk and held up a hand, halting Lees. He took the paper, flapped it open and scanned it without apparent interest. 'Yes,' he said, 'it's a coach. What's the significance?'

'That coach,' Lees panted, 'that coach ran me down this afternoon.'

'Sorry?' Abberline was suddenly alert. 'What did you say?'

'I was in Coventry Street. You know? The new street between Piccadilly and Leicester Square?'

Abberline nodded, impatient.

'Then suddenly, out of nowhere, this coach came hell for leather up Whitcomb Street. One moment it seemed distant and almost still. The next, it was on top of me. The sweat of the horses . . . the hoofs clattering . . . the harness . . . I threw myself to one side, but the hub of the off wheel hit my thigh. I can show you . . .'

'No, no. Please, Mr Lees,' Abberline soothed. 'We'll take your word for it.'

'If I hadn't moved when I did, I'd have been a dead man. Everyone who saw it agreed. They all said . . .'

'Yes, Mr Lees. It must have been a terrifying experience. And where did the coach go then?'

'Up to Piccadilly. I saw it slow down and join the traffic outside Swan & Edgar, as if nothing had happened.'

'But you didn't see the driver's face?'

'No, no, just a flash of white,' Lees snapped, 'but it's not that which matters, it's the coach, man, the coach!'

'The coach?'

'I'll never forget it, inspector. How should I? I've ridden in it, in that very vehicle, when I went to see Her Majesty.'

'Her Majesty?' Abberline stared.

'Yes, yes! It's a royal coach!'

Abberline stood. He walked to the doorway, peered out into the incident room and closed the door. He looked down on Lees like a disapproving dominie. 'You are quite sure?'

'Yes, of course. I wouldn't . . .'

'Have you told anyone else about this?' asked Abberline sharply.

'No.'

'Anyone at all, Mr Lees?'

'No, I came straight here.'

'Well, don't. Not a word. Because I assume you understand the significance of what you've just said.'

'Yes.' Lees, his story told, sat slumped and spent. 'I understand, inspector.' He looked up at Abberline with wide wet eyes. 'I'm scared, inspector. I'm scared . . .'


It was a lovely time, the autumn of 1888. We had the only sort of summer that was tolerable in London then, an Indian summer, brisk, clear and sunny, yet never so warm as to cause the stink of human effluvia to arise from the river and fill the streets.

'Another good scenting day, George,' Abberline would announce each crystalline morning, referring, I think, not so much to the pursuit of the killer as to his memories of hunting the fox with the Cattistock as a child.

The City police have jurisdiction only over the square mile of the City of London. They wore a different uniform to ours and answered to a different master. While we at the Met came within the purlieus of the Home Secretary's domain, the City boys were, and still are, under the control of an independent committee of aldermen.

Major Henry Smith, the Assistant Commissioner of the City police, had declared it to be his ambition to catch 'our' killer on his patch. He had ordered nearly one third of his usually uniformed force into plainclothes with orders, as he later wrote, 'to do everything which, under ordinary circumstances, a constable should not do . . . I have little doubt that they thoroughly enjoyed themselves, sitting on doorsteps, smoking their pipes, hanging about public houses, and gossiping with all and sundry.'

I too had little doubt that they enjoyed themselves. I had seen them doing so, and, as I stood in my best dark suit and bowler in the sungilt royal mews, I frankly envied them.

Abberline, too, looked ill at ease and constantly ran his finger along the inside of his tight starched collar as he chatted to Mr Thackeray, the royal mewsmaster.

I was paying little attention to the conversation. A beautiful gleaming dark blue landau, drawn by a pair of glossy chestnuts, had left the mews just a few minutes ago. Now it waited beneath the arcade for its passenger. Through the railings I saw the Life Guards stiffening to attention by the door, their boots almost as dazzling as their breastplates. A moment later, a tall, slender figure emerged on the doorstep.

Prince Albert Victor, Duke of Clarence and Avondale, was twenty-four years old. He had the look of a high-bred filly; a small head, big, soft, heavy-lidded eyes, a long aquiline nose. He wore a simple high-collared tunic adorned only with braid at the collars and cuffs and with a broad sash fixed by a glistening star. He stood on the doorstep for a moment, sniffing in the sunshine, then a small smile touched his lips. He nodded to the footman who held the carriage door open. He climbed in.

I was, I admit, as thrilled by this close sighting of the second in line to the throne as a detective sergeant would be today by a glimpse of Jean Harlow. 'See who that was, governor?' I enthused. 'The Queen's grandson. Collars-and-cuffs himself.'

'His Royal Highness, the Duke of Clarence,' corrected Thackeray stiffly.

'Quite right.' Abberline nodded. 'A little less of this familiarity with your betters, if you please, Sergeant Godley.' He smiled. 'So, Mr Thackeray.' He held Lees's drawing between finger and thumb like someone else's undergarments. 'You are quite certain there were no royal landaus on the streets yesterday?'

'Quite certain, inspector.' Thackeray blinked through thick spectacles. 'Absolutely beyond doubt. No question. The one that just left was here all day, and the other two are being re-painted. You may see them if you will.'

'Could anybody – how can I put this? Could anybody borrow one, just for a few hours?'

'Borrow one?' Thackeray was affronted. 'Definitively not. Borrow one? Unquestionably not. This is the royal mews, inspector. It is not a cab company.'

'No, no, of course.' Abberline flashed his best consoling smile. 'Well, I'm sorry to have taken up your time. Thank you, Mr Thackeray, and good day.'

'Good day, inspector.' Thackeray hesitated, peered quickly over his right shoulder. 'No, wait. I'll ask a scratch-driver.' He pursed his lips conspiratorially. 'They usually know what's available.'

Thackeray bustled off and beckoned to a tall young man in a round, almost flat hat. Washy dun hair stuck out at his brow and over his ears. He had small, close-set eyes, a snub nose, a brown moustache and no chin whatsoever. His body was thin. He flapped his hands at his side as he spoke as though shaking out excess energy.

'What's he want a scratch-driver for?' I asked Abberline.

'Scratch-drivers are available for hire. You want to look like a lord tonight when you take a bit of cuff to Old Mo's? Find a scratch-driver and leave it to him to find you your personal liveried carriage. Old Thackeray thinks we want to hire a landau. Remind me to strangle Lees. Royal crest, my arse in a bandbox.'

The chinless young man approached us with a broad, tobacco-stained grin. 'Excuse me,' he said, shaking a little more vigour from his fingers, 'I hear you want a landau.'

'Not really, no,' I told him.

'Mewsmaster says you want one,' the young man sniffed deeply.

'No, thank you. It's a mistake. He got it wrong.'

'Wait a second, George.' Abberline fished out the sheet of paper again. 'Could you find one like this?'

'I'm a scratch-driver, governor. Find you anything. For the right money, of course.'

'Splendid,' Abberline smirked. 'You have a word with this informative gentleman, George. I have other business to attend to.'

'Thanks, governor.' I gave him a sideways glance. He tapped his nose, grinned and strolled happily away.

'Got your own horses, have you?' The chinless man spoke in my ear with all the breathy earnestness of a pimp. 'Or will you be wanting the whole rig?'

'Yes,' I considered, 'well, that depends. Why don't we go off and find a drink eh? Somewhere quiet, er . . .?'

'John.' The coachman nodded eagerly. 'John Netley.'


I gave him the soft sop over. I bought him ale and jellied eels and told him that he was the cleverest coachie that I had ever been privileged to meet. Instinctively sensing the approach that would appeal to him, I made much of the importance of his work and of the unworthiness of many of those for whom he worked. He was one of those snobs who was at once thrilled by the distinction of those whom he drove yet affected to despise them.

'Take Prince Eddie.' He chewed and jelly crystals tumbled gleaming from his mouth. 'He's always good for a fiver after a night out. Ooh, he's a lad, though. You wouldn't believe the things he gets up to. I dunno. I feel as royalty should be different from the likes of us. Debasing, it is, that's what it is, debasing, seeing your king-to-be down the East End just like any other vicious person, don't you agree?'

I evaded the question. 'You drive him, too, then? The prince?'

'Not personally, no. I'm a privateer, see. Only there two days a week to help out. Got my own brougham, I have.'

'So who do you drive the rest of the time?'

'Medical profession mostly. Occasionally, you know, senior police officers, foreign businessmen, things like that, but mostly surgeons. I'm on all the lists, see.'

'Lists?'

'Hospitals. Only the big ones, mind. I only do the big ones. Leave the rest to the peasants.'

Astonished, I said something like, 'Hng.'

He did not give me a chance to recover. He spat out an eel-vertebra and casually observed, 'I'm a doctor myself.'

'Er . . .' I said intelligently, then, 'Oh?'

'Yup.' Netley nodded, bending his entire trunk with each nod. 'A good one, too. I've studied it, see. Libraries and things. Oh, yes. You can pick up a lot from books, you know.'

'Indeed, yes.' I bared my teeth.

'I'll tell you,' Netley said, and laid a hand on my knee, 'if I'd been born on the right side of the blanket, I'd have been a top surgeon by now. It's in the mind, you know, all in the mind.'

'And you've got the mind for it,' I assured him.

'And the hands too.' He spread out his fingers before him. I surreptitiously ran my hand over my knee as though to rub away his touch. 'Surgeon's hands,' continued Netley. 'Solid as a rock. See?'

'Indeed, yes,' I said again. 'Remarkable. I don't suppose . . . your duties never took you to Windsor, I suppose?'

'Windsor.' Netley started nodding again. 'Epsom. Newmarket. Lots of gentlemen like to keep their bits of tickle at places like Windsor, you know. Oh, yes.'

'Never meet a man in your trade, name of Chapman, did you?'

'Er . . .' Netley laid down his plate, supped his ale and narrowed his eyes against the sun. 'Chapman, do you say? No, don't think so. Mind, I've met a lot of coachies all over, of course. Can't remember them all.'

'I just wondered. He was a veterinarian, you see. Thought you might remember him, seeing as you shared an interest in medicine.'

'Chapman . . .' Netley frowned and scratched his crotch. 'No, I don't recall the name. Well, now, sorry, and thank you for the ale. Afraid I've got to go.' He stood and straightened his coat. 'Ask for me at the mews. John Netley. "Dr" Netley, they call me. What did you say your name was?'

'George.' I grinned.

'Don't worry, George.' Netley slapped my shoulder. 'I'll look out a landau for you, George. Trust John Netley, eh? Trust good old John Netley.'

'Mad as a buck, in my opinion,' I told Abberline that evening, 'but far from stupid. Disconcerting. Very.'

'Well,' Abberline leaned back in his chair and puffed on a huge cigar. 'While you, my worthy and industrious acolyte, have been enjoying intelligent discourse with Mr Netley, I have been hobbing and nobbing with potentates and panjandrums.'

'What are you talking about, Fred?' I grinned. I liked to see the man happy.

'I was summoned this day to attend upon Sir Charles Warren, no less.'

'Were you indeed?'

'I was, and he confirmed a few minor suspicions of mine. Warren is fighting for his life, George. He's unpopular all round, and he knows it. This madman in Whitechapel could bring him down. Told me he was thinking of taking me off the case, but now that he's talked to me, understood what we're about, he's decided I'm the best man for the job after all. Consoling, isn't it?'

'Most gratifying.'

'He's got a bee in his bonnet about blood-hounds. Thinks we can track the killer that way. What do you think about that?'

I laughed. 'I don't think he's a policeman. It would be like asking someone to pick out a slightly flat second fiddle in a thousand-strong orchestra. I mean, first there's the victim's blood, then all the shit, piss, horse's blood, boiling cat's meat . . . it's impossible!'

'You're right, George.' Abberline nodded. 'He's no police-man. He's a soldier, poor beggar. Bit of a buffoon, bit of a martinet, but I found myself quite liking the man. Felt quite sorry for him when Lord Salisbury tore him off a strip.'

'Lord Salisbury?' I gasped.

'Oh yes. Didn't I mention that? Yes, we did happen to call on the Prime Minister's office. Just briefly, you understand. Henry – Henry Matthews, you know? Home Secretary? He was there, too. Very worried they are. Civil unrest. Bad for the monarchy. Can't have this sort of thing. Unsolved murders are bad for the Empire. They were also deeply perturbed about certain rumours concerning our friend Prince Albert Victor. Seems as he's been sighted in Whitechapel knocking-houses. Not tactful of him. Salisbury is going to have a discreet word with him, and we are going to keep our gobs firmly closed. Prime Minister offered me anything I wanted, short of a peer-age. So there am I, Aladdin's lamp in my paws, and what do I say? "More men, please, sir." Mrs Abberline's boy is never going to die rich and corrupt, but we've got the men, offices, transport, anything we need. All we got to do is ask.'

'They *are* worried.'

'They are indeed, my boy. I wonder if our killer knows that the Prime Minister and Her Majesty herself are concerned about his whereabouts and well-being? Now. I have here the com-pleted doctor's report on Annie Chapman. There's something missing from it. I'm not telling you what, but, just in case I run into a royal coach like friend Lees, or get ripped for murdering said friend Lees, I want you to know. I've asked Phillips to leave out one small detail of the woman's injuries. I let him choose which one. It's not significant, in fact I don't think you'll even notice it, but it's not going to be mentioned in court.'

'What's that for, then?'

Abberline shrugged. 'It doesn't do any harm and it might do some good. When in doubt, do something confusing, something out of the ordinary. May lead somewhere, may lead nowhere. You seen some of these letters we've been getting?'

'No. Haven't been around the station much.'

'Take some of them home with you. Good bedtime reading. It is gratifying to know that in this green and pleasant land there are at least 1,000 people who want to be great detectives and know better than we do and at least 5,000 who would like to be the killer or believe that they are the killer. We've got letters written in blood, letters with pictures of dead women, letters with pictures of bloody knives, letters blaming God, the Prince of Wales, Florence Nightingale and the reincarnation of a mad tiger that apparently terrorized several Indian villages in the sixteenth century. Still, each one has to be examined. One of them may be from our man.'

'Christ, they don't make life easy for us, do they?' I sighed.

'They do not. Now. This man Lusk. Nasty piece of work. Far as I can see, he's got one interest and one interest only, and that's power. I hate men like that, and I care about the people on those streets. If he gets his way, he'll kill a thousand more than our whore stiffener ever will.'

'I've given him a warning,' I said.

'Do more than that, George. Pick a man to join up with Lusk as a volunteer. Tell him to keep his eyes open.'

'What's that for?'

'If I was the killer, I'd join up with Lusk and go out every night looking for myself, wouldn't you? And I'm still interested in all the publicity given to the first killing before they even knew there was a second one. Someone knew something. Lusk is chummy with Bates and is making capital out of these poor dead trollops. Come to think of it, he's the only person so far to have profited by the murders – the only person, you might say, with a definite motive. Have him watched, night and day.'

'Right. And what about this phantom landau?' I asked. 'Still want me to roast John Netley?'

'Young Dr Coachman?' Abberline laughed. 'Nah. His sort piss more than they drink.'

He opened the top right-hand drawer of his desk and again pulled out the squat bottle of whisky. I had been afraid of this. Ebullience is as bad for the drinker as depression. He caught my glance. 'Relaxes the throat,' he said blithely.

'Last time it relaxed your brain.'

'Yes, mother.' Abberline tipped up the bottle and gulped down two fingers' width. I walked glumly towards the door. 'Oh, cheer up, George,' rasped Abberline behind me. 'We're winning.'

I turned, my hand on the door-handle. 'Is that a promise?'

'Yes, my old friend.' Abberline leaned forward, suddenly serious. 'That is a solemn promise.'


The inquest respecting the death of Annie Chapman yielded little that was new. It afforded, however, a few moments of high comedy and a feast of speculation and sensation for the newspapers. A large crowd gathered in the upper room of the Working Lads' Institute, and the heat, coupled with the unpleasantness of the mutilations, caused several women to faint. The comedy was supplied by the testimony of 'The Pensioner', Edward Stanley. Even now, as I read the account of his evidence in *The Times*, the absurdity of the fellow makes me chuckle.

CORONER: Are you a pensioner?

STANLEY: Am I bound to answer this question?

CORONER: You have to answer all the questions affecting this case that are put to you.

STANLEY: I am not a pensioner, and have not been in the Essex Regiment. What I say now will be published all over Europe. I have lost five hours in coming here.

Donovan, the deputy of 35 Dorset Street, then stated that Stanley had been to the lodging-house six or seven times. The last time that he had lodged there was on the weekend before Chapman's death.

CORONER: What do you think of that, Stanley?

STANLEY: The evidence given by Donovan is incorrect. When you talk to me, sir, you talk to an honest man . . .

It was as though there was a conspiracy to make the cases the most sensational in history. On 18 September, at the continuing inquest into Polly Nichols's murder, the foreman of the jury gave the newspapers a treat. 'If a substantial reward had been offered by the Home Secretary in the case of the murder in George Yard [Martha Tabram], these two horrible murders would not have happened.'

'I understand,' said the coroner, 'that there is a regulation that no reward should be offered in the case of the murder of either a rich or poor person.'

Up jumped the foreman again. 'I believe, sir,' he stated bullishly, 'that a substantial one would have been offered if it had been a rich person. I myself, sir, would be glad to give five pounds for the murderer's capture.'

*

Dr Phillips's evidence caused still further consternation and, in certain quarters, unholy glee. At first, he declined to give details of the mutilations found on Chapman's corpse. The coroner, however, insisted and, once the court had been cleared of women and children, the ghastly story was told. The salient details were these: first, the incisions at the throat had started at the left side of the neck. The muscles surrounding the spine had been hacked at 'as though an attempt had been made to separate the bones of the neck'. The injuries could not have been done with a bayonet or a sword bayonet. They could have been done with a post mortem knife (not always to be found in an ordinary surgical case). A slaughterman's knife, well ground down, would have served. There were indications of anatomical knowledge 'which were only less indicated in consequence of haste'. He was positive that the victim entered the yard alive. Her stomach contained a little food, but there was no sign of fluid. Significantly, considering the testimony of the witnesses who had seen her earlier, 'she had not taken any strong alcohol for some hours before her death'.

Phillips avowed that he could not have performed all the injuries inflicted, even without a struggle, in less than fifteen minutes.

It was in the coroner's summing-up that the principal surprises and the richest news items appeared.

He started with a heart-rending summation of the life of the Whitechapel poor. He gave a brief account, too, of Chapman's headlong fall from respectability, the fight with Eliza and the night on which she set off to meet her nemesis. Then came his extraordinary assessment of the medical evidence as to the time of death in relation to that of the 'witnesses' and a vivid reconstruction of the murder itself.

'The wretch must have then seized the deceased, perhaps with Judas-like approaches. He seized her by the chin. He pressed her throat, and while thus preventing the slightest cry, he at the same time produced insensibility and suffocation. Even in those preliminaries, the wretch seems to have known how to carry out efficiently his nefarious work. The deceased was then lowered to the ground, and laid on her back . . . Her throat was then cut in two places with savage determination, and the injuries to the abdomen commenced. All was done with cool impudence and reckless daring . . .

'The injuries were made by someone who had considerable anatomical skill and knowledge. There were no meaningless cuts. The organ was taken out by one who knew where to find it, what difficulties he would have to contend against, and how he should use his knife so as to abstract the organ without injury to it. No unskilled person could have known where to find it or have recognized it when it was found. For instance, no mere slaughterer of animals could have carried out these operations. It must have been someone accustomed to the post mortem room. The conclusion that the desire was to possess the missing abdominal organ seems overwhelming.

'It has been suggested,' he said, with masterly understatement, 'that the criminal is a lunatic with morbid feelings. That may or may not be the case, but the object of the murderer appears palpably shown by the facts, and it is not necessary to assume lunacy, for it is clear that there is a market for the missing organ . . . Within a few hours of the issue of the morning papers containing a report of the medical evidence given at the last sitting of the court, I received a communication from one of the officers of our great medical schools. I was informed that some months ago an American had called on him and asked him to produce a number of specimens of the organ that was missing in the deceased. He stated his willingness to give twenty pounds for each specimen. He stated that his object was to issue an actual specimen with each copy of a publication on which he was then engaged. He wished them preserved, not in spirits of wine, the usual medium, but glycerine, in order to preserve them in a flaccid condition . . . I need hardly say that I at once communicated my information to the Detective Department at Scotland Yard. Of course, I do not know what use has been made of it . . .'

And so, without having ascertained what the police 'had done with' his bizarre intelligence, the coroner, convinced by his own discovery, hastened to his conclusion. Linking the Chapman murder with those of 'Mary Anne Smith' (sic) and 'Ann Tabram' (sic), he pronounced, 'It is not as if there is no clue to the character of the criminal or the cause of his crime. *His object is very clearly divulged. His anatomical knowledge carries him out of the category of a common criminal, for that knowledge can only have been obtained by assisting at post mortems or by frequenting the post mortem room. Thus the class in which search must be made, although a large one, is limited.*'

If only policing were as easy as all that.

Among those who listened to this 'damned penny-dreadful', as Abberline called it, was our friend from Guy's Hospital, Gull's son-in-law, Dr Theodore Acland. He exhibited no desire to pass unseen, but entered halfway through the afternoon in full evening dress and listened rapt to the proceedings.

As the crowd dispersed with much banging and scraping of chairs, I sauntered over to where Acland sat. 'Good evening, sir.'

'Ah!' Acland looked up and grinned. 'Sergeant Godley, isn't it?' He stood and pumped my hand. 'How nice to see you.'

'I didn't know you were interested in this case.' I stepped back so that he and I stood side by side, watching the people leave. We were of the same height, and much the same age.

'Ah, but you have created the interest yourself, sergeant, by coming to the hospital. I know the principals, as it were. And Dr Phillips is an old friend.'

'Off to the opera, are you?'

'What? Oh, the toggery! No, no, not the opera. God forbid.

Squawking fat dollymops taking twenty-five minutes to tell you at the top of their voices that they're dying of consumption. Not for me. No, I'm going down to the Lyceum. Melodrama down there.'

'That's *Jekyll and Hyde*, isn't it?'

'Yes, I've got free tickets, courtesy of the actor.'

'Mansfield?' I hummed casually.

'Mm. Came to me for advice about being a doctor. Showed him round, you know, explained a bit about the physician's life. Charming fellow.'

'Show him an operation, did you?'

'No, no. I have problems enough with students. Don't approve of distraction in the theatre. Showed him an autopsy, though. I don't think I can have helped him much. Still, he sent me the tickets. I must say, I'm mightily looking forward to the drama. Real curdler, so they say.'

'Indeed, yes,' I assured him, 'it is a very remarkable performance. And let me reassure you, Acland. I believe that you were of considerable assistance to Mr Mansfield.'

# 1988

⊙───∞

Godley's avowed aim is, in part, to obfuscate and to introduce 'red herrings'. There would be little purpose, after all, in his posing the riddle of the Ripper if he were to afford credibility only to the true story, whatever that may be. For all the red herrings, however, the essential historical facts that he records are true and can be confirmed by reference to the Home Office and Scotland Yard files and the transcripts of the coroner's inquests.

Much could be made of Wynne Baxter's motives for his really very odd analysis of the evidence given at the Chapman inquest. We have already had cause to cast doubt on his eccentric views regarding the time of the murder. Now we see him conjuring almost from nowhere the most enduring of all the Ripper myths: the Ripper as surgeon.

Dr Phillips's 'there are indications of anatomical knowledge' becomes, in Baxter's version, 'His anatomical knowledge carries him out of the category of a common criminal, for that knowledge can only have been obtained by assisting at post mortems or by frequenting the port mortem room.'

One thing is very plain. Excluding all other motives – such as that, perhaps, established politicians, Radicals or journalists contrived to influence him – Baxter was flattered by the attention of the British public. Like most of us, he was so thrilled with his own great discovery – the mysterious American publisher and his macabre 'free offer' – that he was prepared to assert, without awaiting further police investigation, that this was, this *must* be, the murderer's motive. In doing so, he blithely ignores the fact that, in the cases of Smith, Tabram and Nichols (which he believes to be killings by the same hand) no organs were removed. It can only be, therefore, an irrational delight in his own amateur detective work that allows him to aver with such certainty that the procurement of the uterus was the reason for Chapman's killing.

This is shoddy stuff.

For it is only on the basis of this assumption that the killer's handiwork can be regarded as necessarily that of an expert. And even if for a moment we entertain the (subsequently entirely discredited) idea that the Ripper killed in order to obtain the uterus, the CID Central Officers Special Report of 19 October 1888 shows that the killer excised this organ with no great particularity. For good measure, he took away with him 'part of belly wall including navel, the upper part of vagina and greater part of bladder'.

Hardly a standard hysterectomy.

One of the most enduring and teasing questions about the Ripper killings is 'Just how did he incapacitate his victims?' The logical and obvious way in which to cut a whore's throat silently and without getting covered in blood would be to proposition her – or agree to her proposition – and accompany her to a relatively secluded spot. There she would stand, supporting herself on a fence or a wall, for a 'dog rig' or threepenny upright. Clothes, after all, are expensive, and no tart would willingly have lain on her back. Thus bent forward, however, she would be powerless to defend herself. The murderer would grasp her throat in his left hand and cut with his right, drawing the knife from left to right. The victim would never even see the glint of the blade and have time to cry out before it was plunged into her throat. The initial stream of blood would thus flow away from the killer. Only when she was dead – almost instantaneously and in total silence – and the flow of blood had

139

become a trickle, only then would he lay her on the ground, turn her over and start to mutilate her belly.

Unfortunately, however, in regard to all the Ripper murders, the doctors were unequivocal. The flow of blood showed that the women were lying on their backs when the fatal slash to the neck was made. If this was so, the killer must be assumed to have been left handed, for the cuts were always made from the victim's left to her right.

But how, then, did the killer contrive to make his victims lie down? Bruising around the throat indicates the possibility that they may have been partially strangled. If that is so, a garotte was probably used rather than the bare hands. The trouble with this thesis is that nowhere do the police surgeons – men presumably accustomed to strangulations – note the tell-tale fracture of the hyoid bone, nor, save in this one case, discolouration of the face or swelling of the tongue. Strangulation, too, takes time and inevitably entails struggle and some noise. Godley has some interesting revelations to make about the killer's methods, revelations that I shall not anticipate, save to observe that the killing of Chapman is unique in that she was unquestionably partly strangled before her throat was cut.

# 1888

❦

'Take a look at this.' Abberline tossed a sheet of paper on to my desk. It was the afternoon of 28 September.

I took one look at the letter and groaned. 'Not another one, governor. I can't stand any more.' I waved a sheaf of papers at him. '"My brother done it" ... "It's the Jews" ... "I'm a giant vulture". I'm becoming convinced that there's not a sane man left in London – in the country, damn it!'

'Read, mark, learn and inwardly digest.' Abberline sat squarely on my desk.

'All right.' I scanned the page. 'Red ink. That's standard. Dated 25th inst., postmarked ... 27th. London EC3. Addressee: The Boss, Central News Office, London City. Text reads:

Dear Boss

I keep on hearing the police have caught me but they wont fix me just yet. I have laughed when they look so clever and talk about being on the right track. That joke about Leather Apron gave me real fits. I am down on whores and I shant quit ripping them till I do get buckled. Grand work the last job was. I gave the lady no time to squeal. How can they catch me now. I love my work and want to start again. You will soon hear of me with my funny little games. I saved some of the proper *red* stuff in a ginger beer bottle over the last job to write with but it went thick like glue and I cant use it. Red ink is fit enough I hop *ha ha*. The next job I do I shall clip the lady's ears off and send to the police officers just for jolly, wouldnt you. Keep this letter back till I do a bit more work then give it out straight. My knife's so nice and sharp I want to get to work right away if I get a chance. Good luck.

Yours truly

Jack the Ripper

Dont mind me giving the trade name.

'So, what do you make of that?' asked Abberline.

'Immediately? Well, there are some obviously significant things. The word "Boss", newly imported from America. Fairly current but not universal. The eccentric address "London City". Is the Central News Office in the City itself? If so, this man knows something that most of us, myself included, do not know about the press. If not, the man's a foreigner. No Englishman would write "London City" for "London". An expert on language should be able to make something of the inversion, "Grand work the last job was," and "give it out straight". At a hazard . . .'

'Yes?'

'Well, I know it sounds absurd, and I'm no expert, but some of these words – "Boss", "gave me real fits" as opposed to "really gave me fits", "quit", "fit enough", "trade name" – I'd say it's either someone who's been reading too many Buffalo Bill stories or . . .'

'Go on.'

'Or it's an American. That's just a first impression. Probably a long way off target.'

'Not bad.' Abberline nodded. 'What about the name?'

'Brilliant. Professional, I'd say. No journalist could've come up with anything better. The stuff of legend.'

'Jack significant?'

'Jack, of course, is a sailor, and the letter's posted in dockland, but Jack's also the standard mischievous figure in all the folk stories. I don't know. Where'd it come from?'

'Friend Bates, of course.' Abberline smiled. 'A gleeful Mr Benjamin Bates. This'll be in all the newspapers soon.'

'Why are you so concerned about this one letter, though? There are plenty more as strange, plenty a deal stranger.'

'Hmm, but look at that last line.'

'"The next job I do,"' I read, '"I shall clip the lady's ears off and send them to the police officers just for jolly" ... Strange construction that, "the next job I do". He knows enough to put an apostrophe in on "lady's". "Lady" is a joke, too. That again sounds American to me ...'

'George?' Abberline interrupted gently.

'Hmm?'

'Keep quiet. Shall I tell you what Dr Phillips did *not* reveal at the inquest?'

'Please do.'

'The ears. Our man cut Chapman's ears. Not off, but he did cut them. I knew, Phillips knew, and so did the killer. Now, why should this joker say that he'll cut the next one's ears right off?'

'It doesn't mean that he's the killer, though,' I objected. 'We've seen plenty of threats to cut bits off or out of women.'

'Mmmyes,' Abberline said slowly. Suddenly his eyebrows jerked downward. He hit his thigh with a clenched fist. 'Unless there's another one,' he murmured. Then, louder, 'Unless there's another one.'

'Another what?' I asked, bemused.

Abberline snatched up the letter and two files of similar communications that lay on my desk. 'Now,' he said urgently. 'I want every statement, every file, every report that we have. I'll find it, George. I'll find it if it takes me all week.'

I frowned up at him. 'Find what?'

'Well, don't just sit there,' he yapped. 'Get them!'

When Abberline said 'if it takes me all week', he meant 'if it takes *us* all week'. Throughout that evening and the following day we re-read the letters of madmen and fantasists, the statements of whores, pimps, lodging-house deputies and petty criminals, together with the reports of a thousand constables. We were playing a huge game of Pelmanism.

'Pairs,' Abberline kept urging, 'find me pairs.'

'Pairs of *what*?' I had demanded at the outset. 'They're all single statements.'

'Two butchers in the same pub,' Abberline rapped. 'Two sailors from the same ship, two people who broke the usual patterns of their lives at the same time. Two of anything as long as they tally.'

'You mean . . .?'

'I mean he's got a partner.'

'A partner? Someone who would collude in such madness?'

'There must be. There has to be. How else could he work contentedly in that yard for fifteen minutes? We're going to get this killer, George. I know it now. One of these men or women has personal power over the other. That means that one of them is weak. He'll break. All we have to do is find the bastard!'

By the time that we left the station at seven o'clock on the Saturday evening, we still had not found him. Reports were flooding in at such a rate that there were as many yet to study as there had been when we started.

I walked back to Whitechapel in the gathering gloom. There was a cold sharp edge to the air and the sky was slate. The Indian summer was drawing to its close. A few cold drops of rain fell on my hands and snagged on my eyelashes, misting my vision as I walked along Old Montague Street.

A conspiratorial group of Jews fell silent and huddled closer, their dark eyes swivelling slowly beneath their hat-brims as I passed. I cut through Davenant Street. A pretty, black-haired girl with a two-year-old boy in her arms stepped from a door-step. 'Hello, Mr Devilish!' she called over the child's head. 'Caught the knife, have you?'

'Not yet, Molly.' It was an effort to smile. I was very tired, and the world seemed unfamiliar and unreal. 'Not long now, though. Meanwhile, you look after yourself.'

She placed her left hand on her hip and moved close to me with a curious, half-sideways gait. For a second, her tongue-tip showed between her teeth. 'Why don't you come and look after me for half an hour or so?' She slipped her arm through mine. 'I'd make you feel better.'

For a moment, I seriously considered it. I wanted to say 'yes'. My body ached. My mind seemed cold and hard, an irritant, like a giant pearl within the softness of an oyster. Her hair looked so soft, her throat so warm. I could find solace and succour there . . .

A glance at the child, who studied me seriously, his thumb in his mouth, brought me back to my senses. 'No, thank you, Moll.' I smiled down at her, avoiding her eyes, her lips. I ruffled the child's hair and passed on into Whitechapel Road.

The rain was drifting down now in fine white veils. I wanted to be at home and in bed, but first I needed to get back to these streets and these people. 'Jack the Ripper' and the lives of his victims had become mere academic problems in the smoky atmosphere of the station. I was a copper, not a scholar. If I were to identify this killer, it would be by talking, listening, looking – smelling, even – not by human logarithm tables.

At the corner of Cambridge Heath Road, I stopped and leaned back against the wall, removed my hat and turned my face gratefully up to the rain. To my surprise, I found that my face was stretched by a broad, inane grin.

I crammed my hat back on to my head and sauntered quite jauntily up to the Forester's Arms. It was just after half past six when I pushed open the engraved glass door.

The Forester's was a smaller, gloomier pub than the Britannia, the sort of place that seems to consist entirely of corners. People came here to talk seriously and to drink seriously. They pitched their voices on a confidential, burbling monotone. No individual words were audible to the casual listener, but I would have had to shout to be heard above the thick noise. It filled the room like the constant rush and hush and thunder of the sea.

No one actually turned as I walked in, but I felt rather than saw eyes shifting and I may have imagined a momentary falter in the talk. I squared my shoulders, made my way to the bar and called for a pint of bitter beer.

It may be thought that I exaggerate, but I swear that, of the people there whom I recognized – and I recognized a deal more than half – almost every one was, in one sense or another, a criminal.

Mitchell, the landlord who fetched me my ale, was a retired cracksman. His wife Beryl had served as his canary, bearing the loot and the house-breaking equipment rapidly away from the scenes of his crimes. Now, in common with most 'omees' of Whitechapel carseys, Mitchell was a receiver of stolen goods.

Ten, twenty years ago, this public would have been filled with pickpockets or 'buzzers' and their 'stalls', but that once prosperous trade was now almost extinct. Gentlemen no longer carried silk kerchieves in their tailcoat pockets for the children to learn on. The tailcoat itself was seldom seen; the crinoline was no more. The reformatories, too, now punished young offenders with hard labour. Hard labour destroyed a buzzer's essential manual dexterity for life.

If the swell mobsmen of the past were no longer to be found in Whitechapel, there was no shortage of alternative, if less remunerative, 'lays' for a rogue. The respectable looking

146

middle-aged woman with silvery hair and a kindly expression, for example, worked the 'kinchin lay'. Kinchins were children or young maids and apprentices sent by their parents or their masters to procure goods from the shops. Dear, sweet Sara would lure such children to isolated spots, knock them down, steal their money and sometimes strip them, leaving them to stagger home, bleeding and naked.

Others of her kind, too old, too plain or temperamentally unfit for prostitution, specialized in stealing linen from washer-women's lines or laundry-baskets, 'palming' (shoplifting in pairs) or 'maltooling' (robbing passengers on omnibuses).

As for the men, the lays open to them were many and wide ranging. Two men who sat by the door had at least twice to my knowledge been convicted as 'dragsmen' – thieves who pounced on laden cabs late at night, slashed the straps and ran off with as much baggage as they could carry. Poachers met here, too, to discuss their expeditions into the nearby Essex countryside, and cracksmen to plan their ventures, and there was the usual assort-ment of macers, mutchers, praters, screevers, cash-carriers and proppers or, as we would say today, cheats, robbers of drunks, fake preachers, writers of fake references, testimonials and other documents, ponces and armed street-robbers.

And there, too, beneath the layers of smoke, were the prosti-tutes.

Glass in hand, I strolled slowly around the bar, nodding to those whom I knew without encouraging any intimacy.

'Well, bust a frog!' called a pure clear voice beneath me. 'Why not confess as you're mashed on me and have done with it, Mr Devilish? Can a girl not go nowhere without that a well-favoured sergeant appears at her elbow? Sure, and you may as well sit down and declare your undying passion for me. Have you met my feller, Joseph Barnett? Joseph, say hello to Sergeant Godley.'

A tall young man half stood and extended a hand. He had

fair eyelashes, wide, trusting eyes, shiny red cheeks and a splash of blond hair whose exuberance he had tried in vain to control. He wore a very tight tweed suit buttoned almost to the throat and a badly tied broad brown tie.

'H-h-hello, Mr Sergeant G-G-Godley.' The words came like water from a pump: two or three arduous essays followed by a less than wholly satisfactory spurt.

'Ah, sit down will you, Joe Barnett.' Mary Jane patted the bench beside her. 'And you, Sergeant Godley, sir, come along and tell us what you've been doing about this knife. Can I go out nights without fearing for me life and me innards?'

'Oh, n-no, M-M-Mary J . . . ane.' Joe shook his head vigorously, and I wondered why he had not chosen a girl named Ann. 'He, er, only attacks unf-f-f-fortunates. He wouldn't dare. Not while I'm around.' He smiled at Mary Jane: that smile which is intended to exclude all others.

Mary Jane cast me a wicked glance. She winked. Incredibly, it seemed, Joe did not know – or did not want to know – that she was what he called 'an unfortunate'.

Mary Jane was at pains to explain. 'See, Joe's at work all day down de market, aren't you, Joe? Yes. Fish. Have ye ever shared a bed with a fish-porter, Mr Godley? No, now as I come to think of it, I suppose you haven't. Pongs a bit, I can tell you.' She laid her hand over Joe's. 'Anyhow, a girl's got to go out in the daytime, hasn't she? Specially a girl like me as has seen a bit of the world. And how am I to know as I'm not going to encounter this Dr Jack?'

I started. 'Jack?'

'That's what everyone's saying, isn't it, Joe? That your man's a tar comes up the river and goes away again. Me, of course, I still reckon as he's a Jew.'

'You said. What else are they saying?'

'Ah, sure, there's a hundred stories. Joe was saying yesterday as he'd heard your man hides in the sewers and that's how he gets away so easy.'

148

'Or that he h-hides in the J-J-Jewish ssss-cemetery,' put in Joe.

'"And he shall lay his hand upon the head of his offering, and kill it,"' said Mary Jane suddenly, '"at the door of the tabernacle of the congregation: and Aaron's sons the priests shall sprinkle the blood upon the altar round about. And the two kidneys, and the fat that is on them, which is by the flanks, and the caul above the liver, with the kidneys, it shall be taken away . . ."'

I regarded her with astonishment. 'Sure, Mr Devilish,' she chuckled, 'and wouldn't a good Limerick girl know her Bible? That's what the Jews do when they kill a beast as a peace offering. Says so. Book of Leviticus.'

'Yes, but he doesn't take kidneys,' I objected. 'He takes . . . other bits.'

'"And the flesh that toucheth any unclean thing shall not be eaten,"' Mary Jane quoted and wagged a finger at me; '"it shall be burnt with fire."'

'So you think he takes these things away to burn them?'

She shrugged. 'That's what the Good Book says. As an atonement for sin. And they say as there's never enough blood, right?'

'Some say so,' I admitted. 'Certainly less than I'd have expected.'

'Well, there you are, then,' she said smugly. 'He's taking it away to sprinkle like it says in the Book. Look for a Jew with a bucket, Mr Godley. Look for a Jew with a bucket. And now, in exchange for all me good advice and me good Catholic upbringing, you can buy us a dog's nose. I'm as dry as a lime-basket.'

I bought drinks for both of them, wished them goodnight and worked my way back through the crush towards the front of the pub. I was a mere six feet from the doors when I saw the two men who sat at a small circular table, their heads almost touching. A pair: George Albert Lusk and Benjamin Bates.

Bates saw me at the same moment. He laid a warning hand on Lusk's sleeve. Lusk stopped talking and slowly turned his head. He eyed me up and down. His mouth stretched slowly into a smile. He clasped his tankard in his big fist, raised it and bowed to me before drinking. Bates merely regarded me with anxious eyes. His cheeks burned.

I watched them just long enough for Bates's cheeks to grow redder and for Lusk's assumed composure to degenerate into obvious jauntiness, then I swung round and pulled open the doors.

Outside in the street, I stood still for a minute, thinking and breathing in the cool air. The rain had stopped. There was a light breeze, and a few swagging, red-edged clouds hung low above the city. I glanced at my watch. Half past eight.

I returned to Panton Street and found it difficult to sleep. I was too tired. Too many faces, too many ideas circled in my head.

By three o'clock in the morning, two more whores had been found dead.

The second one, they said, was called Mary Jane Kelly.


The killer had heard the Russian songs and the thumping of dancing feet from above as he slashed Elizabeth Stride's throat and lowered her gently on to the muddy floor of the yard. He saw the flush of light from the first-floor windows, the occasional mothswing shadow as one of the club members passed the window frame, but no light touched him here, behind the gates. He could work in peace.


Fred Abberline lay awake in his room at Anderton's Hotel in Fleet Street, attempting to still his heavy breathing, attempting to still his mind. He had left orders that he should be called at six o'clock. He needed sleep.

In the crook of his right arm, Emma Prentice lay sleeping, her long dark hair splashed across his chest.

He had sought peace, but it was not after all to be found here. Her proximity irritated him. Her sweat-slicked flesh stuck to his. Whenever he moved away, her thigh or her arm also moved to claim him. His body was heavy with fatigue but his mind raced on with startling clarity. Image pursued image in a magic-lantern show behind his eyelids: a black coach, a knife, a face, two faces . . .

He pulled away from her again. She made a little creaking sound and readjusted her head. Her right hand clasped his shoulder. He sighed and stared up at the dappled, watery shadows from Fleet Street that played on the ceiling.

Any one of those shadows might be his man.


Louis Diemschutz, a carter, and the steward of the International Working Men's Educational Club, had had a long day. He had left home at half past eleven this morning, leaving his wife to make the preparations for tonight's meeting. Now it was one o'clock in the morning.

He drove his coster's barrow down Berner Street. He, too, heard with satisfaction the sound of singing from his club. He was sorry to have missed tonight's discussion, but at least he would be able to talk with some of his comrades before retiring.

He turned in through the open wooden gates.

Suddenly, his pony snorted and shied to the left. 'Steady,' Diemschutz soothed, but still the pony pulled to the left and breathed in quick puffs of alarm. 'Steady, girl. What is the matter?'

He peered down to the right. Something lay there. It was too dark for him to be able to see what it was. He prodded it with his whip. Whatever it was gave slightly.

He jumped down from the cart and fumbled for the matches

in his pocket. He struck one, attempting to shield it from the breeze with a cupped hand. The match flared and was almost at once extinguished, but, in that split second, he had seen that it was a woman.

Behind the open gate, the panting killer watched as Diemschutz led the pony and cart across the yard and bustled through the front door of his house. The killer gazed regretfully down at the body beneath him. He quickly bent and wiped his knife on her skirt, then stepped over her, inadvertently kicking the bonnet that had fallen from her head.

He muttered curses of fury and frustration as, covering his face with his sleeve, he scuttled back out through the gates and into the shadows of Berner Street.

'There is a woman in the yard lying,' Diemschutz informed his wife and a few club members who sat in the ground-floor front room. 'Dead or drunk, I do not know.'

He snatched up one of two candles in the room and, shielding the flame with his coat, stepped back out into the yard, leaving the door open behind him.

Shivering now after the momentary warmth inside, he made his way along the wall of the house and so to the gates once more. He bent down. He saw the pool of glistening liquid. He raised the candle, following its course. '*Ach, nein.*' He made a rapid sign of the cross. His whole frame was suddenly gripped by a fit of trembling. '*Nein* . . . please, no . . .'

The woman lay on her side, her head turned towards the wall. Her left arm lay beneath her, her right hand, smeared with an oily film of blood, lay on her chest. Her legs were drawn up before her.

The flickering candle flame showed a black skirt, a long black jacket trimmed with coney fur, unbuttoned at the top, and then, below a tight checked silk scarf, a thick streak of glistening, winking red.

The face was gaunt and very white. The pale grey eyes stared at the wall as though astonished by something that they saw.

They saw nothing.


Diemschutz rushed off, mumbling and crooning to himself, in search of a policeman. He could not find one. He returned with a young man whom he had encountered in Grove Street. The members of the club were alerted. One of them, Morris Eagle, an itinerant vendor of cheap jewellery, at last found two police-men on the corner of Grove Street and led them back to where the woman lay. One of the officers went off in search of the doctor. The other sealed off the yard. Within minutes, the whole area rang with the cry of 'Murder!'


The cause of all the shouts, the lights and the bustle lay still and staring. Her name was Elizabeth Stride, or 'Long Liz'. She was forty-two years old. She had been born Elizabeth Gustafsdotter at Forslander near Göteborg in Sweden and came to England, so she said, at the age of twenty-three 'in the service of a foreign gentleman', though, in fact, she had been registered as a prosti-tute by the Göteborg police for the past year.

In 1869, it was said, she married John Thomas Stride, a ship's carpenter, who drowned with two of their children when the *Princess Alice* foundered. No record of the name Stride, however, can be found on the *Princess Alice*'s passenger list.

For the past three years, she had lived at 38 Dorset Street with a lumper named Michael Kidney. She had on several occasions been charged with drunkenness at the Thames police court but had escaped punishment by claiming that her drunken stupors were, in fact, epileptic fits.

'She was subject to going away whenever she thought she would,' said Kidney. 'During the three years I have known her she has been away from me altogether about five months . . . It was drink that made her go away, and she always returned without my going after her.'

She had gone away on the previous Tuesday. This time, she did not return.


Diemschutz had still been at the other end of Berner Street at two minutes to one. The killer had been crouched over Long Liz's body. At that moment, a prostitute was led from her cell at Bishopsgate police station.

She had been lying in the gutter in Aldgate High Street at eight o'clock the previous evening. Constable Lewis Robinson, in accordance with usual police practice, had picked her up and half carried her to the station to sober up.

Constable George Hutt, our gaoler, visited her every half hour in order to ascertain when she was sober enough to be released. At a quarter past twelve, she had been singing to herself. At half past, she had demanded to know when she would be let out. 'When you're capable of taking care of yourself,' replied George.

'But I am capable,' she had wheedled. 'Honest, constable. Let us out . . .'

It was Sergeant Byfield, however, who had at length decided that she could be released. He had led her from her cell.

'What time is it?' she had asked.

'Too late for you to get any more drink,' Byfield replied.

'No, really, what time is it?'

'Just on one.'

'Huh.' She shrugged. 'I shall get a damned fine hiding when I get home.'

While the alarm was being raised in Berner Street, she was

walking down towards Aldgate. She probably sang to herself as she went. Her friends described her as 'a very jolly woman, often singing'. At twenty to two, just as I arrived at the site of Elizabeth Stride's murder, that 'very jolly woman' died.

I jumped from the cab and nodded curt acknowledgement to the various constables gathered at the entrance. I strode rapidly past them into the yard.

The corpse, now covered, lay ignored on the cobbles. A constable stood guard over it. Some seven or eight other men crouched low, painstakingly scanning the floor of the yard in the swinging beams of their bull's-eye lanterns.

'Who are they, Ernest?' I asked the constable.

'Vigilance Committee, sarge.'

'What? Who the hell allowed them in here?'

'Inspector Spratling,' the constable spoke with poker-faced gravity.

'Did he now? Here, you!' I barked at one of the men.

'Me?'

'Yes, you. Come here.'

An officious-looking middle-aged man with thin orange hair and freckles straightened and marched briskly over to me. 'Yes?'

'How did you hear about this?'

'Same way as anyone else. We was on patrol and we heard the hubbub. Mr Lusk told us to come here right away. Be of assistance to the police, see.'

'No, I do not see. Where is Lusk?'

'Dunno. Probably out hunting the killer like as you ought to be, if I may say so, young fellow. Now, if you'll excuse me. I have work to do . . .'

I grasped the man's shoulder and spun him round. I had a headache and was finding it very difficult to keep my temper. '*I* have work to do, Mr . . .'

155

'Marshall,' he sniffed. 'Well, why don't you get on with it? A woman is dead, sergeant.'

I closed my eyes and muttered a quick prayer for patience. 'I am aware of that, Mr Marshall. Am I to understand that you saw Mr Lusk after this happened?'

'Well, no, as it happens. I was just sent a message. Someone must have seen him though. Stands to reason.'

'Find him,' I ordered.

'What?'

'Find the man who received orders from Mr Lusk to come here. Send him to me.'

'I'm not here to run errands, sergeant. I'll have you know that . . .'

'Constable!' I called to one of the men at the gate.

'Sarge?'

'Place this man under close arrest on suspicion of being an accessory to murder.'

'Yes, sir.' The constable smirked.

'No! I say! Here, do you know who I am?'

'No,' I snapped and walked towards the door of the club. 'Neither do I care. I'll see you in court.'

'Look, no! Look here. If it's so important to you, all right, I'll find out . . .'

'You do that.' I turned in the doorway. 'Constable, you will accompany this man and see that he spares no effort in obeying my orders. In fact, should any of these damned busybodies get in your way at all, arrest them for something and we'll see to their conviction later.'

'Sir.' The constable grinned happily. He saluted.

The front room of the house was bare, lime-washed stone. There was a strong smell of horses, though it was many years since this had been a stable.

Four constables stood at ease by the walls. One guarded the front door. Another stood in the stairwell. Abberline sat at the

156

only table. Spratling sat behind him in a plain ladder-backed chair. A tall man with a shock of grey hair stood facing Abberline. He tightly held the hand of a woman who sat at his side. 'No, no,' he was saying, 'there was nobody. Nobody in the street at all. Why don't you pray for her?' His extended left arm flapped. 'Nobody care, nobody care.'

'We have sent for a priest, Mr Diemschutz.' Abberline acknowledged my presence with a flicker of the eyes.

'Me, I got a wife and two sisters.' Diemschutz put an arm around the woman. She looked up at him and patted his hand. 'All these women killed. So many, so many. Why you *do* nothing?'

'We are doing something, Mr Diemschutz,' Abberline assured him. 'You got his statement down, Lamb?'

'Yes, sir.' Henry Lamb handed him a sheet of paper. I walked around the table and peered over Abberline's shoulder.

'Pony shied . . .' I read in a murmur. 'Prodded the body with my whip . . . blood was still fresh and bright red . . . found between one and two minutes past . . . Jesus,' I whistled, 'he must have missed the bastard by seconds!'

Abberline nodded. 'I'd say our man was standing just inches away in the shadows.'

'*Mein Gott!*' sobbed Diemschutz. 'A woman butchered and all you talk is one and two minutes past and inches and foots. I got a wife and two sisters. Why the police do nothing? Why, why, why?' He keened like a dog and laid his forehead at his wife's throat. His shoulders shuddered. She reached up and, with a long, slender hand, smoothed his hair and crooned some soothing words in German.

I turned quickly to check that Spratling was otherwise engaged. 'Was it him, governor?' I muttered.

'Who's that?' Abberline hummed.

'Our letter-writer. Jack.'

'No. The ears are still there. Everything's still there. Think our friend disturbed him before he could do his business.'

'What the devil is Lusk's mob doing out there in the yard?'

'What?' Abberline started. His eyes suddenly opened wide.

'They're searching the yard.'

'They're . . .' Abberline was speechless.

'Spratling's orders, apparently.'

Abberline stood. 'Spratling!'

'Abberline?' That slow clogged growl.

'My sergeant tells me you've got a load of overgrown school-boys destroying evidence in the yard. I don't recall your consulting me.'

'No, well, Abberline, you had other things to concern you. They're good sorts and they wanted to do something, poor chaps. Their blood was up. Better to keep them quiet by giving them something useful to do, eh?'

'Spratling,' Abberline hissed through his teeth. 'You are to make no further decisions relating to this case without submitting a written proposal to me. If you see this killer at work, do nothing. Give no orders. Write me a report. That is all. Do you understand?'

'Oh.' Spratling nodded. He spoke in a soft, jeering growl. 'Oh, yes. So Inspector Abberline is now so bleeding high and fucking mighty that we poor bloody working coppers ain't good enough for him. Well, just let me tell you, Abberline . . .'

'Write me a report about it, Spratling, there's a good lad.' Abberline patted his shoulder, then, out loud, 'Right, constable.' He raised his eyes to the stairs. 'Bring Mr William West down, please.'

Mr William West, however, was just halfway down the stairs from the club room when there were shouts from outside. Abberline held up his hand. The door swung inward, sending the constable lurching forward off balance.

'Here!' shouted someone.

'What the blee . . .?'

'I've got to talk to Mr Abberline!' called a deep, resolute voice.

'All right!' Abberline barked. 'Let him in!'

A breathless uniformed sergeant in the City uniform emerged from under the constable's arm. His crested helmet was askew. His ears were very pink. 'In-Inspector Abberline.' He removed the helmet and did his best to march in and salute as per regulations. 'I beg to report . . .'

'Get on with it, Fraser,' Abberline droned.

'There's another one, sir. Our patch. Mitre Square. Ripped wide open. We've called the commissioner . . .'

'The commissioner?' Abberline was already shrugging on his coat.

'Yes, sir. This one is terrible. Really terrible.'

'All right,' said Abberline, 'keep your voice down. We'll have a bloody riot on our hands if Spratling's boys out there hear you. Sergeant Godley, come with me. Constable Lamb, get statements from everyone in the club and everyone in the adjacent buildings. You, Spratling, I want statements from every member of the Vigilance Committee out there, then I want you to accompany the body to the mortuary and report to me on everything that happens there.'

Spratling growled. He worked his lower jaw from side to side like an old man chomping on porridge. I flung my coat over my shoulders and followed Abberline and Fraser through the yard, out into the street again and into the waiting cab.

'Have you got an identification for the victim?' I asked Fraser. The cab tilted as we swung right into Back Church Lane.

Fraser righted himself with an outstretched arm, but was still rocking from side to side as he answered. His voice emerged in a rapid, jerking series of staccato sounds. 'Ye-es,' he said, nodding. 'Appa-a-rently-y she-e's called Ma-ary Ja-ane Kelly.'


I did not know P C Edward Watkins, though he had been with the City police for seventeen years. He had an unenviable task to perform. A baby-faced, chubby man, he had to explain how he discovered the body while, just yards away, the doctors and the police performed their own necessary but none the less ghastly rituals.

It was, to say the least of it, distracting.

The woman lay on her back, her head lolling over her left shoulder. The arms lay straight at her sides, palms turned upward, fingers slightly bent as though she were protesting. A thimble still lay glinting on the ground by the right hand. The left leg was extended, the right raised and bent, allowing the killer – and the viewer – grotesque access to the privy parts of the belly beneath the raised skirts.

Yes, plainly she had been a jolly woman. She wore a brown bodice with a black velvet collar and an apron over a skirt of floral patterned chintz. Beneath that again was a green skirt, then a blue one with red frills.

'. . . so the beat takes me – what? – twelve, fourteen minutes at the most,' Watkins was saying.

'Contents of pockets,' droned the doctor, 'two small blue bed ticking bags, two short black clay pipes, one tin box, contents . . . sugar, one tin box, contents . . . tea . . .'

'I'd been patrolling from ten last night until half past one without seeing anything in particular to excite my attention. At half past one, I passed through this square with my lantern at my belt. I looked into all the corners, passages and warehouses. I always do. There was no one about. No one could've been here without my seeing him. Impossible . . .'

My eyes wandered back to the group of men who stood or knelt about the body in the glow of their lanterns. It looked like some vile parody of a nativity. I could not see the woman's head.

'. . . the skirts are ripped, and a piece of the apron is missing. There is no blood on the front of the clothes. The blood from the throat, however, was liquid when we arrived, so I can only suppose that she had not been dead more than a quarter of an hour . . .'

'Which places the death at some point between, say, twenty-five minutes to two and a quarter to, when it was found . . .'

'You are absolutely certain,' Abberline demanded of Watkins, 'that you came through here at half past?'

'Yes, sir.'

'Hmm.' Abberline's eyes dubiously scanned Watkins's face. 'Thank you, constable. We'll have to talk to you at greater length.'

He walked over to the group around the body. I followed.

Three City constables shone their lanterns on the corpse. The two doctors knelt by the victim's head. My stomach lurched as I saw the enormous veined mass of intestines that had been pulled up and placed over the right shoulder. Another section of gut, separated from the body, lay between the left arm and the body.

Abberline afforded the corpse no more than a cursory glance. 'Sir,' he said and nodded to a tall, distinguished-looking man with white moustaches who stood with his hands linked behind his back.

'Abberline! Good to see you!' Major Henry Smith's stentorian tones somehow reduced the tension. Until now, we had all been murmuring as though in a cathedral. 'Well, it looks as though he's moved on to our territory, eh? Be glad to have your help. Messy business. Got half my force after him already. Damned fellow seems to vanish up his own arse, eh? You know Collard, don't you?'

'Of course.' Abberline turned to the man on his right. He had a hooked nose, a high brow and sleek black hair at low tide. 'So, what have we got?'

'Sweet fuck all, begging your pardon, Major Smith.' Inspector Collard smiled. 'He must've stiffened your woman, run like a hare over here, grabbed this one, hacked her up and run away again. Strange, really.'

'What is, old man?' asked Smith.

'Well, you'd think he'd want to stay and enjoy it a bit if he does it for pleasure, wouldn't you? It's strange that the important thing seems to be to do it, not to enjoy the doing.'

'Yes.' Abberline frowned. 'Is Watkins trustworthy?'

'Oh, yes, yes,' Collard said, nodding. Then, 'At least, as far as any old reeler on the beat is trustworthy. Wouldn't put it past him to stop off for a smoke or a cup of tea from time to time, but then, that applies to all of us.'

'Hmm.' Abberline was in pensive mood tonight.

'You know that she was in our custody until one o'clock?' barked Smith.

'What?'

'So, we're told, yes. Poor old troll was intoxicated apparently. One of your constables locked her up in the Bishopsgate cells. Released her as sober just about one o'clock.'

'Dear God.' Abberline raised his eyebrows. 'Well, what did he take this time, then?'

'A kidney.'

'What?' I started.

'A kidney,' said Collard. 'Left one, wasn't it, doctor?'

One of the doctors looked up. 'Yes,' he said. He stood and walked over to us. 'Stabbed the liver a few times, removed the face.'

'Any idea why he'd do that?' I heard Abberline ask, but in my head I was hearing Mary Jane's voice, 'and the two kidneys, and the fat that is on them, which is by the flanks, and the caul above the liver, with the kidneys, it shall be taken away . . .'

'No.' The doctor wiped his hands on his coat, then shook hands with Abberline. 'Frederick Brown,' he said. 'City surgeon. No,' he said, turning back to the body. 'Probably just to disfigure it.'

I had taken two steps forward. Now the corpse's head was

visible. The throat had been gashed clear across just above the red kingsman.

The face was mutilated beyond identity. The gristle at the tip of the nose had been removed, leaving bone visible. The lower eyelids had been nicked neatly off.

'Sweet Jesus Christ,' I breathed.

The murmuring policemen behind me fell silent. 'What is it, Sergeant Godley?' asked Abberline from behind me.

'Two things,' I said slowly, trying to keep my voice even. 'First, that's not Mary Jane Kelly. Those aren't her ears. And second, he's had a damned good attempt to . . .'

'To what?'

'Look.' I pointed. 'Her ears. He tried to cut them off.'


The confusion had arisen because the victim had given her name at Bishopsgate Station as 'Mary Ann Kelly'. She was, in fact, Catherine Eddowes, a hawker and part-time market-dame. She had been 'married on the carpet' to a pensioner and fellow-hawker named Thomas Conway, with whom she had lived for twelve years and by whom she had had two sons and a daughter. Conway had left her some eight years ago.

Soon afterwards, Catherine had met John Kelly and had lived with him ever since, lodging at 55 Flower & Dean Street. Kelly earned his keep by occasional jobs around the market, while Catherine did some charring, or hawked Lucifers, shoe-laces, or flowers on the streets. Street-walking, it seems, they accepted as a last resort when work could not be found.

They appear to have been genuinely fond of one another and, every summer, in common with many a Londoner, went hop-picking in Kent, which explained why the corpse's forearms were found to be bronzed by the sun. This year, they had been working near Maidstone. They had returned to London on foot, arriving back on Thursday, 27 September.

They had no money, so Catherine suggested that she should pawn some of her clothes. Kelly, according to his account, refused, but insisted that he should pawn his boots, or 'bullock his pollies', as he put it. On the Friday, they received two shillings and six pence from the Spitalfields pawnbrokers.

They ate together on Saturday morning and parted amicably at two o'clock in the afternoon. She was off to Bermondsey, she said, to seek her daughter, Annie Philips. She hoped to cadge a few bob off her. This was not abnormal. Catherine's sons' addresses were deliberately withheld from her because of her constant requests for money.

'Don't you worry,' she consoled him. 'I'll be back by four.'

'You take care,' he said. 'Watch out for the knife.'

'Oh, don't fear for me.' She kissed him. 'I'll take care.'

Perhaps she reached Bermondsey (Annie was not there anyhow). Perhaps she had never intended to do so. Either way, she acquired some money from somewhere and went on a bend. By half past eight she was down among the dead men.


The body was taken away. An assiduous search of the square was conducted without result. The streets all around were filled with the clatter of footfalls, the sound of fists hammering on doors, the occasional shout as one officer or another called for assistance.

I was questioning Constable Richard Pearse on the doorstep of his house, 3 Mitre Square. He had pulled a pair of trousers on over his combinations. His hair was unbrushed. His eyes were bleary.

'I heard nuffin, sarge,' he whined. 'I went to bed round twenty past midnight, and slept straight through till you lot comes banging on the door. Thought the house was afire, I did.'

'Neither you nor your wife at any point went to the window?'

'No.' He blinked. 'Just slept straight through.'

'Could the spot where the murder was committed be seen from your bedroom window?'

'Yeah. 'Course. Easy. Give me quite a turn, it did, thinking of him just out there doing it and me asleep just yards away . . .'

'So!' The voice rattled down the rooftiles. 'Two more poor wretches perish because the police do not care! Do they know, the rich and powerful, on what their fortunes and their great houses are based? On filth, degradation and on blood, that is what! Do they know what it is that passes their lips as they sip their fine wines and gorge themselves on their glorious banquets? Do they? They drink the thin blood of the poor! They chew on the offal of poor abandoned women such as these!'

'Here.' Constable Pearse was startled. 'What's he on about?'

Lusk stood at the corner of the square, two henchmen at his back. 'Excuse me,' I murmured to Pearse.

Even as I started moving, I saw Abberline detach himself from a group of women over on my right and stride purposefully towards the Chairman of the Vigilance Committee.

We reached him at the same time.

'Ha!' Lusk's eyes were iridescent in the lamplight. 'Look, friends! The police! The protectors of the people! The people employed to make our streets and squares safe for all! The very people who told us that we were not needed, that they had matters in hand! Oh, yes, they had matters in hand all right. They protected their masters all right, but did they care about the poor? Does it matter to them that yet two more innocent young girls have been driven into harlotry and so to squalid deaths at the hands of a butcher? No, no. Sir Charles Warren merely hacks down the poor when they dare to raise their voices in supplication and in pain, and leaves the streets . . .'

'Mr Lusk,' said Abberline through clenched teeth. 'You will shut your mouth. Now.'

To my astonishment, Lusk laughed defiance in Abberline's face. 'You!' he mocked. 'You're finished, Abberline. You and all your kind. Lackeys. Lickspittles. The people are taking over their own streets. All over the city as the dreadful truth is learned, the people are arming and organizing, men, women, even children, outraged by the abominations performed this night. I tell you, Abberline, if I knew the identity of the man who has done this deed, I would shake him by the hand. At last the politicians and the lords and ladies are aware of what is happening here. At last the people are finding the strength in their poor starved bodies to arise and say, "Enough!" If this is achieved, if the bullying, bungling police are brought to their knees and the world learns of the abject conditions in which we live, these poor women will not have died in vain.'

'Lusk,' Abberline sighed. He made the name sound like an obscenity. His eyes were narrow, his breathing deep. I knew that he wanted to hit the man. 'You talk a lot about the poor, don't you? But you're not poor. You're not even a Londoner. A builder, from Cheltenham, *playing* at poverty. You say you care for these people. You care for no one but yourself, and that is why, Lusk, I am going to nail you. I do not know "the poor". I just know a lot of people, many of whom do not have two brass farthings to rub together, and I care for those people, each poor bloody one of them, while to you they are all dispensable in the cause of your aggrandizement, your great bleeding cause. Constable!' he barked.

'Sir?' A City officer loomed up from the shadows.

'Take a full statement from this man. Bleed him white. I want to know where he's been and what he's been doing for the last two months. In detail. Do you understand?'

'Sir.'

'Are you arresting me, Abberline?' Lusk sneered.

'Don't tempt me,' Abberline snarled. 'No, Lusk. I'm not arresting you. Not yet. But I don't think that you'll be doing your "cause" much good if you are seen not to be co-operating with the police, do you?'

The light of defiance in Lusk's eyes faded. He faltered for a second. 'Oh, no, Abberline,' he said. 'I'll co-operate all right. But I'll be interested to see what the newspapers have to say about your deliberate obstruction of one who seeks to ensure the safety of the common people, one who has shown himself ...'

But Abberline had turned away. 'Whassat?' he demanded sharply of a pair of officers behind him.

'Sir?'

'What did you just say? Writing? What writing?'

'Sorry, sir.' The old constable stepped forward. 'The writing they found on the wall with the bit of apron.'

'What?'

'Well, seems they found a bit of the old girl's apron, sir. In Goulston Street. And there was writing on the wall. Something about Jews ...'

Abberline and I were already running.

We arrived in Goulston Street, a mere six hundred yards away, to find a gathering of the most distinguished policemen in the kingdom. Sir Charles Warren stood at their centre. Around him, Arnold, his chest thrust out more than ever, Major Smith, looking relaxed and gentlemanly and far less military than the bristling Warren, Inspector McWilliam and several others stood gazing at the jamb of an open doorway.

I slowed my pace, but Abberline appeared totally uncowed. He strode up to the group and demanded, 'What's all this, then?'

'Ah,' bleated Warren. 'Abberline. Good. Yes. Bit of woman's apron found here. Fellow had wiped his knife on it. Might be military man. Always clean your sabre, you know? Yes. And this damned writing. Just about to sponge it out. Provocative, you see. Jews. Don't want riots and what not, do we?'

Abberline raised his eyes to the chalked scrawl on the wall. Lanterns were raised to allow us to read it.

> *The Juwes are*
> *The men*
> *That Will not be Blamed for nothing*

'Yes, well, this'll have to be photographed,' said Abberline.

'We have already discussed that, Abberline,' Arnold said briskly. 'Unfortunately, it will not be light enough to photograph it for at least an hour. It is the commissioner's opinion, with which I entirely concur, that it is undesirable that it should be left that long. Within the hour, the street will be filled with people. We cannot have ill feeling against the Jews stirred up by a malicious bit of writing that, in all probability, was not even by the murderer.'

'We can cover it,' said Abberline.

'A decision has been made, Abberline.' There was a warning in Arnold's voice. 'The message has been transcribed and its content noted. It can avail us nothing therefore to retain it.'

'Quite right,' Warren nodded. 'Anti-Semitic filth. What with this other killing, too, you know. Socialist club. Lots of Jews in places like that.'

'Yes, but hold on, Warren,' drawled Smith. 'I still maintain that this is an important bit of evidence and that Inspector Abberline . . .'

'Sorry, Smith.' Warren was becoming irritated. 'I have made up my mind. Our territory, you know, and Abberline our man. Scrub it out, constable.'

'Just wait a moment,' Abberline snapped.

'What do you mean, wait?' Warren almost squeaked.

'I beg your pardon, sir.' Abberline pulled a sheet of paper from his pocket. 'I just wanted to compare the handwriting.'

'What's that you've got there?' demanded Arnold.

'A letter.' Abberline was preoccupied. He glanced from the 'Jack the Ripper' letter to the wall and back again. 'A letter . . . sent to the Central News Office. Interesting . . .'

'We thought that it might be from the killer,' I put in.

Warren and Arnold exchanged a quick glance. They knew something that we did not. 'Come along, come along,' breathed Warren testily. 'Get on with it, constable.'

The constable reached up with his damp sponge and started to scrub.

'Well,' said Warren, relieved now and suddenly genial. 'There we are. That's done. Good. Any resemblance by the way, inspector? Between your letter and – that?'

'No, sir.' Abberline folded the letter. 'None.'

'Well, there we are. Good, yes. Now, yes. Any luck with your investigations, inspector?'

'A couple of possible sightings of the woman with her killer, sir. We'll send you our report.'

'Yes. Right. Well. Got to find something soon, Abberline. One hundred and forty-three plainclothes men, hundreds more in uniform. It won't do, you know.'

'Commissioner,' said Abberline evenly, 'we've taken thousands of statements. There are double patrols on the streets. I've got every known informant with his ear to the ground . . .'

'Yes, yes. Of course. But, none the less, something has got to be done! The Home Department has been receiving letters from this Whitechapel Vigilance Committee. They even wrote to Her Majesty.'

'George Lusk,' pronounced Abberline, 'is a thug.'

'He may be,' said Arnold smugly, 'but he's offering us help.'

'No, Chief Superintendent,' corrected Abberline. 'He's offering us trouble. He's a rabble-rouser, a politician, and he's using this case for his own ends. He as good as told me so.'

'Is he an anarchist?' Warren frowned. 'A Fenian?'

'He *calls* himself a socialist, but if you want a riot, Lusk's your man, and if the Secretary of State accepts his so-called "help", commissioner, I shall be forced to resign. Now,' he said, looking up at the pale grey of the sky, 'I must go back to work. If you will excuse us, commissioner . . .'

He nodded once, turned, and walked wearily back towards Mitre Square.

'All right.' Abberline rested his bum on the desk and held up a hand for quiet.

The incident room at Bishopsgate station was packed with uniformed and plainclothes officers. Behind Abberline's head, a map marked with crosses was drawn on the blackboard. 'Let us look at what we know. All the killings, as you see, occurred within a few streets of each other. All the victims were common prostitutes. Nobody sees anything, nobody hears anything. He kills, and he vanishes.'

'Local knowledge,' growled Spratling. 'We said that from the start.'

'He's tidy,' Abberline said, ignoring him, 'but all the same, there's gonna be a fair amount of blood on him. He's got to get off the streets, so where does he go? We've established that it's not the lodging-houses . . .'

'Someone's hiding him,' said Kerby, 'it's obvious.'

'Why's that obvious?' I frowned. 'He could live alone.'

'Sir?' A young constable at the back raised a hand.

'Yes?'

'What confuses me, sir . . .' The constable stood. His cheeks were pink. 'The thing is, why do these whores keep going with him? The ones I've talked to are too scared even to leave the publics.'

'Good question, Binding.' Abberline awarded him a small smile. 'Do they know him already, or is there some other reason why they feel that they can trust him.'

'A doctor, you mean?' said Binding. 'Or a priest?'

'Or somebody else in authority.' Abberline nodded. 'Could be.'

'Like us, for example?'

'That's not funny, lad,' snapped Spratling.

'Not in the slightest,' Abberline agreed amiably, 'but it is perfectly possible. That is why we are questioning everyone, man, woman or child, in the area. Somebody *must* know something. Now, these last two killings have given us some leads. They're not much, but they are all we've got. The first victim, Elizabeth Stride, née something unpronounceable, was killed at or shortly before one o'clock. At a quarter to twelve, she was seen in Berner Street by one William Marshall with a middle-aged man wearing a small black cutaway coat, dark trousers and a round peaked cap like a sailor's. He was, the witness says, "decently dressed, like a clerk or something". The man was kissing the woman and was heard to tell her, "You would say anything but your prayers." Whether that remark presupposes anything more than casual intimacy, I leave it for you to judge.

'Now, at 12.35, P C 452 Smith believes that he saw the woman Stride with a man five foot, seven inches tall, with a dark complexion and a small dark moustache. He wore a hard felt deerstalker of dark colour, a white collar and tie and a dark overcoat. He held a newspaper parcel in his hand. It was about eighteen inches in length and six or eight inches in width.

'This Stride was a busy lass. At a quarter to one, just minutes before her death, Mr Israel Schwarz saw a man stopping and speaking to her in the gateway where she died. The man tried to pull her into the street, and ended up turning her round and throwing her down on to the footway. The woman screamed three times but not very loudly. Schwarz crossed to the other side of the street, where he saw a second man lighting his pipe. The man who threw the woman down called out – apparently to this second man, "Lipski." Now, there's been a lot of excitement about this, and everyone's been looking for Lipski, but, as some of you know, Lipski was the name of a Jew hanged for murdering a woman back in 1884 and has since become a common insult to Jews. It is my opinion that the man who threw the woman down was insulting Schwarz himself, who is of a strong Jewish appearance.

'Now this business between the man and the woman sounds very like a commonplace domestic quarrel. Had the woman not known the man, surely she would have screamed a great deal louder for assistance. None the less, Schwarz is sure that the woman and the deceased were one and the same, so I'd like you to take down the following descriptions. First man: age, about thirty, five foot five inches; complexion fair; dark hair; small brown moustache; full face, broad shoulders. Dress, dark jacket and trousers, black cap with peak. This tallies with Marshall's earlier evidence, and implies that this fellow had been with Stride since a quarter to eleven or that he had had one encounter with her, and, according to Marshall, quite an affectionate one, and then sought her out again later on. The second man, the man with a pipe, who may be an accomplice in that he chased Schwarz away from the scene, is described as follows: age, thirty-five; height, five foot eleven; complexion, fresh; hair, light brown; moustache, brown. Dress: dark overcoat, old black hard felt hat with a wide brim. Schwarz, I might add, is a perceptive and trustworthy witness.

'Now, for purposes of comparison, here's a description of a man seen at Church Passage, Duke Street, just off Mitre Square, at twenty-five to two. The man was talking to a woman and the three witnesses noticed her black jacket and her bonnet, but didn't see her face. It seems likely, however, that this was Eddowes. The woman had her hand on this man's chest, but not as though she were trying to push him away or anything. He was aged thirty and of medium build. He wore a pepper-and-salt colour loose jacket and a grey cloth cap with a peak. A reddish kerchief was tied in a knot around his neck. He had the appearance of a sailor.

'Right.' Abberline looked up. 'That's all that we have at present. Knock on every door. If anyone comes up with *any-thing*, anything at all, however improbable, write it down and bring it back here. Questions . . .?'

There was silence.

'Right. Wear your boots out.'


Now the fear turned to panic.

Curiously, those most obviously menaced, the women of the streets, showed the greatest equanimity and good humour. They simply postured and cackled and called out, 'I'm next for the Ripper, eh, Mr Godley?' – for the 'Jack the Ripper' letter had now been published and within hours the name was to be heard everywhere. Respectable matrons in their West End houses, however, trembled and fumed. Dollymop nurserymaids no longer took their charges into the squares and gardens but remained in their bolted nurseries, thrilling to the stories and the ghoulish pictures in journals such as the *Illustrated Police News*. From every county, loyal subjects wrote expressing outrage and fury, fear, distress and suspicion of their neighbours.

There was talk of this one man and his knife bringing down the government, even the monarchy. The Prime Minister, Lord Salisbury, quaked. Warren faced an unparalleled onslaught from the press. He did everything in his power to justify himself, even going so far as to answer a charge by the Whitechapel District Board of Works (of which Lusk was a leading light): 'That this board regards with horror and alarm the several atrocious murders recently perpetrated within the district of Whitechapel and its vicinity and calls upon Sir Charles Warren so to regulate and strengthen the police in the neighbourhood as to guard against any repetition of such atrocities.'

Warren's reply was published in the *Daily Telegraph* of 4 October.

*The prevention of murder directly cannot be effected by any strength of the police force, but it is reduced and brought to a minimum by rendering it most difficult to escape detection. In the particular class of murders now confronting us, however, the unfortunate victims appear to take the murderer to some retired spot and place themselves in such a position that they can be slaughtered without a sound being heard. The murder, therefore, takes place without any clue to the criminal being left . . . .*

*I can assure you, for the information of your Board, that every nerve has been strained to detect the criminal or criminals, and to render more difficult further atrocities . . . and the very fact that you may be unaware of what the Detective Department is doing is only the stronger proof that it is doing its work with secrecy and efficiency . . .*

Warren's second-in-command, Sir Robert Anderson, returned from Paris on the day after the double murder to take up his new position as head of the CID. He at once reviewed the steps that we had taken and concluded that our methods had been 'wholly indefensible and scandalous'. The basis of this judgement was that 'these wretched women were plying their trade under definite police protection'. Abberline attempted to explain that prostitution was generally considered a minor transgression as compared with murder and mutilation, but was shouted down. Anderson's proposed solution to the problem was simple. Every prostitute to be found in the open after midnight was to be arrested.

It took a long time to explain to him that this was, to say the least of it, impracticable.

On the very day of the murders, 10,000 handbills were printed and distributed to Whitechapel and Spitalfields households. Within a week, a further 70,000 had been published. 'Should you know of any person to whom suspicion is attached, you are earnestly requested to communicate at once with the nearest police station.'

Meanwhile, Lusk and his Committee wrote to Her Majesty

and to the Home Office, demanding that rewards be offered. Neither deigned to reply.

Benjamin Bates whistled as he sauntered blithely through the incident room on the Tuesday morning.

'Here! You! Bates!' I leaped up and pointed, but Bates was already calmly strolling through the door of Abberline's office.

I wove a path in and out of the desks and the bound piles of papers on the floor. I tapped lightly on the door and pushed it open. 'Sorry, governor,' I said. 'He just stormed through . . .'

'It's all right, George.' One corner of Abberline's lip was tugged hard backward. 'Mr Bates is here to give us information, aren't you, Mr Bates?'

'Indeed I am, inspector, indeed – I – am. Yes, come in, sergeant. You should find this edifying. I have brought you a document. Of course, if you had rather, I shall just take it away with me again and publish it.'

'Come along, Bates,' Abberline sighed. 'We have no time for catch-as-catch-can. Give us the bleeding thing or get out.'

'All right, all right.' Bates sat impudently on the windowsill. He tossed a postcard on to Abberline's desk. 'You will note,' he said smugly, 'that it was postmarked on 1 October, the very day after the murders. You will also doubtless recall that 30 September was a Sunday, and thus that the news of the killings had not then been made public.'

'So?' Abberline dismissively flicked the postcard over to me. 'He reads your journal early yesterday morning and at once sits down and concocts this. Or, if you like, he's a local or even, as Sergeant Godley here believes, a journalist, and therefore knew all the details almost as soon as we did.'

'It looks like the same hand as the other.' I frowned. 'And he does seem . . .'

'Yes, yes,' Abberline broke in impatiently, 'it's the same as the last, but we get a lot of strange letters, you know, especially on murder cases. Check it out, George, before throwing it away.' He picked up a sheaf of papers and pretended to flick through it. 'Thank you, Mr Bates,' he hummed without looking up.

I at last understood Abberline's purpose. 'Oh, yes,' I assured Bates, 'my favourite's the man who thinks he's a giant vulture. He writes to us once a week. I know, why don't I show you those? You could publish them. "Vulture is Whitechapel Killer! The giant bird is said to descend upon the poor unfortunates, kill them with one stroke of its great claws, peck out their vitals and fly away. Four hundred police officers have been equipped with specially designed wings . . ."'

'No, thank you,' spat Bates. His cheeks glowed. 'Well, I only hope you don't think I've wasted your time, *officers* . . .'

'Nah, nah. It's what we're here for, isn't it, George?' Abberline laid down the papers and stood. 'And it's delightful to know the press are on our side.' He shook Bates's hand warmly. 'Good day, Mr Bates. Indeed yes, good day.'

Bates slammed the door behind him so hard that it bounced open and hit the wall.

Abberline leaped forward and grabbed the postcard from off the desk.

I was not codding dear old Boss when I gave you the tip. You'll hear about Saucy Jack's work tomorrow. Double event this time. Number one squealed a bit. Couldn't finish straight off. Had not time to get ears for police. Thanks for keeping last letter back till I got to work again.

Jack the Ripper

'Well?' Abberline leaned back and grinned.

'It's as though he wanted us to catch him,' I said gleefully, then, more hesitantly, 'if this is our man.'

'It could be,' Abberline purred. 'It could be. First one squealed a bit. Had not time to get ears? The squealing, you see, would be the not very loud screams that Schwarz reports as one of them tried to drag her wherever they wanted her to go. No one else knows that she squealed. She certainly didn't after he'd cut her throat, even if she did take more than a minute to die. He cut her windpipe with the first stroke. He "hadn't time" because of poor old Diemschutz. It all makes sense.'

'You still think there's more than one, then?'

'George, he takes a long time – fifteen minutes, they said at the Chapman inquest.'

'So someone's keeping watch, you mean?'

'Would you risk it? Out in the open? Alone?'

'I wouldn't risk the least crime in those circumstances.'

'No. No, it's two all right. Maybe the two that Schwarz saw. At a hazard, I'd say that the taller one, the one with the pipe, is likely to be the killer, while the other is the procurer, but that is pure speculation.'

'This letter, though. As you said, it could still be a journalist.'

'All right.' Again Abberline tossed the card over to me. 'Parse, or construe, or whatever it is you do.'

'Right. "I was not codding dear old Boss" – more cordial, sounds as though he's trying to play the Cockney but he doesn't do it too well. "You'll hear about Saucy Jack's work tomorrow" – contrived, laboriously contrived, I'd say, to make us think that he wrote this soon after the murders. "Saucy" is strangely coy. "Straight off" sounds American to me, though it needn't be. "Had not time to get ears for police" – Hmm. Whoever it is knows that the first corpse was intact, but why isn't he bragging about the second one? Surely the first killing was a failure, and the second, in his peculiar terms, a resounding success, so why's he going on about number one? Because he doesn't know the details? I think so. There's been no post mortem report on the second murder released yet, so he's not going to give himself away by boasting that he has cut the ears off. He's in the dark. A fake, I'd say. Interesting, but a fake.'

'I'm not so sure.' Abberline tapped his teeth with his pen, 'I've got a feeling about this one, George. I think this is our man. And if I'm right . . .' He stood, took the card from my hand and frowned down at it. 'If I'm right, he's just signed his death warrant.'

My memories of those days have merged like the lines of melody in a song. It is hard for me to remember when I questioned this suspect or arrested that.

The grotesque, of course, remains vivid. I know that Lees turned up on the day after the Double Event, claiming to have foreseen the murders. This time, interestingly enough, he had witnesses. At eleven o'clock on the night of 29 September, he had been dining at Simpson's in the Strand. Several diners confirmed that he had leaped to his feet, sending cutlery and glasses clattering to the floor. He had clutched his throat and cried, 'No! No! Again! He walks again! Stop him! He must not again!'

His companions had soothed him, poured brandy and water for him and pressed him to go home and lie down, but he would not, insisting that he must go at once to Whitechapel. 'My guide,' he babbled, brushing them aside. 'My guide will show me where he is. I must go. I must stop him.' And, refusing all company save that of his spirit guide, he had stumbled on to the street.

According to his own account, he had wandered the streets seeking the killer. 'But I was always just behind him. I sensed his presence strongly, very strongly, in Davenant Street: it was at a quarter after midnight, but there are so many streets, so many alleys. I could not find him. And then, now, I hear about these poor, poor wretches, done to death, and I think perhaps, if I had tried harder, if I had pursued with more persistence, if this poor frail frame of mine had been worthier to receive guidance, then perhaps they might still have lived. My gift should have been visited on one worthier than I, for I am feeble and fallible and those women died for my weakness . . .'

'I'm sure they don't hold it against you, Mr Lees,' Abberline had interrupted his ramblings. 'Did anyone see you on your wanderings around Whitechapel?'

'Oh, someone must have done surely.' Lees shook his head sadly. 'I saw many constables, many unfortunate women. Someone will surely have seen me.'

'What were you wearing, Mr Lees?'

'I can stand it no longer, inspector. I shall go abroad . . .'

'Not yet, Mr Lees. What were you wearing?'

'What does it matter, inspector? Those poor, poor lost souls are dead . . .'

'What were you *wearing*?'

'A black cloak.' Lees blinked watery eyes. 'And black trousers, and a top hat.'

'Check it, would you, George?' Abberline handed me two sheets of paper. 'See if anyone saw Mr Lees at or around the time of the killings.'

'Oh.' Lees shifted his weight forward with a little jump. 'Oh, no. By then, you see, I had given up the search and returned home. It was brisk, you see, and my chest . . . No, I must have reached home at – when? Around a quarter to one.'

'Someone will be able to confirm that, I suppose?' Abberline drawled.

'Er . . . well, no. I had given my servants the evening off.'

'I see. Well, well, that is inconvenient, isn't it, Mr Lees? I'm afraid that I cannot allow you to leave the country until your story is confirmed. You will understand that, no doubt?'

'No.' Lees was suddenly, surprisingly assertive. 'No,

inspector. Frankly, I do not. If you are implying for one moment that I, who have given my life to matters of the spirit, might . . . might . . .' His jowls shuddered.

'I imply nothing,' said Abberline, 'but if you were in White-chapel that night, you are suspect. And don't fulminate and stamp and seethe, Mr Lees. Everyone is suspect, even our own officers.'

'I am not one of your officers.' Lees pulled himself to his feet. 'I am a busy man, inspector, an important man, and I have no intention of being bullied by you. If I wish to leave the country, I shall do so, and there's an end of it, and should I in any way be impeded, I shall have no hesitation in lodging a complaint with the highest in the land. I hope that this is understood.'

He sniffed deeply, plucked up his hat and bounced off the door-frame as he attempted to leave with affronted dignity.


The inquest on Elizabeth Stride was again in the hands of Wynne Baxter, and again low comedy found its way into the courtroom.

One Mary Malcolm came forward to identify the body in the mortuary as that of her sister, Elizabeth Watts. With enormous and evident satisfaction, she listed her sister's faults: 'I last saw her alive at a quarter to seven last Thursday evening. She came to me where I worked . . . She came to me to ask me to give her a little assistance, which I've been in the habit of a-doing off and on for the last five years. I gave her a shilling and a little short jacket . . . I couldn't say where she was living except that it was somewhere in the neighbourhood of the tailors and Jews in the East End. I understand,' she said scornfully, 'that she was living in lodging-houses.'

'Did you know what she was doing for a living?' asked Baxter.

'I had my doubts.' She nodded smugly, her plump hands clasped before her belly.

'Was she the worse for drink when she came to you?'

'She was sober, but unfortunately, drink was a failing with her.' She tutted.

The character assassination that ensued was thorough and ruthless. Elizabeth had left her home because she had 'brought disgrace on her husband. Her husband had caught her with a porter . . . I've never seen my sister in an epileptic fit, only in drunken fits. I believe she's been before the Thames police-court magistrates on charges of drunkenness. I believe she's been let off on the ground that she was subject to epileptic fits, but I do not believe that she was subject to them. I believe she once lived with a man who kept a coffee-house at Poplar . . . I knew that she was called "Long Liz" . . . She used to come to me every Saturday, and I always gave her two shillings.'

Mrs Malcolm had, in fact, failed to identify her sister's body on the first occasion that she had viewed it in St George's mortuary. This, however, she blamed on the gaslight. The following morning, however, she had positively identified it.

'Did you not have some special presentiment about your sister?' asked Baxter, alert as ever to a good story.

'Yes. About twenty past one on Sunday morning, I was lying on my bed when I felt a kind of pressure on my breast, and then I felt three kisses on my cheek. I also heard the kisses, and they were quite distinct . . . This disgrace will kill my sister . . . I have kept this shame from everyone.' ('Here,' records *The Times*, 'the witness sobbed bitterly.')

Mrs Malcolm completed her testimony with a glowing tribute. When asked if she recognized the clothes that the dead woman wore, she replied, 'No, I didn't. I never took notice of what she wore. I was always grateful to get rid of her. Once she left a baby naked outside my door, and I had to keep it until she fetched it away. It was not one of the two children already mentioned, but was by some policeman or another. I don't know anyone that'd do her harm, for she was a girl everyone liked.'

This story was recorded and read with much disapproval or amusement throughout the Empire before the poor maligned sister, Elizabeth Stokes of Tottenham, could come forward and clear her name. Meanwhile, to say the least of it, the publicity had caused her no little inconvenience. 'My husband's name is Joseph Stokes, and he is a brickmaker,' she announced to the court. 'My first husband's name was Watts, a wine-merchant of Bath. Mrs Mary Malcolm is my sister. I have received an anonymous letter from Shepton Mallet saying my first husband is alive. I want to clear my character. My sister I have not seen for years. She has given me a dreadful character. Her evidence is all false.'

The coroner was not prepared to judge as to the falsehood or otherwise of Mrs Malcolm's evidence, though it was plainly fantastic and malicious. He recounted with glee the coincidental resemblances in his summing-up. 'Both had been courted by policemen; they both bore the same Christian name, and were of the same age; both lived with sailors; both at one time kept coffee-houses at Poplar; both were nicknamed "Long Liz"; both were said to have had children in charge of their husbands' friends; both were given to drink; both lived in East End common lodging-houses; both had been charged at the Thames police court; both had escaped punishment on the ground that they were subject to epileptic fits, although the friends of both were certain that this was a fraud; both had lost their front teeth, and both had been living very questionable lives . . .'

It never seems to have occurred to Baxter that, as I subsequently ascertained by particularly searching, not to say brutal questioning of Mrs Malcolm, she had known Elizabeth Stride and had recognized her, and, with insane vindictiveness, had attributed Stride's history to the other Elizabeth.

The Eddowes inquest was interesting in three regards. First, John Kelly, Eddowes's common-law husband, testified that, on the Friday before her death, he contrived to earn sixpence. She told him, 'You take fourpence and go to the lodging-house. I'll go to the casual ward.' He objected, assuring her that Fred Wilkinson, the deputy of the lodging-house, would surely not turn them away for want of twopence. None the less, she insisted on going to the casual ward of the Mile End workhouse. He met her early on the following morning – the last of her life – and she explained that there had been 'some bother at the casual ward', which was why she had been turned out so early.

Had she actually passed the night at the workhouse, had she perhaps some rendezvous to keep, or was her conspicuously generous offer to sleep at Mile End merely a means to escape Kelly and go off whoring? Certainly she seemed to have little or no money on the Saturday when she again set off, supposedly to cadge off her daughter in Bermondsey, yet, by late on Saturday afternoon, she had enough cash to get rolling drunk.

If she did reach the casual ward, there is a connection between her last days and those of Annie Chapman who, it will be remembered, vanished from her usual haunts during the last week of her life and declared that she too had admitted herself to the workhouse. Nichols, too, had been away from 'home' for the last eight or ten days before her murder, and Stride for the last five. While these women's lives were scarcely regular, this can unquestionably be regarded as at least coincidental, at most suggestive. It is notable, too, that Nichols, on her return from wherever it was, had a 'fine new bonnet', Chapman had somehow acquired pills and medicines, and Stride, before setting off on her last journey, asked a friend named Catherine Lane to mind 'a piece of velvet' – presumably acquired in her absence – until her return.

Is it possible that, during their stays at the casual ward or elsewhere, these women were wooed with kindness and presents and persuaded to trust their killer?

The second important question raised at the Eddowes inquest was that of the killer's anatomical knowledge or surgical skill. The first dialogue on this point was between the City solicitor, Mr Crawford, and Dr Frederick Gordon Brown.

'Would you consider that the person who inflicted the wounds possessed great anatomical knowledge?' asked Crawford.

Dr Gordon Brown equivocated. 'A good deal of knowledge as to the position of the organs in the abdominal cavity and the way of removing them.'

Again Crawford asked, 'You have spoken of the extraction of the left kidney. Would it require great skill and knowledge to remove it?'

'It would require a great deal of knowledge as to its position to remove it. It is easily overlooked. It is covered by membrane.'

'Would not such a knowledge be likely to be possessed by one cutting up animals?'

'Yes,' said Gordon Brown.

Dr Sequeira, who had been the first medical man to arrive in Mitre Square, was also asked about 'skill'. He did not qualify his answer. When Crawford asked, 'Judging from the injuries inflicted, do you think he was possessed of great anatomical skill?' Sequeira answered, 'No.'

Dr William Sedgwick Saunders, fellow of the Institute of Chemistry, fellow of the Chemical Society, and public analyst of the City of London, was present throughout the post mortem. 'Having had ample opportunity of seeing the wounds inflicted, he agreed with Dr Brown and Dr Sequeira that they were not inflicted by a person of great anatomical skill.'

And, at the last, there was a phenomenon – one of the many that had plagued our investigations of this case. Joseph Lawende, one of the three men who had seen Eddowes with a man just before her murder, was about to describe him when the coroner broke in.

'He had on a cloth cap with a peak . . .' started Lawende.

'Er, yes,' said the coroner. 'Unless the jury wish it, I have a special reason why no further description of this man should be given now.'

Neither Abberline nor I was present at the courtroom on that day, but, as soon as Abberline heard about this extraordinary interruption, he exploded into an unparalleled fury, firing off volleys of telegrams demanding explanations of Major Smith, Arnold, Anderson and Warren. No satisfactory answer was forthcoming.

We saw Mansfield again within a fortnight of the murders. It was just after one o'clock in the morning in the Britannia, and Abberline and I had met up after a long night of scouting around Whitechapél, ensuring that everyone had seen our necessarily vague handbill and the poster reproducing the two Central News Agency letters ('Any person recognizing the handwriting is requested to communicate with the nearest police office') that Abberline had had published the very day after the second letter arrived.

Now we sat, our aching limbs stretched, and drank watered-down whisky. The public was packed as ever. Out at the back, we could hear the snarling and yapping of fighting dogs, the occasional shrill squeak, suddenly drowned by a roar of applause as a rat died. Somewhere upstairs, a woman soulfully sang 'She was Only a Parson's Daughter' to the puddling of a piano.

'There's something that doesn't make sense about all this, governor,' I told Abberline.

'Oh?' His eyes moved constantly, scanning the room. 'And what might that be?'

'Well, if there are two of them . . .'

'Which there are.'

'Well, what's holding them together? I mean, look at us. We

185

work hand-in-glove, but if you started hacking up women, I couldn't promise absolute unquestioning loyalty.'

'George.' Abberline sipped and shuddered. 'You disappoint me.'

'So what are we looking for? There has to be a motive that binds them. It isn't pimps punishing them. We know that. It isn't selling uteruses. That's been ruled out. It doesn't, on the other hand, appear to be pleasure in the conventional sense. As Collard said, he doesn't linger over his butchery. He cuts, grabs and gets out. What does that leave us with?'

'Religion or superstition?' suggested Abberline.

'Possible.' I pursed my lips and nodded. 'But a two-man religion of which no one has ever heard? Solo religious fanaticism we have met before, and the savage frenzy of a unified crowd, but *two* men, prepared to face the hatred of the whole country? It's difficult to believe.'

'Father and son?' Abberline mused. 'Husband and wife? Worse things than this have been done by couples in the grip of libidinous fervour. Or maybe it's not just two people. It could be a secret society of which there are thousands of members to give these two support and sanction.'

'Freemasonry?'

'Could be. It would explain Warren's insistence on cleaning away the writing on the wall. I was looking him up this morning: District Grand Master of the Eastern Archipelago, founder of the Quattuor Coronati Lodge of Masonic Research and Past Grand Sojourner in the Supreme Grand Chapter.'

'What's all that mean?'

'Haven't the slightest clue, but that's what he is. Anderson's another one.'

'All right. That might explain why everyone wants to dispose of the evidence. Don't think Llewellyn's a Mason, do you?'

'Dunno. Or Wynne Baxter. It's possible.'

I considered the possibility. Ritual execution – or, perhaps a conspiracy of silence to protect a demented fellow-Freemason ... It was possible, but that Freemason would have to be very important indeed to be protected and indulged rather than checked. Again the rumours about Prince Eddie were whispered in the dark corners of my brain. Was it possible?

I shook my head at last and smiled. 'This is fanciful.' I sighed. 'It will not do, Fred. There may be some corrupt Freemasons, but no one will persuade me that ordinary, civilized, intelligent, responsible people are conspiring to murder a series of unknown tickle-tails. It's too fantastic.'

'Yes,' Abberline nodded. 'And it's hardly doing any good to the likes of Warren, is it?'

'Nor Salisbury. No. It's no good.'

'Allo ...' Abberline's body retained its languorous posture, but his eyes suddenly narrowed. 'If it isn't dear old Dixie.'

I drained my glass. 'Have another one?' I asked. I stood without awaiting an answer, picked up his glass and swung around, apparently looking for a pot-boy.

Richard Mansfield leaned low over a table at which three girls sat drinking. I recognized Maria Harvey and Mary Jane Kelly, but the other girl's face was unfamiliar. Mansfield said something and the girls laughed. Mary Jane hit his arm with an outstretched hand. He leaned closer to her and whispered in her ear. Her eyes rolled upward. Her lips twisted into a coy little smirk. Maria leaned over, evidently demanding to know what he had said. Mansfield smiled, a smug, cock-of-the-yard sort of smile. He bent and whispered something to Maria too. The two girls looked into one another's eyes and burst into giggles. Mary Jane's hand crept across under the table and clasped Maria's.

Mansfield straightened, beaming, and drained his glass. He ruffled Mary Jane's hair. The backs of his fingers lingered on her cheek for a second, then he waved flamboyantly, turned on his heel and made a dramatic exit, pushing open both double doors. He had not seen us. I was sure of that.

I glanced quickly back to Abberline. He nodded. I carried the glasses over to the corner where a weary moucher sat slumped. His hat was pulled low over his eyes. Two days' growth of beard stained his chin. His kennel coat was filthy, his old boots patched with newspapers and bookbindings.

'See that man who just left?' I leaned against the wall beside him. My crown rested against a portrait of Tom Cribb in fighting stance. The tramp nodded.

'That's Richard Mansfield, the actor. Follow him, all night if need be. Don't let him out of your sight.'

The tramp nodded again, stood with remarkable speed and grace and reached for his crutches. A man can move fast on crutches, with a little practice.

Abberline joined me at the girls' table. 'Hello, Mary Jane, Maria.' He nodded. 'What did our American friend want with you, then?'

'What's it to you?' Mary Jane sniffed. She was willing enough to be friendly with me, but two policemen were a threat. Josephine Butler, who had forced through the Criminal Law Amendment Act of 1885, making all forms of organized whoring illegal, was no doubt a brave and sincere woman, but not only had she forced these girls on to the streets, she had made them the enemies of the police. The Ripper must have been grateful to her.

'Do you know who he is?' Abberline persisted.

Mary Jane shrugged. 'Just a gentleman, isn't he, Maria? Which is more than can be said for some as won't let a girl have a scoopeen in peace.'

'We're trying to help, Mary Jane,' I put in. 'You know we thought it was you got stiffened the other night?'

'Yeah, well.' Mary Jane laid a hand on her friend's forearm and exchanged a quick glance with her. 'That's 'cos Kate gave me name down de lock-up, isn't it? We're all right, thanks a lot, Mr Godley. Got our own place, haven't we, Maria?'

Maria Harvey nodded.

'Where's Joe gone, then?' I asked amiably.

'Dunno,' she sang. 'And don't care.'

'Did that "gentleman" make an appointment of any sorts with you?' demanded Abberline.

Again Mary Jane stiffened. 'What sort of appointment, may I ask?' Then, 'No, of course not. Just a nice gentleman as bought us a lush, that's all, isn't it, Maria?'

Maria nodded again and scowled darkly up at us.

They were lying.


Six days later, the killer sent us a present. It was brought into Abberline's office by a jaunty Benjamin Bates.

'Well, well,' he drawled. 'You're not doing too well, are you, boys? Seems you depend on me too much to bring in the evidence. And our friend Jack is doing everything in his power to help. Look what he's brought us today.'

'What is it?' I sighed.

'Something you'd never have dreamed of, sergeant.' Bates pushed his hat back on his head and grinned. 'And it arrived in the afternoon post, addressed to George Lusk, for whom, it seems, the killer has considerably more respect than for you.' He proffered the small cardboard box to Abberline, who sat studying some papers. Throughout this, Abberline had not looked up. He did not do so now. Somewhat discomfited, Bates turned back to me. 'Just look at that, sergeant.'

I took the box, opened it, looked down and dropped it as though it had burned me. The box fell to the ground with a dull, wet sound, and toppled. 'Oh, no!' I groaned, and stared gulping down at the shining red thing on the boards.

'What is it?' Abberline leaped to his feet and walked around the desk, pushing Bates unceremoniously out of his way. 'Oh,' he said. He, too, gulped. 'Considerate of him. If it's real. Is there a covering letter?'

'There is indeed.' Bates pulled a sheet of paper from his pocket with a proud flourish like that of a prestidigitator. 'Just read that, gentlemen.'

Abberline took the letter, scanned it quickly and said blithely, 'Thank you for your assistance, Mr Bates. I'm sure that this will turn out to be yet another little prank, but we'll look into it.'

'We've already taken a facsimile of the letter,' Bates crowed. 'This should be the best copy yet. Sorry to have given you a little surprise, sergeant. You turned quite white.'

'Goodbye, Mr Bates.' I opened the door, averting my eyes from the thing that still lay on the floor, speckled with dust.

Bates smiled and strolled past me. 'Cheer up, sergeant,' he said. 'It couldn't have tasted that bad. He probably had it with sage and onion.'

I slammed the door.

'Pick it up, will you, George?' Abberline returned to his desk.

I nodded sadly, picked up a sheet of cardboard and knelt, trying to keep my gaze upon Abberline's shoes beneath the desk. I flicked at the thing, and, as the cardboard touched it, was overtaken by a violent fit of coughing. I picked up the box and, screwing my eyes up, placed it quickly on the desk.

It contained half of a kidney.

'Can I see the letter?' I croaked.

Abberline handed it to me. It was written in a bolder, more aggressive hand than that in which the Jack the Ripper letters had been penned:

*From Hell*

*Mr Lusk*

Sir

I send you half the kidne I took from one woman

prasarved it for you tother piece I fried and ate it was very nise I may send you the bloody knif that took it out if you only wate a whil longer

Signed

Catch me when you can<br>Mishter Lusk

'Oh, God.' I winced. 'Whether this is our man or not, he should be hanged. What are we going to do with it?'

'Take it to a medical man.' Abberline shrugged. 'Tell you what. We'll follow procedure. You get it taken down to London Hospital, then we'll go and see our friend Sir William Gull for a second opinion. I've been wanting to have a word with friend Gull.'

I nodded and leaned out of the door to summon Constable Wensley. 'Oh, yes,' said Abberline. 'What happened to friend Mansfield last night?'

'Brand lost him, I'm afraid.'

'Not like Brand. What happened?'

'Mansfield went to a brothel off Cable Street. He stayed in there so long that Brand called in Constable Robinson and asked him to go in and look for him. Robinson searched the house. No Mansfield.'

'Back entrance?'

'Yes, if he'd climbed the garden fence.'

'Did anyone else leave while Brand was watching?'

'Hmm. We're thinking the same thoughts,' I said grimly. 'Let me fetch you the descriptions. Ah, Wensley,' I said as he stood back to allow me through the door, 'Inspector Abberline has a mission for you.'

By the time that I returned from my desk, the kidney had, thank God, gone, and there was only a small dark patch on the dusty boards to remind me of its existence.

'Here we are.' I flicked through Brand's report. 'Mansfield

entered the knocking-house at twenty-five to two. At a quarter to two, a sailor left with a trollop. Man described as five foot eleven, dark hair, sailor's cap, tattoos, about twice Mansfield's weight. At two o'clock, a smaller man emerged on his own. About five foot four, five foot five, dark hair, small brown moustache, broad build, dressed in a dark coat and a dark cap. Moved rheumatically, says Brand.'

'That's him.' Abberline's mouth was set in a rictus. 'That's Mansfield, and it could be the man Schwarz saw with Stride, too. Right. I want three men assigned full time to Mansfield, and they're to follow him wherever he goes at night. They're to be told that Mansfield can change his appearance better than any of those damned lizards you read about, and if they see anyone of the right height and build coming out of a building that Mansfield has entered, they're to watch him. In fact . . .'

'Yes?'

'Have we got a well-favoured, cunny-haunted lad on the force? Someone as doesn't mind too much about propriety or the risk of disease so long as he's serving Queen and Country?'

I grinned. 'I'll find one.'

'Oh, and one more thing, George?'

'Yes?'

'Did Brand stay on after Robinson had completed his search?'

'No, but you're right. Robinson saw Mansfield, dressed as Mansfield, leaving the knocking-house at twenty-two minutes past five.'

'Keep him in view, George.' Abberline nodded, well satisfied. 'Keep the bastard in view.'


Dr Openshaw's verdict on the kidney reached us that afternoon. It was, he believed, a human kidney. Having read the autopsy report, he concluded that it had belonged to Catherine Eddowes.

Either that, or some very knowledgeable – and very mischievous – medical man had sent it in as a practical joke.

Gull confirmed this view on the following morning. Peering down at the dissected kidney through his microscope, his hands at his waist, pushing back his frock coat, he announced, 'Female kidney, woman of middle age in an advanced state of alcoholism. Suffering from Bright's disease.' He pushed the microscope across to his son-in-law. 'Take a look, Theo.'

Acland leaned over the table and squinted down the microscope. 'Indeed yes,' he hummed. 'Is this from the Mitre Square corpse, then?'

'That's what we want to know,' replied Abberline.

'Autopsy report?' Gull held out a hand.

Abberline handed it to him immediately as though in a practised routine. Suddenly Gull winced. His right hand arose to his brow. He closed his eyes tight and squeezed the bridge of his nose between forefinger and thumb.

'Are you all right, Sir William?' Abberline bent forward.

'Just tired.' Gull leaned back and blinked at the ceiling for a second. Then, 'Now, let's see . . .'

'This kidney's been preserved in alcohol,' said Acland suddenly.

'The way a medical man would do it?' inquired Abberline.

'Alcohol's easy enough to obtain, inspector, as this woman could have told you. Anybody can get it, not just doctors. And it's not charged with fluid, as it would have been had it been destined for the dissecting room. Probably came from a post mortem room. A student could have obtained it, or a porter . . .'

'Yes.' Gull's voice made me jump. He slammed the report down on the table. 'I'd say it belonged to this poor woman.'

'You're quite sure, sir?'

Gull grunted. 'How long's a renal artery in an adult human, Theo?'

'Three inches.' Acland's eye was still at the lens. He was smiling. 'As you very well know.'

'There. Two inches were left in the body, and there, if I'm not very much mistaken, is the missing inch.'

'Was it removed in a professional manner, Sir William?'

'By a surgeon, you mean?'

'Why all this sudden emphasis on surgeons?' snapped Acland suddenly. 'You don't need a medical degree to take hold of a kidney and cut it out. Butchers do it every day, for goodness' sake.'

'I was only asking, Dr Acland.' Abberline's eyebrows were raised.

'Ah, well.' Gull smiled. 'Ever since the day when you consulted me about mental instability, inspector, my son-in-law has been following this case avidly, haven't you, Theo? Can't talk or think of anything else. I'm afraid all this talk of doctors has hurt his professional pride,' he teased, 'hasn't it, dear boy?'

'No, of course not,' said Acland testily. 'It's just so − so ridiculous, that's all.'

'I have already given the inspector my opinion as to the likelihood of a doctor committing these bestial murders, haven't I, inspector? A doctor, as I have said, would derive no pleasure from anything so commonplace.'

'Nor does the killer,' said Abberline, glancing up at Acland. 'Nor − does − the killer.'

As we trotted down the steps outside Guy's Hospital, Abberline laid a hand on my left shoulder. 'Look, George,' he said and nodded towards the street, 'a dear old friend of yours.'

I looked, and groaned.

John Netley had already seen me and was walking forward, a broad smile stretching his moustache. 'Remember me, George,' he called, 'from the royal mews?'

'Of course.' I took his hand. 'John Netley. You remember John Netley, don't you?'

'Indeed, yes. Weren't you going to keep your eyes peeled for a coach – a black landau, like the royal one?'

'Yeah, well.' Netley shrugged, smirked and looked down at his outstretched fingers. 'I been busy.'

'Lots of doctors, eh?' I prompted.

'Only the best.' He nodded eagerly. He explained to Abberline, 'I'm a crack driver, see. Waiting for a famous surgeon now, matter of fact.'

'He's driven royalty, too, haven't you, John?' I cajoled.

'Highest in the land. Oh, yes. Not in this one, mind.' He tapped his little brougham with a knuckle. 'When you work for the Palace, they give you a beauty.'

'Tell him about the prince.'

'Oh, Prince Albert Vee.' Netley was blasé, plainly the Prince's best friend. 'Oh, he's a lad is Prince Albert Vee. I could tell you a thing or two – not that I would, of course. Not I. Soul of discretion. They rely on that.'

'What sort of a lad?' asked Abberline.

'Oh, no.' Netley grinned and winked with odious overfamiliarity. 'You won't catch me like that, inspector. No, no. Discretion is my byword. I know how to keep my mouth shut, I do. Ooh.' He straightened his hat and picked up his whip. 'Here's my surgeon. Tar tar, gents.'


Warren, meanwhile, was pursuing his absurd conviction that bloodhounds would save the day, despite the criticism, cavilling and downright mockery of the police, the press and the public.

He acquired on loan from Mr Edwin Brough of Scarborough two magnificent specimens by name Burgho and Barnaby and, while we were combing the stinking streets of Whitechapel and Spitalfields, our commissioner was to be found galloping about Regent's Park of a frosty morning, hotly pursued – and on one occasion lost, it is said – by two lugubrious, slavering hounds.

*

If, as the saying goes, rumours concerning Prince Albert Victor 'spread like wildfire', it was not for want of arsonists. Bates and Lusk had both been seen shooting blazing arrows into the scrub, and I had had occasion to warn both of them. Other Radicals, too, climbed on to their soapboxes and, in the midst of their rantings about 'If Polly Nichols had been Lady Nichols, the Prime Minister would have been down here! Rewards of thousands of pounds would have been offered! If Annie or Cathy had been duchesses, they'd have brought the army in. But oh, no, they're only our women, so no one cares, no one gives a damn . . .', in the midst of such ululations, none, it seemed, could resist a reference to royalty. 'Oh, yes, they come down here, all right. You've seen them! We all have! They have uses enough for the likes of Annie Chapman when it comes to their own corrupt vices. They, who are wealthy, will take enough from our poor children – our girls *and* our boys – but will they give anything in return? When those whom they have exploited and corrupted raise their little hands, their little eyes to them in supplication, will they heed them? Oh, no, brethren. They stay safe in their grand houses – their palaces even – and occasionally deign to visit us of a night. You've seen their carriages, haven't you? Coachies sitting waiting as their ever so high and mighty masters do some not very high and mighty things to our wives, our daughters, our friends, our sons. You've seen them, my friends, have you not? Coaches emblazoned with crests, with coronets, even – and yes, I dare to say it – even one that bears a crown!'

The queen, of course, was down at Osborne in her mournful mausoleum, surrounded by relics of her beloved consort, but she read the newspapers and knew full well the agonies suffered by her people. It was all that we could do to prevent these slanders – if slanders they were – from appearing in print.

'You know, George,' said Abberline as we walked briskly

towards Buck's Row on the freezing night of 20 October, 'if there's any truth in these rumours, we're sailing without a map. You realize that?'

'I'm not stupid, Fred.' I tried to stop my teeth from chattering. 'I know what royalty means.'

'What I'm saying is, if things get nasty, you don't have to stay.'

I smiled. Abberline was obviously depressed. 'I know what you're saying, governor. How long have we been working together?'

'Dunno,' said Abberline. Then, 'Four years.'

'Then you should know me by now. I only become anxious at midnight. I'll let you know when it's chiming. Now,' I said as we turned into Buck's Row, 'what did you want to show me?'

We walked, puffing steam into our greatcoat collars, to the place where Polly Nichols had lain. 'Number one,' said Abberline, 'Mary Ann Nichols. Feet this way, head there.'

'Right.'

'And not much blood. A pint, maybe. No more.'

I wrapped my arms about my chest and shifted from foot to foot. 'How d'you know that? They'd washed it away by the time we'd arrived.'

Abberline pointed. 'Look at all those windows, there, there, there – all around us.'

'Y-yes.' I nodded. 'What have windows got to do with blood?'

'I'll show you.' Abberline said softly. 'Come on. Hanbury Street.'


'Number two, Annie Chapman.' Abberline peered up at the windows surrounding the yard. 'Dragged in here, killed, then slowly taken to bits. Do you believe it?'

I looked down at the cracked flagstones and, for a moment, saw again the splayed and ravaged body as it had lain there that night. You may get inured to horror, but you never forget. 'Believe it?' I frowned. 'I saw her. Seeing is believing.'

'Yeah? Watch this.' Abberline took one small step forward and rapped out a sharp, 'Hey!'

Almost at once, faces appeared at two of the windows, then a third. A window creaked open, 'Who's that?' croaked a voice that might have belonged to an old woman or an old man.

'Police,' said Abberline. 'Goodnight. Come on, George.'


'Back to Duffield's Yard, I suppose?' I asked, sidestepping a small group, a family perhaps, who slept soundly on the pavement despite the cold.

'That's right.' Abberline marched with more vigour now. His depression had passed.

'Has it occurred to you to wonder why Whitechapel?' I asked.

'Easy pickings.' Abberline shrugged.

'Yes, but why Whitechapel? Why not Southwark, on the other side of the river? Plenty of easy pickings there, too, and nothing like so many coppers and Vigilance Committees. Or St George in the East? I mean, if you were planning a campaign like this, you'd kill a few – two, perhaps, three – in this area, then when the streets are crawling with reelers, you'd move, surprise everyone with another killing somewhere down by Guy's Hospital or something. These murders have all taken place within – what? Half a mile of one another?'

'So our man has only a limited time,' mused Abberline, 'or perhaps he's superstitious . . . damn it,' he said, 'nothing's logical in this case.'

We were in Berner Street now. 'All right.' Abberline swung into Duffield's Yard. 'So here there's a change of pattern. Long Liz won't play along with these men's game. They want her to come with them, but she resists. Not much, mind you. Her screams aren't the sort you'd expect from someone who thinks she's about to be murdered, which implies that she already knows this man or these men but suddenly gets suspicious. So maybe she's going to report her suspicions. Maybe one of the men has given himself away. One way or another, they've got to kill her, even if she's not, like the rest of them, a willing lamb to the slaughter. So. You're Long Liz, right? Dunno if you've read the inquest report, but you'll have noticed if you had that Dr Phillips discovered bluish marks on the shoulders and round the collar-bones. What's the quickest way of incapacitating someone while leaving them alive, Sergeant Godley?'

'Cut off the supply of oxygen to the brain,' I said. 'Block off the carotid artery.'

'Right, and that takes a little medical knowledge because the right spots on which to put pressure aren't that easily found. Still, that's what our friend does. Reaches over her shoulders, so . . .' said Abberline and bent me backwards, 'and presses with his fingers here.' He jabbed at the two points, just within the clavicle, at which the flow through the carotid arteries can easily be stemmed. 'Or maybe,' he said, spinning me round, 'maybe he does it from in front, so, because in the case of Chapman there were two distinct bruises at the same point, each the size of a man's thumb. Either way, she wouldn't have known it was happening. Just a caress with a bit of pressure, then out go the lights. No chance to struggle, scratch or claw, as there would be with strangulation, just sudden unconsciousness. So then he lays her down on her back. Lie down, George.'

'Must I?' I winced. I knew what the answer would be.

'Yes. Order from a superior officer. Don't question, man. Yours but to do or die. That's better. Right. And he slashes her throat, but not very efficiently because he's interrupted. All right, get up, George. We've got some running to do. Mitre Square. At the double.'

I made it in seven minutes, Abberline in nine. Both of us were impeded in our progress by suspicious cries of 'Hey!' and the necessity to prevent pursuit by shouting back, 'It's all right! Police!' as we ran along Commercial Road and Whitechapel High Street (Abberline chose to go by Braham Street) and so to Aldgate and Mitre Square.

I was leaning on the fountain, trying to look casual and to control the heaving of my chest when Abberline ran wheezing into the little square. 'Stop for a chat with someone, then?' I asked.

'You – you obviously want to stay a-a sergeant,' puffed Abberline. He gulped down a pint of cold air. 'All right, Hermes. You don't have to spend all your life tied down behind a desk. How long did you take?'

'Seven minutes.'

'Eight,' volunteered Abberline hopefully.

'Nine.'

'Yeah, well. But our man's not gonna run like us, draw attention to himself, is he?'

'So, say, the better part of a quarter of an hour.'

'At the least.' Abberline nodded. He slumped down on to the step below the fountain. 'At the least, because, if he had blood on his hands or clothes or simply didn't want to be seen in the area, he would have had to go by the little back streets. Say he gets here round twenty past one. But, hold on, he doesn't get here, does he? Because he's not seen by P C Watkins. So he goes a little further, perhaps, and meets our Kate somewhere on her way down from Bishopsgate. He talks to her, takes her to Church Passage where they're seen standing still and talking at twenty-five to two. He then waits a minute until the three witnesses from the Imperial Club have gone away, leads her into Mitre Square, kills her and starts hacking away. He's started his job at, say, twenty to, and he's finished it and vanished into thin air by a quarter to. It could be done.' Abberline was talking to himself now. 'It could be done, but I don't believe it. It's cutting it too fine. I think . . .'

'Yes?'

'I think he had a coach.'

'A *coach*?' Now I had to sit down, too. 'But how . . .? I mean, what . . .?'

'I do like a cogent man on the case.' Abberline grinned. 'A man who grasps the essentials with the speed of lightning. Gives one confidence.'

'Well, explain, damn it,' I snarled. 'I mean, it makes sense, sort of, but there are a thousand problems about a coach.'

'No, there aren't. We're agreed there are two men involved in this?'

'It seems so, yes.'

'Well, a coach doesn't drive itself, does it? And you can't see the man inside it. And it can move fast and almost unnoticeably through the streets. So. One of them drives, one of them goes out hunting. I don't know which does which. Perhaps the driver goes procuring for the passenger. Perhaps the passenger goes out, leaving the driver on the box. Anyway, whatever the case, the man who approaches the girl is probably known to her. He could be a doctor working for one of the charities, or one of these students that come to aid the poor unfortunates, or maybe a coachman who already does a bit of procuring for a better class of customer, so they know him and come with him, expecting to be taken somewhere nice and paid royally. Only on this occasion, the better class of customer ain't taking them anywhere. He kills them, or half kills them, in the coach, safe from prying eyes. Maybe he actually mutilates them there . . .'

'That's going a bit far, isn't it, Fred?' I objected. 'I mean, the blood! You'd never be able to free a coach of that stink. It could never be used for any other purpose again.'

'Well? That's possible, isn't it? In a private carriage.'

'Just possible,' I admitted, 'But very, very dangerous. What if we stopped the coach?'

'Ah, yes.' Abberline stood. 'But there are some coaches that we would never dream of stopping, aren't there?'

'God almighty,' I breathed as the import of his words became clear. It was prayer, not profanity. 'It can't be.'

'Maybe not, maybe not.' Abberline started to pace back and forth. 'But the coach has to appear to be important, like Lees's precious coach with the crest on its side. It doesn't follow that the passenger has a right to that crest, does it?'

'No.'

'And all right, maybe he doesn't actually kill in the coach. Maybe I'm wrong about the quantity of blood. Some of the doctors seem to think that there wouldn't be much anyhow. Maybe they're right. But what matters is, he incapacitates them out of sight, then, perhaps, drags them out, unconscious, and does the rest, all the time guarded by his coachy, then climbs back in and can be away in seconds. Another thing. If he kills or incapacitates them by this carotid method, it would mean that there'd be very little blood in any case, because the blood flow's been staunched!' Abberline was almost shouting in his excitement. Only now, as the echoes of his last few words came back to him in the walls of the square (and, incidentally, I saw a light come on in PC Pearse's bedroom. He evidently slept a little lighter these days), only now did Abberline raise a hand to his mouth and lower his voice.

'Let's go home, George.' He grinned happily. 'Warn the women. Two men and a coach. And give orders throughout the force. Every coach out after dark is to be stopped, no matter who is riding in it. I'll take responsibility for that.'

Abberline's happiness was short-lived. Coaches were stopped and complaints accordingly received, but we discovered nothing new. Suspects were found, dragged to the station and questioned, then released. And worst of all, we were constantly besieged.

'Out! Out! Out!' came the persistent ragged barrage of cries from outside the station. 'Warren resign! Warren resign!' And always at the centre of the crowd stood Lusk, roaring, waving a club or a torch and conducting the rioters like an orchestra. Always too, on the verges, stood Bates, smugly taking notes, compiling new copy for the 'War on Warren' that the *Star* had declared in a banner headline.

Warren, however, was not the only butt. All of us were wary. We were jostled on the streets. People spat as we passed. The revolution that Lusk and Bates so ardently desired seemed just days away.

The tales about Prince Albert Victor, too, had ceased merely to be rumours whispered in corners and were now shouted on the streets. This despite the fact that we had shown that the poor silly, maligned prince had been in Scotland for the past ten weeks. This, in fact, was one of my duties. I checked every last guest list, shooting party and speech on the royal itinerary. He had never left Scotland, even for a day.

Bates was informed of this, but merely smirked and told us, 'Court circulars are the concoctions of the Palace. Why should we believe them?' He continued in his increasingly triumphant and hysterical articles to cast suspicion on 'the close associates of the royal family'.

Of Mansfield, however, there was news, and less than edifying news at that. *Dr Jekyll and Mr Hyde* was another of the Ripper's casualties. The theatre-goers of London, it seemed, were sated with blood, and it was claimed that Stevenson's demented doctor might serve as an example to the real murderer. Mansfield was playing to half-empty houses, and soon the play was taken from the stage.

On 27 October, Mansfield once more ventured down to the

brothel in the dockland. Once again, he emerged in a different guise, in a short dark jacket, dark trousers, a blue scarf and a sailor's blue cap. He was followed.

He visited the lowest and roughest haunts of that lowest and roughest of areas. Whitechapel was near to the city and, although peopled by many criminals and many poor, was none the less policed. The area where Mansfield wandered was governed by its inhabitants, lumpers and publicans, rude visiting sailors and whores who catered only for them. I would not have ventured into that world alone.

Mansfield, however, always the actor, appeared to enjoy himself enormously. Posing as a coarse foreign sailor, he spent liberally, enjoyed a brief dog rig with a pocked trug-moldie and then, incredibly, made his way to the Mile End workhouse where he spent the remainder of the night.

Two days later, he visited Robert James Lees for a 'consultation'. That evening after rehearsals for his new production, *Richard III*, he again ventured on to the East End streets, this time in his own guise – or, at least, in what we took for his own. And he slept with Mary Jane Kelly.

On 6 October, I called on Lees at his home. The drawing-room into which I was shown was very dimly lit. All the furniture was covered with oriental cloths. Everything was fringed or tasselled. There were crystal balls, an astrolabe, astrological charts and tarot cards scattered on the table at the centre. The curtains were drawn, although it was only two o'clock in the afternoon.

In the corner, a large chair, ornately carved with twisted shapes and grimacing faces, was canopied over with dark gold brocade. This, evidently, was the throne from which Lees made his pronouncements.

Lees greeted me brusquely. He walked quickly from a side room and did not even look at me or shake my hand, merely walked to the table and started to snap books shut and replace them on the shelves.

'What is it this time, sergeant?' He studied a title-page, nodded to himself and returned to the book-case. 'I was just going out.'

'This sketch you drew for us, Mr Lees.' I held out his drawing. 'The coach you saw in a vision, the one you say nearly killed you in the street.'

'Er ... yes.' He glanced at it quickly, then looked away again. 'What about it?'

'You said it was a royal coach.'

'Very like a royal coach, certainly.'

'Ah. *Like* a royal coach. But you said you'd ridden in it, when you went to see Her Majesty. Is it royal property or is it not?'

Lees flapped a hand impatiently. 'It has a sort of crest on the side, as I've drawn it there. I never looked at it closely. Perhaps I was wrong.'

'Perhaps you were wrong?' I feigned disbelief. 'Perhaps you were wrong? Mr Lees, we like people to be clear, concise and truthful. We are trying to apprehend a murderer. Was this coach royal property or was it not?'

'Probably not. I travel in a lot of coaches, you know.'

'I understand that Mr Richard Mansfield has been visiting you recently?'

'Yes, yes, he has. He is a most charming and talented man. I think that I have been of some assistance to him.'

'Did he mention his curious nocturnal habits?'

'I don't know what you can mean,' said Lees quickly. 'Really I don't.'

'Hmm. And how is it we haven't seen your name in the popular press of late, Mr Lees? No further interest in advertising your skills through the medium of Mr Benjamin Bates?'

'That is enough, sergeant.' Lees decided to be firm. 'These implications, these imputations ... I tried to help you. I try to help humanity, and I get treated like a common criminal. I won't have it.'

'Yes, well, I'm sorry about that, sir,' I said meekly, 'but we do not very much like or trust the company that you keep, and you have an unfortunate habit of knowing too much about these murders after the event.'

'Nothing, sergeant' – Lees became the lecturer – 'nothing in the realms of the spirit is ever simple and easily explained. It is the will of some other being, one beyond my control, that I should see these things, just as, no doubt, it is his will that I should be visited by Mr Mansfield and others. Oh!' He stopped suddenly and held his left hand up to his ear. 'Oh, listen! She's singing!'

I frowned and looked around me.

'Listen, listen!' There was a rapt look upon Lees's face. His jowls trembled. 'Oh, no.' He spoke like a child imitating his own disapproving mother. 'Oh, no. You must stop him. Somebody must stop him, now.'

I had by now realized that I was privileged to watch a display of Lees in the grip of a vision of some sorts. To be honest, it looked very fraudulent to me, but I had never seen anyone having such a vision before. It was quite entertaining, however, so I just stood and watched.

Suddenly, Lees reeled backward as though struck hard on the jaw. 'Oh, my God!' he keened. 'Oh, my God! He's doing it! He's cutting! No! No! Stop him!' Lees covered his head with his arms and flung himself down to his knees, apparently sobbing.

I placed a hand on his shoulder. 'Mr Lees?' I said, torn between a desire to laugh and curiosity. 'Mr Lees, sir, are you all right?'

'Yes, yes,' Lees whimpered and shook. 'Yes. You must stop him, sergeant.' He lowered his arms and stared up at me with eyes that showed a lot of white. 'You must stop him!'

'What was it?' I helped him up and into a chair. 'What did you see?'

'Long hair. I saw long, yellow hair. Such beautiful yellow hair. And a man, wearing armour.'

'Er . . . armour?'

Lees nodded and stared blindly ahead of him, his eyeballs swimming from side to side. 'Yes, like a knight. With a sword. A knight in armour. And she's got lovely yellow hair.'

'A knight in armour,' I repeated and my voice wavered a little, 'with a sword.'

Suddenly, Lees squealed and again covered his face. His knees arose, his head descended. 'No!' he drooled. 'He's cutting her, cutting her to pieces! Oh, my God! Somebody stop him. *Please!*'


'So,' I told Abberline, 'we're to look for a knight in armour and a girl with lovely long yellow hair.'

'Could be difficult to spot among the crowds.' Abberline shook his head. 'Anything more obvious?'

'Well, he's got a sword, apparently. That's all there is to go on.'

'Very difficult.' Abberline grinned. 'God! When I think how much of our time that man has wasted!'

'I know. Anything else for today, governor?'

'No. Get a good night's sleep. You look as though you need one. Me too. Got to see the commissioner at eleven o'clock tomorrow morning.'

'You coming with me, then?'

'No. You go on.' The office was thick with dusk. Abberline had not lit the lamps. 'I'm going to sit and think for a bit.'

'You did say, "Think" didn't you, not "drink"?'

Abberline's heavy eyes sagged. The lines from his nostrils to the corners of his mouth were deep and dark. 'Goodnight, George,' he said, and laid his forehead on the palm of his hand.

\*

Friday, 9 November, the day of the Lord Mayor's Parade, was bright and cold and cloudy. The streets shone after the persistent heavy rain of the previous night. The sky was a stack of fleeces. London smelled fresh.

In the West End, no doubt, children were being dressed up in their best suits in preparation for the big parade.

In Spitalfields, too, children were dusting themselves down and flexing their fingers in anticipation. There would be rich pickings to be had of the crowds today.

Some few enterprising and public-spirited East Enders had even strung bunting across one or two of the roads.

And Mary Jane Kelly's body lay stripped to the skeleton in a little ground-floor room in Miller's Court, Dorset Street.

'About twenty years ago,' wrote Henry Mayhew back in 1862, 'a number of narrow streets thickly populated with thieves, prostitutes and beggars were removed when New Commercial Street was formed, leading from Shoreditch in the direction of the London docks, leaving a wide space in the midst of a densely populated neighbourhood, which is favourable to its sanitary condition, and might justly be considered one of the lungs of the metropolis.'

But healthy as such a new development may then have seemed, the cancer that the surgeons had sought to cut out had merely reformed about this 'lung'.

Dorset Street was a short and narrow thoroughfare running from Commercial Street to Crispin Street. Between Nos. 26 and 28, there was a passage entered through an archway. This passage led into a little yard known as Miller's Court.

On the right-hand side of the passage, there were two doors. The first led to the upper rooms, the second directly into Mary Jane's room, fifteen feet square, with no furniture save a bed (parallel with the window and behind the door), a table and two chairs. A plain, unadorned room. Until now.

Mary Jane had shared this room with Joe Barnett until 30

October when, according to him and to her friend Julia Ven-turney, she had decided that she was so poor that she must resort – or revert – to full-time prostitution.

Poor stuttering Joe blamed himself for not earning enough to keep her, but none the less could not stand to live with her, know-ing that she came to him each night from off the streets. He had left her, apparently amicably, and Maria Harvey, another prostitute, had moved in. Maria had stayed for just two nights, Monday and Tuesday, before finding lodgings of her own just down the road. She left an overcoat, two dirty cotton shirts, a boy's shirt, a white petticoat and a black crêpe bonnet in Mary Jane's care.

On Thursday evening at five to seven, Joe called on Mary Jane. Maria Harvey had also dropped in for a chat, but thought it tactful to leave them together.

Joe stayed for about an hour. The principal purpose of his visit – aside, perhaps, from intimacies of which we will never know – was to express again his remorse at being unable to find work and his rancour at her taking Maria in. As to why she did so, we can only guess. Mary Jane was hard up. She owed her landlord, John McCarthy, one pound and nine shillings – over seven weeks rent – and was perhaps at once offering a fellow 'unfortunate' shelter and doing a little part-time brothel-keeping on her own account.

Friday was rent day, and at a quarter to eleven John McCarthy, a chandler, and as unpleasant a character as I have encountered, dispatched his man Tom Bowyer to collect.

Bowyer walked down the passage and rapped on the door. There was no reply. Suspecting that Mary Jane was hiding, he hammered harder and called, 'Mary Jane! Are you in there? Mary Jane!'

Still there was no reply.

Bowyer walked around the corner and into the yard. He bent and peered in through the window.

He jumped back. He turned away, looked at anything else – the clouds above him, the gutter pipe, the roofs of the little whitewashed houses that surrounded the yard. He mumbled something to himself, took a deep breath, and took one more quick glance through the window.

He walked quickly and quietly back to Dorset Street. He nodded and mumbled as he went. He walked like a man desperate for a piss yet afraid to run.

John McCarthy was drinking coffee in his shop. His back was turned towards the door. The sweet smell of wax was strong and suddenly revolting to Bowyer.

'There's been a murder.' Bowyer spoke quietly.

'Eh?' McCarthy turned.

'The Kelly woman. There's been . . . There's blood and . . . It's everywhere.'

McCarthy frowned and stood. He was a heavy man and his stomach strained his waistcoat, but he moved with the lumbering power of a fighting man. 'What you talking about?' he growled, brushing past Bowyer.

'It's everywhere.' Bowyer followed his master down the passage. 'Look in through the window. It's fucking everywhere!'

McCarthy placed his hands on either side of the window frame and leaned forward, pressing his nose against the pane. 'Je–sus Christ.' He blinked. 'What's he wanna do it here for? Je–sus Christ. This is gonna mean trouble, this is. Oh, Jesus. Poor bitch. It's bleeding . . .' He pulled himself upright. 'Come on, then, Tom. Suppose we'd better get the reelers in.'


The trouble was that we had been told that we were to wait for the bloodhounds. Warren's theory was to be put to the test, and no one was to venture on to the scene of the crime and spoil the scent until the dogs arrived. What no one had told us, of course, was that the dogs were now back in Scarborough and that, the previous day, Warren, now damned on all sides and pilloried as though he had been the killer, had tendered his resignation.

We arrived at the scene at half past eleven or thereabouts. Inspector Beck and Dr Phillips were already there and expressed their reluctance to force the door. We waited, therefore, and waited, while telegrams sped across the city. 'Found at 10.30 am, a woman cut to pieces in a room on the ground floor at 26 Dorset Street, Spitalfields.'

Abberline had already looked through the window. I had not. Abberline's first reaction had been enough for me. He had straightened and turned away with a hiss. 'When I find whoever did that,' he said, and his eyes were hard and cold, 'I will kill him, George.'

So we sat or slouched and waited and waited. We took McCarthy's statement and Bowyer's and sent constables into the other houses in 'McCarthy's Rents' in search of evidence.

Elizabeth Prater, who had a room in No. 27, testified that, between half past three and four, she was awakened by a kitten walking across her neck. At that moment, she heard three distinct cries of 'Murder!' 'I didn't take much notice,' she said. 'I often hear such cries from the back of the house.'

Another constable brought Mary Ann Cox over to us. 'I am a widow and an unfortunate,' began her statement. 'I've known Mary Jane for about eight months. As I was telling the officer, it was about a quarter to twelve last night when I came into Dorset Street from Commercial Street and there was Mary Jane in front of me with a man. They turned into the Court ahead of me, and just as I came into the Court, they went indoors. I says, "Goodnight, Mary Jane," but she was sort of hanging on to the door-frame and so 'toxicated that she could scarcely answer. Still, she says, "Goodnight," only it was more like, you know, "Gny." Oh, and the man was carrying a quart can of beer . . .'

'What was that?' I pulled myself up from where I was sitting. 'What did you say?'

She took two quick, nervous steps backward. 'Sorry,' she said softly. Then, as I smiled, 'He was carrying a quart can of beer.'

'Did you see the beer?' I demanded.

'Yes . . .' She frowned. 'I think so.'

'*Look for a Jew with a bucket, Mr Godley*,' I heard Mary Jane's admonishment. '*Look for a Jew with a bucket.*'

'Can you describe this man?' I demanded.

'Yes, yes. I think so. He was about – what? Thirty-six years old, I'd say. About – oh, I'm no good at heights – same as him over there, perhaps a little taller.'

'Five foot five, six.' I nodded. 'And? Complexion?'

'Dunno.'

'Fresh, swarthy, dark?'

'Fresh, I'd say, perhaps a few blotches on his face. Could've been the drink, of course. Small side-whiskers and a sort of thick carroty moustache.'

'And dress? How was he dressed?'

'Shabby.' She closed her eyes and nodded. 'Definitely shabby. Dark sort of clothes, dark overcoat, black felt hat.'

'Doesn't sound like our man,' said Abberline behind me.

'No, but . . . How long do you think he was there, Mrs . . .?'

'Cox. I don't know. I heard her singing soon after that. I went out soon after twelve and returned about one o'clock and she was still singing. Then I went out again shortly after one o'clock and returned about three, and there was no light in her room and all was quiet.'

'I see. Presumably you were not alone each time that you went backwards and forwards. Someone was with you, several people, perhaps, who could confirm your evidence?'

Despite her initial statement that she was an 'unfortunate', this question offended her. She refused to add anything more. No wonder that we could discover nothing. Prostitutes did not know their clients and the clients, in most cases, would not come forward and declare themselves.

'Constable?' I hailed an officer who was fidgeting and was plainly in need of something to do.

'Sergeant?'

'See if you can find me a Bible, would you?'

'A . . .?'

'A Bible. You know? Book, found in churches and decent Christian homes. Remember? I want one, quickly.'

'You feeling like repenting and saying your prayers, George?' asked Abberline as the constable scampered off. 'God knows, I might join you.'

'Really bad?' I glanced at him sideways.

'I said the man was playful, remember?'

'Yes.'

'Well, this time he got angry and broke all his toys.'


It was not until half past one that Arnold arrived, in full dress uniform bedecked with medals. 'Well now, yes,' he said. 'So what is happening, Abberline?'

'Nothing, sir,' drawled Abberline.

'What? Why not?'

'Because we were told to wait for the blee . . . for the blood-hounds, sir.'

'Ah, yes. No bloodhounds any more. So you haven't forced the door, eh?'

'No, sir. Nobody's been in there at all.'

'Right, well, come along, then. Let's get to it. Have we a photographic camera?'

'Yes, sir.'

'Well, let's force the door and then photograph the room before anything else, right? Yes. Oh, and the eyes, too.'

'What?'

'They say the eyes of a dead person record the last thing they

see. Commissioner Warren suggested it to me. Photograph the
 es, just in case it's true, eh?'

'That's if she still has eyes,' mumbled Abberline. 'All right,
lads. Clear the way!'

And we forced the door.


Enough has been written of the appearance of that room. Some
ghoulish screevers, dissatisfied even with the extent of the horror
that we found there, have exaggerated it still further, claiming
that entrails were festooned over the pictures on the walls and
such grotesque fancy. They reveal more of themselves, these
so-called historians, than of the scene that met our eyes that
afternoon. There were no pictures on the walls. Had there been
any such things, Mary Jane would scarcely have needed to go
on the game for want of money.

The scene was simple and sparse.

The body lay sprawled on the bed. The face had been cut
off, the stomach ripped wide apart to the breastbone exposing
ribs – everything. The flesh of the right thigh, too, was ripped
off, completely baring the bone. The corpse still wore a thin
linen undergarment. The breasts and the kidneys lay on the
table. Various other, bits were scattered about the room.

Two constables, including the photographer, vomited as soon
as they saw the body. Two others did so later as they came
upon – or, in one instance, trod upon – items that had once been
part of Mary Jane Kelly. The stench in the room was appalling.

I, to my surprise, did not vomit. Anger – cold, dangerous
fury – had supplanted all other emotion. I had known Mary
Jane Kelly. She was no close friend, no saint, and if she had had
a heart of gold she would have cut it out and sold it for scrap,
but she had been a person and I had known her. I wanted to kill
whoever had done this.

Everyone talked very quietly as they went about their business in that room. Somewhere a long, long way away, a band was playing a jaunty marching tune.

'There's been a big fire in here,' murmured one officer from the grate. 'So big it even melted the spout of the kettle.'

'What'd that be for?' frowned Abberline.

'So that he could see what he was doing, I suppose,' said Phillips, who was measuring some part of the erstwhile face with a pair a callipers.

'But what did he burn?'

'Dunno,' said the constable. 'There are some scraps of stuff here.'

'Clothes?' Abberline squatted. 'Hmm. Yes. Women's clothes. But hers are still here.' He nodded at the chair, where Mary Jane's clothes lay neatly folded. 'And a few clothes wouldn't be enough to create that sort of blaze. It must've been one great oven in here as he went about his work.'

'Hell,' said the constable.

'Exactly. Could've been his clothes, I suppose. You got any idea, Sergeant Godley?'

'Yes,' I said softly. 'I'll tell you about it later. Outside.'

A few moments later, as we were about to leave the medical experts to their business, Abberline picked up a small etching in a wooden frame that had stood on the table.

'Good God,' he breathed. Then, looking up, 'George, you ready?'

'Yes.' I followed him out into the yard. I breathed in as much cold air as my lungs could hold and blinked up at the consoling and permanent sky. Abberline still held the etching.

'What's that, governor?' I asked.

He handed it to me without a word.

It was a familiar picture, to be found in parlours throughout the land. Lancelot and Guinevere. A man in armour, with a sword. A girl with long blonde hair.

'More things in heaven and earth, eh?' Abberline's voice

cracked. He sounded as though he might cry for anger. 'Unless, of course, Lees knew that this was here. From friend Mansfield, for example. Anyhow,' he said, shaking himself, 'what was it you wanted to tell me?'

'Let's sit down.' I indicated the stone base of the water pump and pulled the octavo Bible from my pocket. Listen.'

First I read the passages that Mary Jane had quoted to me – Leviticus, chapter 3 – relating to the 'peace-offering'. Then, glossing a little, I moved on to the 'sin-offering.'

And if a soul sin, and hear the voice of swearing, and is a witness, whether he hath seen or known of it; if he do not utter it, then he shall bear his iniquity.

Or if a soul touch any unclean thing, whether it be a carcase of an unclean beast, or a carcase of unclean cattle, or the carcase of unclean creeping things, and if it be hidden from him; he also shall be unclean, and guilty . . .

Or if he touch the uncleanness of man, whatsoever uncleanness it be that a man shall be defiled withal, and it be hid from him; when he knoweth of it, then he shall be guilty.

And he shall bring his trespass offering unto the Lord for his sin which he hath sinned, a female from the flock, a lamb or a kid of the goats, for a sin offering; and the priest shall make an atonement for him concerning his sin.

'And then, moving on a bit, listen.'

Command Aaron and his sons, saying, this is the law of the burnt offering: it is the burnt offering, because of the burning upon the altar all night unto the morning, and the fire of the altar shall be burning in it.

And the priest shall put on his linen garment, and his linen breeches shall he put upon his flesh, and take up the ashes which the fire hath consumed with the burnt offering on the altar, and he shall put them beside the altar.

And he shall put off his garments, and put on other garments, and carry forth the ashes without the camp unto a clean place . . .

In the place where they kill the burnt offering shall they kill the trespass offering: and the blood thereof shall he sprinkle round about the altar.

And he shall offer of it all the fat thereof; the rump, and the fat that covereth the inwards,

And the two kidneys, and the fat that is on them, which is by the flanks, and the caul that is above the liver, with the kidneys, it shall he take away:

And the priest shall burn them upon the altar for an offering made by fire unto the Lord: it is a trespass offering . . .

His own hands shall bring the offerings of the Lord made by fire, the fat with the breast, it shall he bring, that the breast may be waved for a wave offering before the Lord.

And the priest shall burn the fat upon the altar: but the breast shall be Aaron's and his sons'.

And the right shoulder shall ye give unto the priest for an heave offering of the sacrifices of your peace offerings.

'Atonement for sin,' Abberline mused, 'or for touching the uncleanness of man . . . It's possible, isn't it, but he seems to have got it all a bit wrong. I mean, yes, he left the breasts and the right shoulder, but he's meant to have burned the kidneys and all the fat, isn't he?'

'Yup. But I'm not saying that this is a rabbi, I'm saying it could be someone tormented with guilt about something, Jew or Christian, and that, at the back of his mind is this set of images. This is the sort of thing he's got to do in order to expiate. It's demented, of course, but it is possible. Supposing that our man's contracted syphilis from a whore and regards the disease as God's punishment. Now, he's got to go through some sort of strange sacrificial ritual in order to appease God and cure himself. He knows about the kidneys. He knows that you leave the breasts. And why did he go to all the trouble of stripping that thigh bare? He was after the fat to burn. It is possible.'

'It's very possible,' Abberline nodded. 'But what's he told his partner?'

'Ah, but supposing his partner is the one who *enjoys* it? Supposing his partner had fed all this stuff into a madman's burning brain simply so that he can satisfy his loathing for whores or his bloodlust? There's a bond deeper than any we've ever mentioned before – the bond between the madman and his master who persuades him that his life depends upon his doing these things.'

'And it wouldn't have to be a master in the literal sense, would it?' Abberline grinned. 'I mean, the person controlling could be the pox-ridden feller's servant, his social inferior . . .'

'Easily.'

'Yes. Yes, I find it persuasive, George.' Abberline clapped me on the shoulder and stood. 'Or rather, I find it suggestive. I think you're right about one thing. Whoever is doing this has read or has heard those bits from the Good Book. No doubt about that. Whether you're right about motive, though . . .' He shrugged. 'Come on. There's work to be done.'

He cast a quick glance back through the open door into Mary Jane's room. A shudder shook his shoulders. We walked back on to the street again with our heads bowed.

'There he is, the bastard!' came a raucous, too familiar voice. We looked up. A small crowd had gathered in the street and there, inevitably, straining to break through the line of constables who stood with linked arms, was George Albert Lusk. 'That's Abberline!' he called to the crowd, many of whom, I noticed, had red eyes from weeping. 'String the bastard up! The police are your enemy! They're protecting a monster! They don't care about ordinary working people. No police! No police! No police!'

The two henchmen who flanked him joined in the chant.

The rest of the crowd, mostly women, moved away. Abberline was already halfway across the street before I noticed it. He half walked, half ran straight for Lusk. The constables unlinked their arms to allow Abberline to pass.

One of Lusk's henchmen was quicker than his leader. He stepped in Abberline's way. I was running as Abberline's elbow came back. His fist caught the henchman clean on the point of the jaw. The man's head jerked backward. He spun into the crowd behind him.

'Fred! Fred, no!' I bellowed. I grabbed his arms and pulled him back. 'Leave it, Fred!' I pleaded as he struggled to tear out Lusk's throat. 'For God's sake, leave it!'

'There!' Lusk released a great triumphant guffaw. 'You see? There is your enemy! No police! No police! No police!'

Abberline, whose breathing was just steadying, made another move towards Lusk, but I checked him and bundled him into a cab.

As the cabby whipped up his horses, I caught a glimpse of Bates at the back of the crowd. He scribbled fast in a notebook. He looked euphoric.


'It's there somewhere, George.' Abberline stood in the wash-room shaving. 'One more try.'

'If you say so,' I mumbled through foam.

'All the killings are within a very small radius.'

'So could be local.' I nodded. 'But they use a coach.'

'Organs are removed.'

'So could be medical, but no proof.'

'Anatomical knowledge is demonstrated.'

'But not necessarily surgical skill.'

'There's going to be a fair amount of blood on their clothes.'

'So they wash their own clothes or are slaughterers and so arouse no suspicion . . .'

'Where would a slaughterer get a coach?'

'True. Or, of course, they burn them.'

'And if they burn them, they're not poor.'

'Right.' I finished shaving and dabbed my face dry with a towel. Abberline was still stropping his blade.

'So.' He stood once more before the looking-glass, blade poised. 'Let's look at a few of the friends we've made in the course of all this. Llewellyn. Our own police surgeon. Local, uncooperative – downright obstructive – and he's got medical knowledge.'

'True, but he's got an alibi for the Chapman murder. Well, a sort of alibi. Question mark. Frankly, I don't believe it.'

'Pity. Lusk, now. Political, violent, knows the area *and* he has a very good motive.'

'Stirring up the people, you mean. Sacrifice a few whores for the greater good?'

'God knows, George.' Abberline washed his razor. 'Politicians have done many, many worse things than this in order to change the established order. Jack the Ripper might turn out to be the most merciful revolutionary in history.'

'Hmm.' I buttoned my shirt and considered. 'But has he got the medical knowledge?'

'Dunno. It's not necessary, you know. I mean, he'd have to know where a kidney was, but in general, he's shown no great skill. Any ex-soldier's used to butchery on forced marches. We'll leave him on the list.'

'All right. Lees, now. No medical knowledge, and he's got an alibi for Chapman's murder.'

'Yes. I can't think it's him, but it wouldn't surprise me if he knew more than he's revealing. The man's a journalist and I reckon he's got a source other than his spirit-guide. It is just feasible that someone's been dropping clues to him. Half a question mark.'

'Acland. He's a doctor, attended Chapman's inquest just out of interest.'

'Leave him on. Goddam it, leave half of London on. Then there's your friend the actor. Alibi for the Chapman killing, if we believe that bang-tail, but none for the rest of them. Knows about autopsies because Acland showed him one. Likes to hang around the East End in disguises. Even likes to pretend that he's sunk so low that he stays in the casual wards. You ask him about that?'

'Yes. Says it helps his research. Acting is essentially animal communication, he says. Everyone that he meets in the ordinary course of things is too polite. We all conceal our animal traits too much. That sort of thing.'

'So while he's down there, he meets a market-dame, charms her, gives her a present – nothing too grand – makes an appointment and kch!' Abberline drew his razor across his throat. 'He can reveal his animal traits to his heart's content.'

'What about motive?'

'I dunno.' Abberline shrugged. 'Maybe he's your Frenchified madman looking to purify himself. America's full of mad religious maniacs. Run the bleeding country, so far as I can see.'

'It's no good, Fred,' I sighed. Abberline shrugged on his coat and we turned to walk back to the incident room. 'As you said, it could be you – you're pretty good with a razor – or me or Sir Charles Warren himself!'

'Now, there's a thought!' Abberline smiled. 'You know that he's resigned, don't you? Don't tell any one.'

'Has he now?' I whistled. 'Which, of course, puts Anderson on top.'

'Yup.'

'Well, well. The revolution draws nearer. The House that Jack Built – on the foundations of a few dead harlots.'


The house grew ever taller and more imposing.

*The public will wait with painful eagerness for some intimation that the police are on the wretch's track, and that now at last there is a chance of running him down. Should they fail here, as in the other previous crimes in this dreadful series, to obtain any real clue to the perpetrator, they will undoubtedly add, whether justly or unjustly, to the mass of discontent which has been steadily gathering for a long time past in the public mind with respect to the guardianship of life and property in the Metropolis. For our own part, we may frankly say that we need no such evidence of fresh failure, and indeed we would think it scarcely fair to allow ourselves to be influenced by any such evidence, in declaring that the whole condition of the Force is absolutely deplorable. The fact is patent, and the mind of the Metropolitan community is deeply impressed by it. As to the men who compose the Force, they have never had, and they have not now, any firmer friends or warmer advocates than ourselves. They are not highly paid, and they are not drawn from a class generally educated to the exercise of authority, of patience, or of discipline; yet, as a body, they have for years past displayed all these qualities in ample measure, and have thereby earned the respect — we might almost say the friendship – of the people . . .*

*The legal, constitutional, intellectual element in the administration of the police was always intended to be supreme, and to find representation in a high functionary, whose watchful office it would be to see that it prevailed. This element, however, has almost entirely died out, and the Force has drifted into the hands of a mere soldier, with results which we see only too plainly today in the deplorable condition to which it has sunk, and in the miserable record of undiscovered murders which stands to its account.*

\*

On the Monday, our old friend turned up again. We had been waiting for him.

While the inquest into Kelly's death proceeded with unseemly haste at Shoreditch Town Hall, George Hutchinson wandered listlessly into the police station and stated that he had 'matters of importance and some delicacy to relate with regard to the death of the woman Kelly'. Hutchinson was a wiry little man with leathery wrinkled skin like that of a jockey. He walked and talked with an air of continuous weariness.

'At two o'clock on Friday morning,' he deposed, 'I was coming by Thrawl Street, and just afore I reached Flowery Dean Street, I meet the woman Kelly. She says, "Hutchinson, can you lend us sixpence?" I says, "I can't. I've spent all me money going down to Romford." She says, "Well, good morning, then, I must go and find some money." So then she goes off towards Thrawl Street, doesn't she? Now there's this man coming in the opposite direction, and he taps her on the shoulder and says something and they both burst out laughing. Then she says, "All right," and he says, "You'll be all right for what I've told you." Then he puts his right arm round her shoulders, doesn't he? He had a kind of small parcel in his left hand, with a kind of strap round it.

'Well, I stands against the lamp of the Queen's Head – that's the public down there, and I just watches them. They come past us and this cull's got his head held down and his hat pulled over his eyes. I stoops down and looks him square in the face. He looks back at me, stern. So, they both goes into Dorset Street and I follows them. They stand at the corner of Miller's Court for about – I dunno – about three minutes. He says something to her and she says, "All right, my dear, come along, you'll be comfortable." So then he puts his arm on her shoulder and gives her a kiss. She says she's lost her handkerchief, so he pulls out his stock – a red one – and gives it to her. Then they both goes up the Court together. So I goes to the Court, don't I? And I wait to see if I could see them come out. And I stands there for all of three quarters of an hour to see if they come out, but they don't, do they? So I just scarper.'

This stranger, who had presumably been with Mary Jane after our anonymous carroty friend had left her, was described in all too familiar terms: 'Age about thirty-four to thirty-five. Height, five foot six. Complexion, pale. Dark eyes and eyelashes. Slight moustache curled up at each end. Hair dark. Very surly looking. Dress: long dark coat, collar and cuffs trimmed with astrakhan and a dark jacket beneath, light waistcoat, dark trousers, dark full hat turned down in the middle, button boots and gaiters with white buttons.' He also wore, so Hutchinson said, a thick gold watch-chain, a white linen collar and a black tie with a horseshoe pin. He was of Jewish appearance.

And if any man dressed as square-rigged as that had *walked* all the way through Spitalfields, without being assailed, I, as I told Abberline, would eat my boots.

If, however, this was our man, then, according to Mary Ann Cox's evidence, he had been doing something with Mary Jane, or with her corpse, in the dark at three o'clock. The fire, therefore, must have been lit later. Medical evidence indicates that Mary Jane died between half past three and four o'clock, though the warmth in the room as the fire blazed and died will certainly have contributed to a delay in the onset of rigor mortis and she may, in fact, have died earlier.

There is one story sillier than most concerning the Ripper that I would like for once and for all to refute. Those who favour conspiracy theories have maintained that Mary Jane was three months' pregnant at the time of her murder. Even had she been – of which there was no evidence either from the doctors or from her acquaintance – there would have been precious little left of a three-month-old foetus by the time the Ripper had finished playing about with her puddings.

This myth in part owes its existence to the evidence of Caroline Maxwell who, extraordinarily, claimed that she had met

Mary Jane in Dorset Street at half past eight *on the morning of her murder*.

'What brings you up so early?' Caroline had asked.

'Och, I've the horrors of drink on me,' replied Mary Jane. 'I've been drinking for some days past.'

'Why don't you go down Mrs Ringers and have half a pint of beer?' suggested Caroline.

'Sure, and I've been there and had it.' Mary Jane summoned a faint smile. 'But I brought it all up again.' She pointed to some vomit in the roadway.

Caroline then went to Bishopsgate and, according to her evidence, returned to Dorset Street at nine o'clock to find Mary Jane standing outside the Britannia, chatting to a man who looked to be a market-porter.

Caroline's evidence is plainly false, though strangely convincing. I can only think that, in the usual drunken haze through which lodging-house keepers and their wives well-nigh permanently wandered, she confused one morning with another.

Abberline, of course, incredulous that any member of his species could conceive of, still less desire and execute such carnage, had to rush off to his pet medical expert, Sir William Gull. This time, we called on his home in Finsbury Square.

It was a burly building of deep-red brick, characteristically English, assertive without being aristocratic, expensive without elegance. It spoke of sturdiness, seriousness and wealth.

The interior, too, was predictable. Lady Gull, a thin, nervous-looking woman with a charming smile, showed us into a dark hall. Stained-glass above the carved staircase split and softened the bright autumn light. Dutch landscapes hung in heavy gilt frames on the green stuff that covered the walls.

'Good afternoon.' Lady Gull spoke in a soft voice that none the less echoed in the stairwell as though in a tomb. 'I'm afraid that Sir William is resting. He'll be down in a moment no

225

doubt. Any excuse to ignore doctor's orders.' Her hand was cold and limp. 'Would you care to take some tea?'

'Er, yes,' said Abberline, who loathed the stuff.

'We will take it in the library, Moore,' she told the butler.

'Doctor's orders?' asked Abberline. He held open the library door for her. 'Has your husband been ill, then, Lady Gull?'

'No, no, not really.' She swept gracefully into the room and sat upon the sofa. I remembered that Gull, though by then successful, had married money. 'As you probably know, he had a small stroke some time ago, and our son-in-law insists on a nap. He is a doctor, too. Dr Acland. He has quite a battle on his hands, I can assure you.'

'A stroke?' Abberline frowned. He sat upon a high-backed chair as though afraid that it would break beneath his weight. 'I'm sorry. I hadn't realized.'

'Oh, yes. He hardly practises at all now. Just a day or two at the hospital because he is so voracious for knowledge. He does get very depressed and tired, so . . .' She looked up from her lap with a plea in her tired blue eyes. 'You won't tax him too much, will you?'

'Of course not, Lady Gull.' Abberline soothed and smiled.

'Sergeant.' Lady Gull gestured with a thin white arm. 'Do come and sit by me.'

I tiptoed to the sofa and sat on the very edge as though I had dysentery. Moore came in with the tea-tray and for a few minutes there was silence save for the tattoo of the tea-cups on their saucers, the gurgle of tea, the 'plop' of sugar cubes, the ticking of the clock and the murmurs of 'Sugar, inspector?' 'Some sandwiches, sir?' It was a ritual as old and consoling as a liturgy. It seemed strange, in this room of golden oak panels, books and chintz that, just yards away, people were living as Mary Jane had lived.

Moore evanesced. I sipped my tea and gazed into the puddering fire. I even sat back a little bit. I could have stayed there, in that cosy stillness, for a very long time.

The door was flung inwards and Gull swept in like a storm. He wore a dressing-gown of Japanese design. 'Ah!' he boomed. 'Thank the Lord someone's come. Inspector. Sergeant. No, no. Please sit down. How about some tea, my dear? No, I can see you've already thought of that.'

'I hope we're not interrupting, Sir William.' Abberline resumed his seat.

'Good heavens, man, no. When you grow old, you know, they treat you as a baby and send you to bed. Now you're here, I shall be allowed some cake. Splendid.' He carved himself a large slice of Genoa sponge and, opening his mouth wide, bit into it. Crumbs tumbled down his chin. 'Mmmmm.' He chewed, then blinked as he swallowed. 'My dear,' he said and gestured towards his wife with the bit of cake between forefinger and thumb, his other fingers extended, 'I have a feeling that these gentlemen wish to discuss certain matters – unpleasant matters – ill fitting the ears of a lady.'

Lady Gull was already on her feet. 'If you will excuse me, gentlemen.' She smiled at each of us in turn. The door closed softly behind her. The flames of the fire bucked.

'Now, sit down, sit down,' Gull said again. He spread himself out on the sofa where his wife had sat. He drank his tea with an inelegant slurp. 'What can I do for you?'

'Sir William.' Abberline pulled the photographs of Mary Jane from an envelope. 'Can you surmise what sort of man could do that to a young girl?'

Gull fumbled in his pocket for his spectacles, placed them on the end of his nose and peered fiercely down at the pictures that balanced on the tea-cup in his lap. 'Good God,' he murmured as he placed one photograph on the bottom of the pile. 'Good God,' he said again. 'Oh, dear, oh, dear . . .' At last he blinked up at us. 'Er, when did this happen?'

'The night before last, Sir William. What kind of a man am I looking for?'

Gull looked back at the photographs. 'He is a pathologically deranged person. No doubt about that. In this case, I imagine, with a chronic sexual problem. The mutilations all centre, as in your previous cases, on the genital organs.'

Gull took another large bite of cake as Abberline said, 'According to the police surgeons, there's never any actual . . .' He looked down at his hands.

'No intercourse?' supplied Gull. 'Hmmm,' he said, chewing. 'Yes, you surprise me.'

'Have you ever seen anything like it before, Sir William?'

'Never. I've engaged in vivisection, of course. Necessary. Spoken about it a great deal, as a matter of fact. Some people disapprove, but it's the only way in which medical science can be advanced. But there can be no purpose in this – none. The total destruction of a healthy human being – I'm at a loss to understand.'

'How do we recognize him, then?' Abberline laid his cup and saucer on the table.

'Ah, now. That won't be easy. He'll probably appear quite normal. It's clear that this man – or woman – could not live with himself or others if this insanity was a permanent state. No, it's intermittent. He'll probably have a regular employment. Likely, perhaps, to be a little bit of a bully to his womenfolk or to talk about them indiscreetly to his male friends, you know? I say that because I assume, if there is no intercourse, that he is incapable of intercourse. This is his substitute. In that case, in public at least, he'll be anxious to show that he is a normal, virile man. A Lothario without a *penis intrans*. Unpleasant for him, poor chap.'

'We think there may be two of them,' I put in. 'May I have another cup of tea?'

'Of course, of course, sergeant! Can you pour? And for me. My right arm's not what it was. Inconvenient for a surgeon, eh? Now. Two of them, you say? Now that *is* interesting. They'd

have to be very sure of one another, to share a thing like this.'
He handed the photographs back to Abberline. 'Oh, yes. Very
sure indeed.'

'A family tie?' suggested Abberline.

'Possibly. More likely to be a sexual bond. There's no lasting
human relationship, you know, that doesn't know dominance
and submission to some extent. Essential, otherwise we'd always
be fighting for our place in the hierarchy. In a case like this,
we'd be looking for exceptional dominance in one partner. There
have been cases of such abominations being performed by husband and wife, you know. A sort of grotesque sexual indulgence
– and, of course, the trouble with such indulgence is that it is
never enough. Next time you seek something worse, something
still more horrible – like doses of opiates, really.'

'Sounds like our men.' Abberline nodded.

'Some exotic religion, perhaps? Politics?' Gull mused. 'Anything that will make one person submit to the will of another.'

'I'm interested that you should mention politics.' Abberline
leaned forward on his elbows.

'Oh, certainly, certainly. Convince a little man that he's serving some great cause, some grand experiment, and he'll do
practically anything for you.'

'Kill people?'

'Oh, come, inspector. You speak as though killing people
were such an extraordinary thing. Yes, he'll kill people, burn
witches for you, torture your enemies for you, and he'll do it
with a smile, too, if he thinks he's right. The history books are
full of it.'

'Convince a little man . . .' Abberline repeated to himself.
Then, 'Sergeant Godley has a theory.'

'Yes?' Gull turned to me and laid his left hand on my forearm.
'What's that, then, my boy?'

'Er, well,' I said nervously, 'um. I thought, what if the person
who actually enjoys this, the person who hates whores or

whatever, what if he's manipulating another, weaker man to do all the killings, by exploiting his fears, or religious mumbo-jumbo or something like that?'

'An evil thought, sergeant.' Gull squeezed my arm. 'And if you're right about there being two of them, as likely a thesis as I've heard so far. Oh, yes. Perfectly possible. God knows, I've met enough people, in and out of Bedlam, whom I could have persuaded to do such things by the means that you suggest. This, in fact, would account far better for the extent of the mutilations. The man doing it may be an idiot. The man causing it to be done, however, may merely be someone with an interest – even a rational interest – in seeing the deed done. That is a horrible thought. Whatever the case, however, you are not looking for partners. You are looking for one master and one slave. And the good thing about that, from your point of view, of course, is that the slave, because he is a slave, can be as well enslaved by you, by the force of your will, as by that of his master. And then, as we doubtless all know in the everyday experience of romance, the converted slave will hate his previous master and will betray him with glee. Yes, my dear?' Gull pulled himself to his feet with a grunt. I turned. Lady Gull stood in the doorway, smiling and wrapped in a fuzzy aura of light from the gasolier behind her.

'I think, William, that you have exhausted your energies quite enough for one day,' she said.

'Rubbish, woman!' Gull waved her away. 'Just starting to enjoy me self. I told you, it's just like being an infant again.'

'No, no.' Abberline stepped forward and extended his hand to Gull. 'You've been a great help to us, Sir William, and we must be on our way, mustn't we, Sergeant Godley?'

'Yes, yes, indeed.'

'Ah, well.' Gull was resigned. 'Very well, but come back whenever you feel that I may be of some assistance. As I have said, we medical men can be of little assistance because this sort of thing doesn't properly fall within the medical field. It will, though. It will. Persist, gentlemen, and you will find the truth. That's always been my way, hasn't it, Susan? Persist!'

'Yes, my dear.' Lady Gull saw us into the hall. 'Thank you so much for coming, gentlemen. Sir William does enjoy the chance to discourse. I fear that I am a little dull and ignorant for him . . .'

The footman held out our coats for us. We mumbled good-byes and thanks and walked out on to the doorstep. The door closed behind us.

We stopped. And stared.

Dr Theo Acland was climbing from a coach. He handed down his wife, Gull's daughter, then an expensively dressed little boy with long brown curls. He picked up the boy and they started up the steps towards us.

'Ah, inspector!' I heard him as though he spoke from another room a long way away. 'Caroline, this is Mr Abberline. You remember I . . .'

I was looking at the coach behind them. It was a black landau. On the door, there was a white patch where, pre-sumably, a crest had been. It was the coach that Lees had drawn for us, and, on the box, sat John Netley.

'So, you've been to see my father, inspector?' said Mrs Acland in a pleasant voice.

'Yes, er, yes, Mrs Acland.' I knew that Abberline's gaze, too, was on the coach. 'Yes, we've just been, um, talking to Sir William . . .'

'I hope you left him in a good mood. He can be quite a tyrant at times, can't he, Theo?'

Netley had seen us now. He watched us furtively and tried to pretend that he wasn't there.

'Well, good day to you gentlemen,' said Acland, 'and good fortune in your quest.'

'Good day, Dr Acland. Mrs Acland.'

Netley had picked up the reins. For a moment, I thought that he would whip up his horses and try to escape. He appeared agitated. He bit his lower lip, making his chin seem still smaller.

'Well,' said Abberline casually as we strolled down the steps. 'That was agreeable, wasn't it, George?'

'Oh, very.' I looked away from Netley. We swung round to the left. 'And instructive. Isn't Lady Gull delightful?'

'Enchanting,' said Abberline. 'Pity we couldn't have stayed longer . . .' We rounded the corner into Christopher Road. 'It's such a pleasure . . .'

Suddenly he flung himself backward against the wall.

'That's it, George,' he hissed. 'That's the coach. The one that tried to run Lees down. It's true. It's *there*!'

'But no royal crest on the side.'

'There was, though. The patch is still there. And that's Netley, scratch-driver from the royal mews, large as life on the box. Convince a little man, eh?'

'Governor.' I peered around the corner. 'We're going to lose him.'

'Bring him in, George.' Abberline grinned nastily. 'We'll break him. We've got them, George. We've got them *both*! Move!'

And, as he spoke, I was moving fast back into the square and Netley was staring back at me, his face white, his eyes wide. He released the brake and raised his whip. I threw myself forward and grasped the reins just as the horse started to move.

'Whoah, there,' I coaxed, then smiled up at the coachy. 'Good evening, Mr Netley,' I said.


He fought all the way. He jumped from the coach and wriggled like an eel. He swore and scratched and bit – I still have the mark between the thumb and the forefinger of my right hand.

I dragged him to City Road and summoned the aid of a

copper – Walter Dew, as a matter of fact, who would later become famous as the man who caught Crippen – and still Netley kicked and protested. When at last we got him to the cells – the same cells as those in which Abberline had lain on the morning of Mary Ann Nichols's murder, the same cells as those in which Catherine Eddowes had crooned her own dirge – his shrieks rang through the walls.

'Let go, you fuckers! You'll regret this! I'll see that you do! I work at the royal mews, I do! I'll tell all about your precious Prince Albert Victor, I will!'

I slapped him with a full swing of the arm across the face. Blood spurted from his nose. 'Shut your mouth, Netley!' I barked.

'Bastard bleeding reelers!' Netley squealed. 'Let me go! Let me g . . .'

His protests were temporarily drowned as he gurgled on his own blood. We opened the door and, with greater force than was strictly necessary, flung him in. I slammed the door and sighed.

'Who was that, then?' PC Dew removed his helmet and mopped his brow.

'A coachman.'

'I gathered that.' Dew grinned.

I turned away and walked down the corridor towards the washroom. At the door, I looked back at Dew. 'And half of Jack the Ripper!' I called.

I washed and dressed the wound on my hand very carefully. If Netley was who we thought he was, I wanted none of his venom in my veins. When at last I returned to Abberline's office, he was sitting smiling very happily, a sheet of paper in his hands.

'He's here, then?' he said.

'Yup. Little bastard fought like a salmon, but he's here.'

'Good. Look what I've got.' He was almost hugging himself with pleasure and pride. I took the paper from him. Of all the extraordinary things that I had seen in the course of this investigation, this was unquestionably the most astonishing:

MURDER – PARDON. Whereas, on 8 or 9 November in Miller's Court, Dorset Street, Spitalfields, Mary Jane Kelly was murdered by some person or persons unknown, the Secretary of State will advise the grant of Her Majesty's pardon to any accomplice not being a person who contrived or actually committed the murder who shall give such information and evidence as shall lead to the discovery and conviction of the person or persons who committed the murder.

It was signed in the bottom left-hand corner, 'Sir Charles Warren'.

'A – a pardon?' I gasped. 'For an accomplice to five murders? A *pardon*? Why did – how *could* he sign this? A . . .?'

'Calm down, George,' Abberline instructed, 'and sit down.' He got up and shut the door behind me.

'Now listen.' He returned to his seat. 'All right. We got Netley. And all right, he can be broken. Matter of fact, I reckon if I left him alone with you, he'd break within twenty minutes. He'll tell you who the Ripper is – and then what? We have *no* evidence, George. None at all, save the testimony of a dirty little, slightly barmy scratch-driver. Whoever employs him is strong-willed and has some power. He'll just deny the whole damned thing. We could wait and watch, of course, and, even without his driver, he's probably now so caught up in this murdering business that he'll do it again one day. But we can't wait till one day. We've got to get him now. Look at this – where is it?' He rummaged through the stacks of papers on his desk. '"This new and most ghastly murder shows the absolute necessity for some very decided action . . ." Those words, George,' he said and laid down the telegram, 'are those of Her Majesty the Queen. You've heard the crowds outside? Warren's already had to resign. Who's next? Matthews? They're already baying for his blood. Salisbury himself? The monarchy? We can't wait years until the next murder, George. We can't wait months. We can't even afford days. We must get him *now*.'

'But is this bleeding document even binding? I mean, as you say, Warren's resigned . . .'

'But his resignation doesn't come into force until the twelfth, George, and that's tomorrow.'

'How in God's name did you get that thing out of him anyhow?' I demanded.

'Explained that there must be an accomplice.' Abberline shrugged. 'Would never have got it otherwise, that's for sure.'

'All right,' I said sulkily. 'So what's the plan?'

'You want your pound of flesh, don't you, George?' He grinned.

'Pound be damned.' I smiled. 'I'll take a full stone and roast it before his eyes.'

'You'll get it, old friend. Don't you worry. You'll get it. Right.' He pulled out his watch. 'It's a quarter to seven. We haven't long. First, fill friend Netley with the fear of God and of the hangman. I want him gibbering by, say, eight o'clock, and resigned to his fate by nine. If you can do it any faster, so much the better.'


It followed a pattern. Most interrogations do. Netley started out abusive and foul-mouthed. We dealt with that. He then decided that cockiness would serve him better. He sneered at us, struck poses and laughed at our every suggestion. Gradually, however, we wore him down.

'What route did you take from Berner Street to Mitre Square?'

'I . . .'

'Oh, of course, you weren't in Berner Street, were you? You'd have been seen. Where did you wait?'

'I . . .'

'Commercial Road? Ellen Street?'

'I . . .'

'Here, take this chalk. Write, "The Jews are the men . . ."'

'I can't write.'

'You can read medical books. You can write. Write. "The Jews are the men . . ." '

'Shan't.'

'Oh, yes, you will, my friend, I think you will. Where's your friend now, Netley? Where's your protector and your paymaster now? He's not going to hang with you, is he? He's not wielding influence to save you, is he? Will he feel the noose tightening around his neck as you kick and choke? Will he? He dragged you into this, didn't he?'

'Him? Drag me?' Netley snorted.

'Write.'

'No.'

'Write, Netley. "The Jews are the men . . ."'

'All right.' Netley's upper lip was cracked and swollen. He took the chalk and confidently wrote in capital letters, 'THE JUW —' He stopped, frowned, and rubbed at the last two letters with his sleeve.

'Leave it!' I yelled.

'Jews,' I said, forcing him back into his chair, 'is spelled J-E-W-S. You are going to hang, *Dr* John Netley, if, that is, the crowd allows you to reach the gallows.' I bent and spoke into his ear, 'You seen a hanging, have you, Netley? Have you? Less merciful than the Ripper, you know. Oh, yes. There'll be the trial first, of course, and everyone in the kingdom'll hate you. That'll go on a good while. You got a mother, have you, Netley? Well, you won't have by the time this is finished. It'll kill her. No question. And then there are the days of waiting in gaol. All the other prisoners will want to get at you and rip you to pieces, of course. Maybe some of them will be allowed to succeed, at least

236

partially. Then the day of the execution. The people gathered outside, all full of hatred for one man: John Netley. Takes quite a long time, you know – the walk to the scaffold, the last futile prayers for one who is already in hell, the placing of the noose around the throat, the grin of the executioner because he's doing the world a service in ridding it of a speck of turd called John Netley. And then the drop. You'll evacuate your bowels, you know that, don't you, Netley? Oh, and you'll have an issue of seed, not that you'll enjoy it. Messy, and very undignified. And then, when you're dead, the hatred won't stop. Oh, no, your name will be despised throughout history. John Netley – not heroic Jack the Ripper, but the man who was so frail and impotent that he couldn't even jerk jelly without slashing up a worn old tickle-tail. That, my friend, is the fate of John Netley. That is the result of all these years. They'll laugh at you. Pathetic little John Netley who thought he was a doctor. Ha!'

'No . . .' Netley was sobbing as I straightened. 'No. You can't do that to me. I know important people. They'll have me out of here.'

'Oh, no, they won't, John Netley. We can hang you, but your testimony ain't enough to hang them, and they know it. They'll let you drop and rot and burn in hell and they'll pour themselves another brandy and soda and they'll smile. Poor old *Dr* Netley. We had our jollies and now he's six foot under.'

'You're codding.' Netley shook his head slowly. He punched away tears on his sleeve. 'You can't hang me.'

'Shall I tell you something, Netley?' I laughed. 'We could hang you ten times over with what you've given us. And it's not going to take long to find whores who'll identify you as a pimp, and then there's Schwarz. You don't know Schwarz, do you? But he knows you, Netley. You chased him away in Berner Street, remember? After your friend said, "Lipski"? No, Netley, you're as good as dead, and your friend's not coming to help you. You may as well accept it.'

237

'It wasn't me!' he shouted. 'I didn't do it!'

'No one's going to believe that, Netley,' I said casually. I nodded to PC Robinson. 'You'd better take him back to his cell,' I said. 'If he stays here any longer I might want to hit him again.'

'But I'll tell you . . .' Netley gabbled. He broke free of PC Robinson and scrabbled at the lapels of my coat. 'I'll tell you everything! It wasn't me. I was forced. I didn't know . . .'

I very slowly detached his fingers from my coat and pushed him back into Robinson's arms. 'I don't even want to hear it, Netley,' I sighed. 'You're of no account. You'll hang. He won't. There's an end on it. Take him away.'

'He's longing to sing,' I told Abberline. 'Now what?'

Abberline looked at his watch. 'Half past eight. Good. Well done, George. Right. Now give him twenty minutes to sit and sweat, then go and offer him a pardon. Yes, I know, George. It turns your stomach and mine, but don't worry. We'll find something on him and make sure they throw away the key. As for you, I want you to rush down there and find out who the next victim was to be. Here's ten pounds, George. Buy yourself a girl.'

'You!' I pointed.

'Sir?'

'Your boots.'

'Yes, sarge?'

'Yes, sir. They're shining.'

'Yes, sir.'

'Well, do something about it, man. This is the police, not the fucking parade ground. Our man'll see you a mile away.'

'Yes, sir.' The constable bent and rubbed dust into his toe-caps. 'Sorry, sir.'

'Right. You lot stay here and be invisible, and I mean totally invisible. Understood? You are not to move unless you're called by name.'

'Right sar . . . sir.'

'You.' I turned to the girl behind me. 'Come with me.'

She followed me with rapid, nervous steps to a doorway further up Old Montague Street. 'Right.' I stood behind her in the darkness and pointed over her right shoulder. 'He'll be coming from up there, in a coach, a big black coach with a coat of arms on its doors. He won't be coming too fast, so I want you just to stroll back and forth along that wall hawking for trade and, without any hasty movements, try to be as near opposite this doorway as possible when the coach draws alongside you. Understood?'

'Yes.' I felt rather than saw the girl's nod. There was a rustle of clothing, then her breath was on my chin and her eyes shone like moonstones. 'You are sure it'll be all right?'

'I swear.' I made my voice deep and hoped that I sounded more certain than I felt. 'We'll be here. There's no danger. Just pass your time in thinking what you can do with those twenty pounds. Give up this business. Find yourself a house in the country. Think about that, not about danger. You'll be all right. Now.' I squinted downward at my watch face. 'We've got five minutes before we need to be in position. They may arrive ten, fifteen minutes after that. You might as well take up your post now. I've got a few more constables to talk to. Chin up, Molly. There'll be twenty crushers charging like bulls before he can make a move.'

'I just want to get the bastard,' Molly said softly. 'I'd like to kill him.'

'You're playing your part,' I said and clasped her shoulder, 'and I promise you a front seat when he hangs. To work, my girl, and, if anyone else approaches you, just whisper to them that you've got a meat and two veg under that skirt and a dose of clap to boot. All right?'

'All right.' She nodded and sauntered out into the dim moon-light. A moment later, she was strolling up and down the wall on the other side of the street, her red shawl pulled tight about her shoulders.

I dealt with the other constables, one hundred yards further back. For fear of lynch mobs, this was to be a quiet operation. The policemen at either end of the street were simply there in order to block off any avenue of escape. I returned briskly to my doorway and, with a wave for Molly, settled down to watch and wait.

The street was frosted with fog. There were moments when I could not even see the girl, just fifteen or twenty feet away from me. I knew that Abberline would reprove me for selecting a young girl, when the Ripper had hitherto shown a marked preference for the old and ugly, but I liked Molly and she had a small child and I was never again going to have the chance to give twenty pounds to a prostitute. If I had given such a sum to someone like Mary Ann Nichols, she would have been dead within the week, either of the gin or of a knife in the back. Molly, I believed would put the money to good use.

Foghorns boomed from the distant Thames. Somewhere in an adjacent street some industrial machine purred and clattered through the night. Occasionally you heard the rasp of a coster's cart, a distant scream or laugh, the barking of a dog. Otherwise all was still.

At twenty past one, Molly stiffened and glanced quickly over her shoulder. I heard the clopping of hoofs and the jingle of harness a moment later. I stood. My right hand reached into my pocket and momentarily gripped the butt of the revolver. I had no intention of using it if I could avoid it, but the feel of it was as consoling as the touch of a mother's hand.

'It's all right, George,' – Abberline's voice – 'he's on his way.'

The fog cleared for long enough for me to see Abberline's

240

silhouette against the wall. He exchanged a few murmured words with Molly, then retired into the shadows on the other side of the road.

I crouched down again, and waited. Molly's feet clicked back and forth once more. The city clocks struck the half hour. Still our man did not come. Molly sighed deeply and leaned back against the wall. The sudden cessation of her rhythmical footfalls made the silence seem intense.

I thought of the man who would be coming here. I knew him, yet I did not know who he was. In one of his guises, I supposed, he might be a doctor, a clerk, a sailor, a priest, but in the guise in which he visited these streets, he had ceased to be any such thing. He was Jack the Ripper, vengeful, amused, sexually aroused, politically motivated or devoutly religious, his identity and his full-time profession were the same: killer.

I remembered the women, their ragged bodies ripped and torn in a grotesque parody of defloration, their throats . . .

'Damn it,' I muttered. 'Their throats!'

Maybe it was coincidental. Maybe it was irrelevant, but I suddenly felt sure that we had broken the pattern. Every one of the killer's victims had worn a kingsman about her throat. There was nothing extraordinary about that, of course. Kingsmen were common enough in the East End of London. They were not, however, universal. Could it then have been the sight of this gash of colour that triggered the killer's urge to replicate it in blood? If so, our goat would not draw the tiger. Molly's throat was bare.

I had a red snuff handkerchief in my left-hand pocket. It was crumpled but more or less clean. It would suffice, but dare I show myself for any hunch so trivial when, at any moment, the killer might appear on the scene?

I told myself that it was foolish at least three times before at last I succumbed to my conviction. I crouched low and scampered across the street. 'Here, Molly,' I whispered urgently.

She jumped and let out a little yelp of alarm.

'Shh!' I hissed. 'Take this. Quickly. Wear it round your throat.'

She took the handkerchief from me. I turned to return to the shelter of the doorway.

It was then that I heard the oncoming carriage, and it was moving a deal faster than I had supposed.

To anyone looking eagerly forward from the coach, I must have been no more than a rapidly moving, fuzzy blue shadow, indistinct yet unquestionably human. The walls of my chest were heaving as I flung myself back into the shadows.

Molly was still tying the scarf as she stepped off the pavement and into the street. The diffuse light from the carriage lamp crept along the cobbles, touched her boots then climbed, up her black skirt and her black jacket to the white of her throat with the red streak across it. Then suddenly she was hidden from my view by the horse that burst from the mist, trotting fast. I stood flattened against the wall as horses and carriage rattled past. A breath of wind lifted my hair from off my brow. Molly stood once more alone in the darkness.

We had failed.

I was about to step forward when suddenly Netley's voice called, 'Whoah.' The clatter of the hoofs slowed and stopped. There was a 'click' as somebody jumped down from the coach on to the street.

This was it. To judge from the sounds, the coach must have stopped some twenty yards past Molly. I could see nothing, and twenty yards was a long way to run if by chance I should be compelled to get there fast.

The footfalls approached slowly, casually. I risked a peek around the corner. The fog split, and a drunkard's shadow – three men, as it seemed, in one – stepped through. I recognized the shambling gait of John Netley. He walked straight past Molly without a word. I frowned, uncomprehending. Then another, taller man seemed to emerge from the wall.

242

Abberline.

He took her arm and led her back down the street towards the coach. 'You'll be all right, my dear.' He did a fair imitation of Netley as they passed me. 'Ever so generous, he is . . .'

'Are you sure?' Molly's voice wavered. 'I mean, the reelers have been saying as Jack the Ripper's got a coach . . .'

'Not a coach like this one. Just you wait till you see who my gentleman is . . .'

The fog swallowed them. Their voices burbled on.

I could not stay here. I had to get closer to the coach, even if it meant disobeying orders. If the killer saw that Netley had changed into Abberline, if Netley's rituals on such occasions were in some small degree different from those that he had described, the knife could claim both Abberline and the girl within seconds. I had to be nearer.

I bent low and, very slowly, crept down the street, rowing myself along with my right hand on the damp wall. I was perhaps ten yards from my hiding place when Abberline's roar seemed to push the fog-billows like a wave towards me. *'George!'*

I threw myself forward, regardless of what I might find in my way. I saw the coach, heard Molly's scream, and then I was upon them. Molly stood whimpering by the coach door. I pushed her aside. 'Run, girl!' I yelled. 'Run!'

Abberline was half in, half out of the coach. His right hand held the Ripper's extended arm. I saw the dull glimmer of a blade. I reached up for the arm, but at that moment, the man flung himself out of the coach with a snarl. His cloak slapped my face, his shoulder hit my chest and sent me staggering backward.

'The knife, George!' Abberline croaked desperately. 'Get the knife!'

In the dim light, I could make out nothing but the bulk of the man who lay over Abberline. His spreading cloak made him look like some giant basking bird. His knife was poised and trembling above Abberline's face.

I threw myself over the man. I grasped his hair in my left hand, his wrist in my right. I pulled, and, for a moment, as though in some ghastly orgy, we just lay there, and the only sounds were Abberline's rapid breathing and the low prolonged grunts of the killer, then the man's head came backwards. A strangled whimper of pain and frustration bubbled up from his stomach and seeped from his throat. His arm shook violently against the combined pressure of Abberline's grip and of mine. The hand swung sideways. The knife clattered on to the cobbles. The man rolled over beneath me, sandpaper air rasping through his lungs. I hit him, just once, for the sake of it.

We had the Ripper.

Lusk.

'You're too late,' Lusk sneered up at me, 'you stupid bastards are too late! Too late, too late, too late!'

I pulled him to his feet. Abberline stood and dusted himself down. 'All right!' I called down the street. 'All officers will return to normal duties!'

'Warren's gone.' Lusk wiped blood from his mouth and spat. 'The people are up in arms. Your precious world of privilege has been destroyed. By one man! One man! Even her fucking majesty has now taken notice of the London poor. You and your type – lackeys and lickspittles – you're things of the past.'

'Are we now?' Abberline, too, spat. 'And what happens when we tell the world that the man who preyed on the most defence-less and the poorest of the poor was a radical and a so-called rebel? What then?'

'Ah, but you won't reveal it, my friend.' Lusk's teeth glowed like eyes in the soft light, his eyes like teeth. 'That's the joy of it. That's the beauty. You won't reveal it because I, Mr Bastard

Policeman, am the cousin of the Marquess of Salisbury, Prime Minister of Her Majesty's corrupt and cruel government. Only a second cousin, it's true, and "on the wrong side of the blanket" – "Now God stand up for bastards", eh? – but my friends in the journals know of it. *Jack the Ripper was Prime Minister's Cousin* makes a better headline than *Jack the Ripper was Radical*, don't you think? The government will fall. The people will say that I was protected all this time by the aristocracy and the police. They will take revenge. Either way, I have won! I have won!'

I shook my head, incredulous before the inexorable logic of lunacy. 'You killed . . .' I panted. 'You killed all those women . . .'

'Whores!' Lusk roared in my face. 'They were already dead in spirit, prepared to sacrifice their most precious possession for nothing more than your filthy money. Whores! I did them a favour. I didn't hurt them. I killed just four more than you killed on Bloody Sunday. Hundreds more are killed as cannon fodder in wars. But wars are intended to perpetuate the oligarchy, aren't they, Abberline? I sought to destroy it. Just think. I alone achieved what war and bloody revolution could not, merely by the death of five old whores. They were martyrs, necessary casualties, that's all. There is genius for you, Abberline! There is something for you to fear. More than five people are killed or maimed each day in mines and mills and factories. More than 50,000 slave each day for a pittance and return to weeping wives and children. What do five whores matter? How do they count in the balance, ha, inspector?'

I could hear the grinding of Abberline's teeth. He wanted to kill. So did I.

The man was right, of course. He was unquestionably, logically right. But he was obsessed with silk purses. We dealt with sows' ears. He was talking of theoretical possible worlds. We were thinking of real people in the real world. People who, perhaps, mattered not a jot *sub specie aeternitatis*, people of whom, it might be said, the world was well rid, but people none the less who depended upon the same laws as we and felt the same needs. Even 'monsters', if they be human, must sometimes weep, feel hunger, fear death. This man was talking like a god. We were thinking only as poor lonely frightened human beings.

And we found ourselves atheists.

'I've heard enough of this crap.' Abberline grabbed Lusk's collar and twisted it, hard.

Lusk's eyes rolled upward. He bent backward. 'Oh, yes,' he croaked. 'Do your worst. You know that you are beaten. You'll have to let me go. I will be a hero of the people, a saviour . . .'

'I'll kill you sooner,' Abberline hissed.

'No!' Lusk suddenly yelled, whether in panic or in the same sudden outburst of manic rage in which he had carved up Mary Jane. 'No! Oppressors, murderers! An individual life is cheap . . .'

Abberline covered Lusk's mouth with his hand. Lusk's last words ran shouting down the street and knocking at the windows.

Lusk's head jerked forward. Abberline growled. His hand flew away. He looked down at it for a second. Blood broke from the index finger. It was a moment's inattention only, but Lusk had already started to move. His handcuffed fists swung round, catching Abberline in the diaphragm. Then before I knew what was happening, Lusk's shoulder caught me just above the collar-bone and I was reeling backwards against the coach.

'Ha!' Lusk barked. He was running fast towards Valance Road. Abberline's hand arose. His revolver glinted blue like kidney iron-ore.

'No, Fred!' I shouted. I lowered my head and ran off in pursuit. The fog engulfed me like the sea. I could see Lusk now in the light from the coach, just five yards ahead of me, then four, three . . .

I dived at his feet and took him hard and low. He could not put out his hands to protect himself. He was flung forward like a caber. There was a crack as his head hit the pavement. I pulled myself to my feet. Abberline walked up, a lantern in his left hand, the revolver in his right. Very calmly, he raised the revolver and aimed it at Lusk's head.

'No, Fred!' I cried. I knelt in his line of fire. 'No, governor. They'll hang you!'

Abberline's eyes were cold. For a moment he looked down at me with hatred, then his lips twitched. He lowered the gun.

'All right,' he said. 'Is the bastard still alive?'

'I don't know.' I looked down at the staring white face. The whites of the eyes were hard and cold as alabaster. I threw back the black cloak and reached beneath Lusk's velveteen jacket. There was still a faint movement there. 'Yes,' I said, 'he's still breathing. He's still alive. Just.'

Gull.

'Well, inspector. Sergeant.' He grinned up at me. 'I was right, wasn't I? Two minds in one. One man, two faces. They won't laugh now.'

'God almighty,' I panted.

'Handcuffs!' snapped Abberline.

I reached into my pocket. Gull suffered himself to be hand-cuffed without protest or struggle. I stood and pulled him to his feet. My world had turned upside down. I still could not believe it. Gull. The saviour of life, the tireless labourer for human health, the man who had told us that no doctor could derive any pleasure from mutilation . . .

'You see,' Gull said, nodding, 'the healer, the great destroyer, the doctor, the killer, the scalpel, the sword, Jekyll, Hyde, two minds in one. I said so, didn't I? No one believed me, but I said so, and I've shown it.'

I shook my head, incredulous before the inexorable logic of lunacy. 'Those women. You killed all those women . . .'

'For science, yes! Don't you see, sergeant? They were worthless creatures with no value in themselves, but I made them valuable. They are important because they were part of my experiment. Martyrs, you might say, to a greater cause. Others will be healed thanks to their deaths. You must understand. It is very important that you understand. I didn't enjoy what I had to do. Really I didn't, any more than I enjoy vivisection, but it had to be done. You see, it isn't life that is sacred, it is health and happiness and truth. To attain those, much must be sacrificed. You do see that, don't you? I have always known, just as you do, that there is in my mind much that is, shall we say, bestial – bloodlust for example. The sort of thing that normally we exhibit only in the brothel or in battle, as I seem to remember telling you before. But we repress it in the course of our normal lives, don't we? I wanted to see if it was possible that both could coexist, and they can, gentlemen, they can!'

'You're mad,' I gasped.

'Yes, yes, in one sense, maybe.' Gull nodded smugly. 'But in that sense, we are all mad, aren't we? There will be learned papers written, books and monographs. It is established. One man can be two people. Don't you see how important it is? You do see, don't you?'

'I've heard enough of this crap,' Abberline snapped. 'You're going to hang, Gull, for all your fancy theories. Come on.' He pushed Gull roughly towards the coach.

'No!' Gull suddenly bellowed. 'I am a scientist, a distinguished scientist, not a common criminal! I did this for mankind! Get your hands off me, inspector, please. The Royal Society will protect me, you'll see . . .'

And suddenly his handcuffed fists swung round. They caught Abberline in the diaphragm. Before I knew what was happening,

Gull's shoulder caught me just above the collar-bone and I was reeling backward against the coach.

'It's no good,' Gull barked. He was running fast towards Valance Road. Abberline's right hand rose. His revolver glinted blue like kidney iron–ore.

'No, Fred!' I shouted. I lowered my head and ran off in pursuit. The fog engulfed me like the sea. I could see Gull now in the light from the coach, just five yards ahead of me, then four, three . . .

I dived at his feet and took him hard and low. He could not put out his hands to protect himself. He was flung forward like a caber. There was a crack as his head hit the pavement. I pulled myself to my feet. Abberline walked up, a lantern in his left hand, the revolver in his right. Very calmly, he raised the revolver and aimed it at Gull's head.

'No, Fred!' I cried. I knelt in his line of fire. 'No, governor. They'll hang you!'

Abberline's eyes were cold. For a moment he looked down at me with hatred, then his lips twitched. He lowered the gun.

'All right,' he said. 'Is the bastard still alive?'

'I don't know.' I looked down at the staring white face. I threw back the black cloak and reached beneath Gull's velveteen jacket. There was still a faint movement there. 'Yes,' I said. 'He's still breathing. He's still alive. Just.'

❧

Spratling.

'Leave me alone, Abberline.' His jaw worked furiously. 'Take this man off me! So pleased with yourself, aren't you? Such a clever policeman. Five fucking murders done right under your noses, and you finally catch your man, ha!'

'Handcuffs,' Abberline snapped.

Spratling struggled furiously and spat in my face, but I finally clamped his hands together and handcuffed him. I also hit him again, once in payment for the gob of saliva and because I had never hated anyone so much in my life.

I got up and pulled him to his feet.

'You little bastard.' Abberline spoke in a menacing monotone. 'You're a policeman, for Christ's sake!'

'Don't you pose as the great moralist to me, Abberline,' Spratling snarled. 'You talk to these women. You indulge them. You protect them. At least I have done something constructive to curb their evil. At least I have rid the world of a few of them.'

'You've murdered them,' said Abberline.

'Murder? You call it murder? I call it execution. They are the murderers, Abberline. They with their filthy, stinking diseased fiddler's halls, killing innocent men and women and children. Oh, I sinned once, I sinned and God punished me, and it's not just me that suffered for my weakness. Oh, no, it's my wife, my children, my son born blind, Abberline, blind, do you understand? And all because those whores had the devil between their legs, the devil that lures good men to damnation, which turned me, a police officer and a Christian, into a gross rutting beast. And I was punished, and the Lord says, if a man has sinned, he must sacrifice. Not bread and wine, but blood. It's in the Bible, Abberline, for anyone to see, but of course, you wouldn't read those parts of the Good Book, would you? You read the nice love-thy-neighbour parts and omit the Word of God if it doesn't suit you, that's right, isn't it, sergeant? Oh, yes. But not I. I do as I am bidden. I went astray, but the Lord showed me the error of my ways. He punished me cruelly, even as he punished Job, but I have expiated. I have killed the succubi, the devil's agents, the tempters, and I have sprinkled their blood on the altar and burned their unclean organs.'

'They trusted you.' Abberline grabbed his collar and twisted hard. 'They trusted you and you hacked them up.'

'They!' Spratling croaked. 'Beasts that lie with other beasts! I am to concern myself with such creatures? They killed me and they have killed thousands of others, like me. Poor fallible sinners whose souls are for ever doomed because of their wiles. I have done what is right. I have maintained the law. How many lives would the Kelly woman have destroyed by the alluring poison in her twat? Tell me that, Abberline. I saved those lives. And you call yourself a policeman! Ha!'

'I've heard enough of this crap.' Abberline shoved Spratling roughly up against the coach. 'You'll hang, Spratling, like the common criminal and bully that you are.'

'What do I care?' Spratling laughed without a trace of humour. 'I am dying anyhow. At least I have done some good. At least I have redeemed myself in the sight of God.'

Abberline was about to bundle Spratling into the coach when suddenly he stopped.

'George?' he said softly.

'Yes?'

'I think that I left my gloves in the yard back there. Get them for me, would you?'

'All right.' I think that I knew what he was saying. I think I can say that I was a knowing accessory. I turned and pushed open the wooden gate into the yard. I spent some time in searching for non-existent gloves. There was no sound from the street beyond the occasional snort from the horses, the click of impatient hoofs on the cobbles.

When at last I returned to the street, Abberline was alone. 'I'm afraid,' he said, 'that there's been a dreadful accident. Poor old Spratling's dead.'

I nodded and bit my lower lip and looked where he shone his lantern. Spratling, now unhandcuffed, lay flat on his back on the opposite pavement. His eyes were closed. His lower jaw had dropped on to his chest. His right hand lay across his chest. A little blood mingled with spittle glistened at the corner of his mouth. Otherwise there was no sign of any injury.

'Oh,' I said intelligently.

'I think we'd best take him back to Bishopsgate, Sergeant Godley,' Abberline said briskly. 'We don't want any speculation about the police, do we? Result in rebellion, lawlessness. Bad thing.'

'Yes, governor,' I said solemnly, and bent to pick up Jack the Ripper's feet.

❧

'Dear God,' I murmured, 'Dear God, no . . . It can't be . . .'

His dark doe's eyes rolled. A faint scent of violet cachou emerged from his snarling mouth. Beneath me strained and struggled the man born to be our king.

'Get off me!' he croaked. 'Get away from me! Don't you realize who I am? Get away, get away, get away!'

I turned imploring eyes to Abberline. Even now, knowing what I did, the commands of a royal prince had the power to make me question my evident duty. 'Governor,' I wheezed, 'it's the prince! What . . . what do we do?'

'Get him up,' snapped Abberline. 'Get him up and handcuff him.'

I pulled him to his feet. Abberline grasped him in an unceremonious armlock, but it was still a struggle to bring his wrists together and to attach the bracelets. All the while Prince Albert Victor bucked and kicked like a wild filly who knows for the first time the restraints of saddle and bridle. As he did so, he gabbled and drooled. 'Get your hands off me, damn you! They're going to die, understand? They're going to die. They're traitors, all of them, filthy, corrupt traitors, do you hear me? They killed me, and what do you call someone who kills the heir apparent to the throne, eh? Eh? Well, my good man? Traitors. And what do we do to traitors? We kill them! An eye for an eye, a life for a life – no, a hundred whores' lives, a *thousand*, for that of a prince!'

'You . . .' I almost wept, 'you killed all those women . . .'

252

'Women? What women? How dare you refer to them as women? My mother is a woman. These were whores, *whores*, do you hear me? Not women! And they took my life! I am going to die because of whores! How shall they deserve to live while I die? Whores! Ah, now could I drink blood!'

'Oh, Christ,' I breathed, 'you're mad . . .'

Suddenly his whole manner changed. He pulled himself up and strutted and sneered like a spoiled and slighted child. 'I am Albert Victor, Duke of Clarence and Avondale. I will be king. You know that, don't you? You know me, don't you? I will be king, and emperor of India, defender of the faith, you know that, don't you?'

'You'll never be king, your highness.' Abberline sighed and pushed him roughly towards the coach. 'Oh, you may not hang, but you'll die one way or another. I'll see to that.'

'No!' the prince suddenly shrieked. 'I am the . . .' Abberline's hand was rapidly clamped hard over his mouth, smothering the protestation.

The prince's elbow jerked backward into Abberline's diaphragm. His head jerked forward. Abberline's hand flew away. Blood broke from the index finger. Before I could move, before Abberline could recover his grip, the prince had started to move. His handcuffed fists swung round, catching Abberline on the left temple. His shoulder caught me just above the collar-bone and I was reeling backward against the coach.

As I struggled to retain my footing, I saw the prince charging, head down, into the mist. I also saw Abberline's arms swinging upward. The revolver glinted blue like kidney iron-ore in his hands.

'No, Fred!' I shouted. I lowered my head and ran off in pursuit. The fog engulfed me like foaming breakers. I could see the prince now, running fast towards Valance Road. He was just five yards ahead of me, then four, three . . . I had to stop him before he met anyone else . . .

I dived at his feet and took him hard and low. He could not put out his hands to protect himself. He toppled forward like a caber. There was a loud crack as his head struck the pavement. I pulled myself panting to my feet. Abberline walked up calmly, a lantern in his left hand, the revolver in his right. Very slowly, like a duellist, he raised the gun and aimed it at the prince's white face.

'No, Fred!' I half knelt, half lay across the prince in Abberline's line of fire. 'No, governor! They'll hang you!'

Abberline's eyes were cold. For a moment he looked down at me with hatred, then his lips twitched. He breathed out through his nose. He lowered the gun.

'All right, all right,' he said sourly. 'Is the bastard still alive?'

'I – I don't know.' I looked down at the staring eyes. With trembling fingers I loosened the high braid collar beneath his cloak. There was still a faint pulse in the long throat. 'Yes,' I said, 'he's still alive. Only just, I'd say.'

'Well, we can bring in no help. Let's get him into the carriage and hope he dies before we reach a doctor. You take the legs. Come on, man. Stop fidgeting. This is no prince, whatever his birth-certificate may say. This – this carrion – is less worthy of your respect than the likes of Catherine Eddowes. Pick him up. He's only Jack the Ripper.'

# *1988*

❦

 From Godley's account and his statement to my father that
Sir Charles Warren had known the truth about the Ripper,
it must be assumed that it was Warren who commanded
Abberline and Godley to maintain secrecy.

Of the four stories, the Lusk tale certainly seems the most
cogent. It is hard to conceive of any logical motive for the
Ripper murders, but they did have considerable political con-
sequences and drew the attention of the world to the plight of
the East End poor and unemployed. Lusk would have to have
been some sort of revolutionary genius, but his explanation
does make a grotesque sort of sense. He would have had means,
motive and, as a trusted Whitechapel resident, ample opportunity. The extraordinary publicity afforded to the Ripper
murders, particularly in the Radical press, argues that certain
journalists were tipped off that these killings were somehow
special.

Gull (or indeed any surgeon) seems at first sight a less likely
candidate. As he himself said, it is difficult to see how a surgeon
could take pleasure in such mutilations as the Ripper performed.
The thesis that Gull committed the killings in order to prove
his theories about split personality at first seems equally absurd.
The only factor that makes it possible is the stroke that Gull
suffered in 1887. This is precisely the sort of obsessive, twisted
logic that could be expected in a powerful mind distorted by dementia.

If indeed the Ripper used a coach, Gull is one of the few

citizens who would at any time have access to a coach and whose presence in Whitechapel in the early hours of the morning would arouse little or no surprise. Gull died two years later of a cerebral haemorrhage. The signature on his death certificate was that of his son-in-law, Dr Theodore Acland.

Little is known of Inspector Spratling, so it is difficult to analyse this theory. Certainly a policeman would have a better opportunity to murder these women than anyone else in Whitechapel. He could pass through the streets without hindrance and, again, would be trusted by his victims. This thesis would also explain why the Ripper confined his operations to so small an area, despite the risks implicit in doing so. Given the strength of anti-monarchist and anti-police feeling at the time, I have no hesitation in asserting that a police Ripper would unquestionably never have been brought to trial but would have been quietly, discreetly disposed of in much the way that Godley describes.

After one more notable case, the Cleveland Street Scandal, Detective Inspector Frederick Abberline retired. He died in 1928.

Sir Charles Warren went on to fight in the Boer War, and died in 1927.

John Netley died beneath his horses' hoofs when he was thrown from his coach in 1903.

Robert James Lees published several books on telepathy and reincarnation and, on this occasion, died in 1931.

Richard Mansfield returned to America, where he married his leading lady, Beatrice Cameron. He died in 1907.

Chief Inspector George Godley died in June 1941. He was eighty-five.

# The Ripper Murders
## Prevailing Weather Conditions

❧

*30–31 August 1888. Mary Ann Nichols*
Partly cloudy but dry and becoming fine during the night.
Second day of moon's last quarter.

*7–8 September 1888. Annie Chapman, a.k.a. Siffey*
Partly cloudy but dry, and becoming fine during the night.
Second day of new moon.

*29–30 September 1888. Elizabeth Stride, a.k.a. Kidney ('Long Liz') and Catherine Eddowes, a.k.a. Kelly (Also used the names Mary Jane and Mary Ann)*
Cloudy with rain, clearing after midnight. A chilly night with minimum temperature 43°F (6°C). Second day of last quarter.

*8–9 November 1888. Mary Jane Kelly, née Davies*
Overcast with rain all night. Cold, with minimum temperature 38°F (3°C). Fourth day of new moon.

# Note on Street Names

For the benefit of those who would follow in the Ripper's footsteps, Buck's Row is now Durward Street, while Berner Street has been renamed Henriques Street.

# Glossary

❦

bang-tail (*n.*)   prostitute
bend (*n.*)   drinking-bout
Berkshire hunt (*n.*)   female genitalia (rhyming)
bionk (*n.*)   a shilling (parlyaree)
bit of cuff (also 'crumb', 'jam', etc.) (*n.*)   girl, woman
blow (*vb*)   to inform
bottom (*n.*)   character, soundness
bread-basket (*n.*)   stomach
break a lance (with) (*vb*)   to copulate
buckle (*vb*)   to arrest
bugger's grips (*n.*)   sideboards
bug-whiskers (*n.*)   sparse whiskers
bullock (*vb*)   to pawn
buzzer (*n.*)   pickpocket


canary (*n.*)   thief's assistant
carman (*n.*)   driver of carts
carsey (*n.*)   public house (parlyaree)
cash-carrier (*n.*)   pimp
Cattistock (*n.*)   the Cattistock Hunt (Dorset)
cod (*vb*)   to joke, humbug
crabshell (*n.*)   shoe
cracksman (*n.*)   safe-breaker, house-breaker
crusher (*n.*)   policeman
cull (*n.*)   a man, mate, policeman
cunny-haunted (*adj.*)   (of man) obsessed with sex, concupiscent
cunny-warren (*n.*)   brothel, red-light area

daffy (*n.*)   gin
dewey (*adj.*)   two (parlyaree)
dinarlee (*n.*)   money (parlyaree)
dip (*n.*)   pickpocket
dog's nose (*n.*)   gin and beer mixed
dollymop (*n.*)   loose woman (loosely classed by Mayhew as a prostitute)
dook (*n.*)   (of Kent) rent
dot on the boko (*n.*)   punch on the nose
down among the dead men (*adj.*)   falling down drunk
downy (*adj.*)   artful, 'street-wise'
dragsman (*n.*)   robber of baggage from cabs
drum (*n.*)   house, premises
dumpling-depot (*n.*)   stomach

fancy-cove (*n.*)   a favourite man friend
feldscher (*n.*)   medical auxiliary
flash house (*n.*)   tavern frequented by villains
flophouse (*n.*)   low brothel
Frenchify (*vb*)   infect with pox

gay house (*n.*)   high-class brothel
gonoph (*n.*)   thief
growler (*n.*)   four-wheeled cab
grumble and grunt (*n.*)   female genitalia (rhyming)

hallelujah stew (*n.*)   soup distributed by Booth's Salvation Army
High Mettled Racer Shortly Before Its Demise   run-down old horse.
   From a popular engraving of that title

It's called Pete   you owe me (parlyaree)

jerry (*n.*)   watch

kinchin (*n.*)   child, children
kingsman (*n.*)   kerchief worn as neckscarf
knocking-house (*n.*)   brothel

let go the painter (*vb*)   to strike out, punch hard
letty (*n.*)   bed (parlyaree)
Lucifer (*n.*)   match
lumper (*n.*)   dock labourer
lush (*n.*)   alcoholic drink

macer (*n.*)   swindler
maltool (*vb*)   to rob passengers on omnibuses
mashed (on) (*adj.*)   infatuated with
masher (*n.*)   dandy (or, as *adj.*) dandified
market-dame (*n.*)   prostitute
meat and two veg (*n.*)   male genitalia
mivvy (*n.*)   marvel, wonder
moucher (*n.*)   tramp
mutcher (*n.*)   robber of drunks

nants (nantee) (*n.* and *adj.*)   nothing, no (parlyaree)
nemmo (*n.*)   woman (back-slang)
nose (*n.*)   informer

omee (*n.*)   man, master, landlord (parlyaree)
out of twig (*adj.*)   shabbily dressed, in disguise

palm (*vb*)   to shoplift in pairs
peroon (*adj.* & *adv.*)   each (parlyaree)
phossy-jaw (*n.*)   phosphorus necrosis of the jaw
pinchgut (*n.*)   miser
pinch-prick (*n.*)   prostitute
polly (*n.*)   boot
pot-boy (*n.*)   publican's assistant
prater (*n.*)   fake preacher
pretty horsebreaker (*n.*)   high-class courtesan
propper (*n.*)   street-robber
prosser (*n.*)   ponce, hanger-on
public (*n.*)   public house

reeler (*n.*)   policeman

roast (*vb*)   to arrest, also as in 'to roast brown', to watch closely, to harass

rookery (*n.*)   overpopulated slum

saddle (*n.*)   loaf

screever (*n.*)   writer of fake testimonials, etc.

serve out (*vb*)   to take revenge (on)

skin-the-pizzle (*n.*)   female genitalia

snot-box (*n.*)   nose

snow (*vb*)   to steal linen

social evil (*n.*)   prostitute (euph.)

soft sop over (to give someone the) (*vb*)   flatter, cajole

soldi (*n.*)   money (parlyaree)

soused (*adj.*)   drunk

square-rigged (*adj.*)   smartly dressed

stall (*n.*)   pickpocket's assistant

stew (*n.*)   low drinking house

stiffen (*vb*)   to kill

still-sow (*n.*)   prostitute

tar (*n.*)   sailor

toke (*n.*)   bread

trug-moldie (*n.*)   prostitute

typewriter (*n.*)   stenographer

unfortunate (*n.*)   prostitute (euph.)

# FOR THE BEST IN PAPERBACKS, LOOK FOR THE 🐧

In every corner of the world, on every subject under the sun, Penguin represents quality and variety – the very best in publishing today.

For complete information about books available from Penguin – including Pelicans, Puffins, Peregrines and Penguin Classics – and how to order them, write to us at the appropriate address below. Please note that for copyright reasons the selection of books varies from country to country.

**In the United Kingdom:** For a complete list of books available from Penguin in the U.K., please write to *Dept E.P., Penguin Books Ltd, Harmondsworth, Middlesex, UB7 0DA*

**In the United States:** For a complete list of books available from Penguin in the U.S., please write to *Dept BA, Penguin, 299 Murray Hill Parkway, East Rutherford, New Jersey 07073*

**In Canada:** For a complete list of books available from Penguin in Canada, please write to *Penguin Books Canada Ltd, 2801 John Street, Markham, Ontario L3R 1B4*

**In Australia:** For a complete list of books available from Penguin in Australia, please write to the *Marketing Department, Penguin Books Australia Ltd, P.O. Box 257, Ringwood, Victoria 3134*

**In New Zealand:** For a complete list of books available from Penguin in New Zealand, please write to the *Marketing Department, Penguin Books (NZ) Ltd, Private Bag, Takapuna, Auckland 9*

**In India:** For a complete list of books available from Penguin, please write to *Penguin Overseas Ltd, 706 Eros Apartments, 56 Nehru Place, New Delhi, 110019*

**In Holland:** For a complete list of books available from Penguin in Holland, please write to *Penguin Books Nederland B.V., Postbus 195, NL–1380AD Weesp, Netherlands*

**In Germany:** For a complete list of books available from Penguin, please write to *Penguin Books Ltd, Friedrichstrasse 10 – 12, D–6000 Frankfurt Main 1, Federal Republic of Germany*

**In Spain:** For a complete list of books available from Penguin in Spain, please write to *Longman Penguin España, Calle San Nicolas 15, E–28013 Madrid, Spain*

# FOR THE BEST IN PAPERBACKS, LOOK FOR THE 🐧

## A CHOICE OF PENGUINS

### Castaway  Lucy Irvine

'Writer seeks "wife" for a year on a tropical island.' This is the extraordinary, candid, sometimes shocking account of what happened when Lucy Irvine answered the advertisement, and found herself embroiled in what was not exactly a desert island dream. 'Fascinating' – *Daily Mail*

### Out of Africa  Karen Blixen (Isak Dinesen)

After the failure of her coffee-farm in Kenya, where she lived from 1913 to 1931, Karen Blixen went home to Denmark and wrote this unforgettable account of her experiences. 'No reader can put the book down without some share in the author's poignant farewell to her farm' – *Observer*

### The Lisle Letters  Edited by Muriel St Clare Byrne

An intimate, immediate and wholly fascinating picture of a family in the reign of Henry VIII. 'Remarkable . . . we can really hear the people of early Tudor England talking' – Keith Thomas in the *Sunday Times*. 'One of the most extraordinary works to be published this century' – J. H. Plumb

### In My Wildest Dreams  Leslie Thomas

The autobiography of Leslie Thomas, author of *The Magic Army* and *The Dearest and the Best*. From Barnardo boy to original virgin soldier, from apprentice journalist to famous novelist, it is an amazing story. 'Hugely enjoyable' – *Daily Express*

### India: The Siege Within  M. J. Akbar

'A thoughtful and well-researched history of the conflict, 2,500 years old, between centralizing and separatist forces in the sub-continent. And remarkably, for a work of this kind, it's concise, elegantly written and entertaining' – Zareer Masani in the *New Statesman*

### The Winning Streak  Walter Goldsmith and David Clutterbuck

Marks and Spencer, Saatchi and Saatchi, United Biscuits, G.E.C. . . . The U.K.'s top companies reveal their formulas for success, in an important and stimulating book that no British manager can afford to ignore.

# FOR THE BEST IN PAPERBACKS, LOOK FOR THE 🐧

## A CHOICE OF PENGUINS

### Adieux: A Farewell to Sartre   Simone de Beauvoir

A devastatingly frank account of the last years of Sartre's life, and his death, by the woman who for more than half a century shared that life. 'A true labour of love, there is about it a touching sadness, a mingling of the personal with the impersonal and timeless which Sartre himself would surely have liked and understood' – *Listener*

### Business Wargames   James Barrie

How did BMW overtake Mercedes? Why did Laker crash? How did McDonalds grab the hamburger market? Drawing on the tragic mistakes and brilliant victories of military history, this remarkable book draws countless fascinating parallels with case histories from industry worldwide.

### Metamagical Themas   Douglas R. Hofstadter

This astonishing sequel to the best-selling, Pulitzer Prize-winning *Gödel, Escher, Bach* swarms with 'extraordinary ideas, brilliant fables, deep philosophical questions and Carrollian word play' – Martin Gardner

### Into the Heart of Borneo   Redmond O'Hanlon

'Perceptive, hilarious and at the same time a serious natural-history journey into one of the last remaining unspoilt paradises' – *New Statesman*. 'Consistently exciting, often funny and erudite without ever being overwhelming' – *Punch*

### A Better Class of Person   John Osborne

The playwright's autobiography, 1929–56. 'Splendidly enjoyable' – John Mortimer. 'One of the best, richest and most bitterly truthful autobiographies that I have ever read' – Melvyn Bragg

### The Secrets of a Woman's Heart   Hilary Spurling

The later life of Ivy Compton-Burnett, 1920–69. 'A biographical triumph . . . elegant, stylish, witty, tender, immensely acute – dazzles and exhilarates . . . a great achievement' – Kay Dick in the *Literary Review*. 'One of the most important literary biographies of the century' – *New Statesman*

# FOR THE BEST IN PAPERBACKS, LOOK FOR THE 🐧

## A CHOICE OF PENGUINS

**An African Winter** Preston King   With an Introduction by Richard Leakey

This powerful and impassioned book offers a unique assessment of the interlocking factors which result in the famines of Africa and argues that there *are* solutions and we *can* learn from the mistakes of the past.

**Jean Rhys: Letters 1931–66**
Edited by Francis Wyndham and Diana Melly

'Eloquent and invaluable . . . her life emerges, and with it a portrait of an unexpectedly indomitable figure' – Marina Warner in the *Sunday Times*

**Among the Russians** Colin Thubron

One man's solitary journey by car across Russia provides an enthralling and revealing account of the habits and idiosyncrasies of a fascinating people. 'He sees things with the freshness of an innocent and the erudition of a scholar' – *Daily Telegraph*

**The Amateur Naturalist** Gerald Durrell with Lee Durrell

'Delight . . . on every page . . . packed with authoritative writing, learning without pomposity . . . it represents a real bargain' – *The Times Educational Supplement*. 'What treats are in store for the average British household' – *Books and Bookmen*

**The Democratic Economy** Geoff Hodgson

Today, the political arena is divided as seldom before. In this exciting and original study, Geoff Hodgson carefully examines the claims of the rival doctrines and exposes some crucial flaws.

**They Went to Portugal** Rose Macaulay

An exotic and entertaining account of travellers to Portugal from the pirate-crusaders, through poets, aesthetes and ambassadors, to the new wave of romantic travellers. A wonderful mixture of literature, history and adventure, by one of our most stylish and seductive writers.

# FOR THE BEST IN PAPERBACKS, LOOK FOR THE 🐧

## A CHOICE OF PENGUINS

### The Book Quiz Book  Joseph Connolly

Who was literature's performing flea . . .? Who wrote 'Live Now, Pay Later . . .'? Keats and Cartland, Balzac and Braine, Coleridge conundrums, Eliot enigmas, Tolstoy teasers . . . all in this brilliant quiz book. You will be on the shelf without it . . .

### Voyage through the Antarctic  Richard Adams and Ronald Lockley

Here is the true, authentic Antarctic of today, brought vividly to life by Richard Adams, author of *Watership Down*, and Ronald Lockley, the world-famous naturalist. 'A good adventure story, with a lot of information and a deal of enthusiasm for Antarctica and its animals' – *Nature*

### Getting to Know the General  Graham Greene

'In August 1981 my bag was packed for my fifth visit to Panama when the news came to me over the telephone of the death of General Omar Torrijos Herrera, my friend and host . . .' 'Vigorous, deeply felt, at times funny, and for Greene surprisingly frank' – *Sunday Times*

### Television Today and Tomorrow: Wall to Wall Dallas?
Christopher Dunkley

Virtually every British home has a television, nearly half now have two sets or more, and we are promised that before the end of the century there will be a vast expansion of television delivered via cable and satellite. How did television come to be so central to our lives? Is British television really the best in the world, as politicians like to assert?

### Arabian Sands  Wilfred Thesiger

'In the tradition of Burton, Doughty, Lawrence, Philby and Thomas, it is, very likely, the book about Arabia to end all books about Arabia' – *Daily Telegraph*

### When the Wind Blows  Raymond Briggs

'A visual parable against nuclear war: all the more chilling for being in the form of a strip cartoon' – *Sunday Times*. 'The most eloquent anti-Bomb statement you are likely to read' – *Daily Mail*

# FOR THE BEST IN PAPERBACKS, LOOK FOR THE 🐧

## A CHOICE OF PENGUINS

### A Fortunate Grandchild   'Miss Read'

Grandma Read in Lewisham and Grandma Shafe in Walton on the Naze were totally different in appearance and outlook, but united in their affection for their grand-daughter – who grew up to become the much-loved and popular novelist.

### The Ultimate Trivia Quiz Game Book   Maureen and Alan Hiron

If you are immersed in trivia, addicted to quiz games, endlessly nosey, then this is the book for you: over 10,000 pieces of utterly dispensable information!

### The Diary of Virginia Woolf
Five volumes, edited by Quentin Bell and Anne Olivier Bell

'As an account of the intellectual and cultural life of our century, Virginia Woolf's diaries are invaluable; as the record of one bruised and unquiet mind, they are unique' – Peter Ackroyd in the *Sunday Times*

### Voices of the Old Sea   Norman Lewis

'I will wager that *Voices of the Old Sea* will be a classic in the literature about Spain' – *Mail on Sunday*. 'Limpidly and lovingly Norman Lewis has caught the helpless, unwitting, often foolish, but always hopeful village in its dying summers, and saved the tragedy with sublime comedy' – *Observer*

### The First World War   A J P Taylor

In this superb illustrated history, A. J. P. Taylor 'manages to say almost everything that is important for an understanding and, indeed, intellectual digestion of that vast event . . . A special text . . . a remarkable collection of photographs' – *Observer*

### Ninety-Two Days   Evelyn Waugh

With characteristic honesty, Evelyn Waugh here debunks the romantic notions attached to rough travelling: his journey in Guiana and Brazil is difficult, dangerous and extremely uncomfortable, and his account of it is witty and unquestionably compelling.

# FOR THE BEST IN PAPERBACKS, LOOK FOR THE 🐧

## A CHOICE OF PENGUINS

### The Big Red Train Ride   Eric Newby

From Moscow to the Pacific on the Trans-Siberian Railway is an eight-day journey of nearly six thousand miles through seven time zones. In 1977 Eric Newby set out with his wife, an official guide and a photographer on this journey. 'The best kind of travel book' – Paul Theroux

### Star Wars   Edited by E. P. Thompson

With contributions from Rip Bulkeley, John Pike, Ben Thompson and E. P. Thompson, and with a Foreword by Dorothy Hodgkin, OM, this is a major book which assesses all the arguments for Star Wars and proceeds to make a powerful – indeed unanswerable – case against it.

### Selected Letters of Malcolm Lowry
Edited by Harvey Breit and Margerie Bonner Lowry

Lowry emerges from these letters not only as an extremely interesting man, but also a lovable one' – Philip Toynbee

### PENGUIN CLASSICS OF WORLD ART

Each volume presents the complete paintings of the artist and includes: an introduction by a distinguished art historian, critical comments on the painter from his own time to the present day, 64 pages of full-colour plates, a chronological survey of his life and work, a basic bibliography, a fully illustrated and annotated *catalogue raisonné*.

### Titles already published or in preparation

Botticelli, Bruegel, Canaletto, Caravaggio, Cézanne, Dürer, Giorgione, Giotto, Leonardo da Vinci, Manet, Mantegna, Michelangelo, Picasso, Piero della Francesca, Raphael, Rembrandt, Toulouse-Lautrec, van Eyck, Vermeer, Watteau

# FOR THE BEST IN PAPERBACKS, LOOK FOR THE 🐧

## BIOGRAPHY AND AUTOBIOGRAPHY IN PENGUIN

### Jackdaw Cake  Norman Lewis

From Carmarthen to Cuba, from Enfield to Algeria, Norman Lewis brilliantly recounts his transformation from stammering schoolboy to the man Auberon Waugh called 'the greatest travel writer alive, if not the greatest since Marco Polo'.

### Catherine  Maureen Dunbar

*Catherine* is the tragic story of a young woman who died of anorexia nervosa. Told by her mother, it includes extracts from Catherine's diary and conveys both the physical and psychological traumas suffered by anorexics.

### Isak Dinesen, the Life of Karen Blixen  Judith Thurman

Myth-spinner and storyteller famous far beyond her native Denmark, Karen Blixen lived much of the Gothic strangeness of her tales. This remarkable biography paints Karen Blixen in all her sybiline beauty and magnetism, conveying the delight and terror she inspired, and the pain she suffered.

### The Silent Twins  Marjorie Wallace

June and Jennifer Gibbons are twenty-three year old identical twins, who from childhood have been locked together in a strange secret bondage which made them reject the outside world. *The Silent Twins* is a real-life psychological thriller about the most fundamental question – what makes a separate, individual human being?

### Backcloth  Dirk Bogarde

The final volume of Dirk Bogarde's autobiography is not about his acting years but about Dirk Bogarde the man and the people and events that have shaped his life and character. All are remembered with affection, nostalgia and characteristic perception and eloquence.

# FOR THE BEST IN PAPERBACKS, LOOK FOR THE 🐧

## PENGUIN CLASSIC CRIME

### The Big Knockover and Other Stories   Dashiell Hammett

With these sharp, spare, laconic stories, Hammett invented a new folk hero – the private eye. 'Dashiell Hammett gave murder back to the kind of people that commit it for reasons, not just to provide a corpse; and with the means at hand, not with handwrought duelling pistols, curare, and tropical fish' – Raymond Chandler

### Death of a Ghost   Margery Allingham

A picture painted by a dead artist leads to murder . . . and Albert Campion has to face his dearest enemy. With the skill we have come to expect from one of the great crime writers of all time, Margery Allingham weaves an enthralling web of murder, intrigue and suspense.

### Fen Country   Edmund Crispin

Dandelions and hearing aids, a bloodstained cat, a Leonardo drawing, a corpse with an alibi, a truly poisonous letter . . . these are just some of the unusual clues that Oxford don/detective Gervase Fen is confronted with in this sparkling collection of short mystery stories by one of the great masters of detective fiction. 'The mystery fan's ideal bedside book' – *Kirkus Reviews*

### The Wisdom of Father Brown   G. K. Chesterton

Twelve delightful stories featuring the world's most beloved amateur sleuth. Here Father Brown's adventures take him from London to Cornwall, from Italy to France. He becomes involved with bandits, treason, murder, curses, and an American crime-detection machine.

### Five Roundabouts to Heaven   John Bingham

At the heart of this novel is a conflict of human relationships ending in death. Centred around crime, the book is remarkable for its humanity, irony and insight into the motives and weaknesses of men and women, as well as for a tensely exciting plot with a surprise ending. One of the characters, considering reasons for killing, wonders whether the steps of his argument are *Five Roundabouts to Heaven*. Or did they lead to Hell? . . .'